Fireflies in December

FIREFLIES

IN DECEMBER

Jennifer Erin Valent

TYNDALE HOUSE PUBLISHERS, INC.

Carol Stream, Illinois

Library of Congress Cataloging-in-Publication Data

Valent, Jennifer Erin.
   Fireflies in December / Jennifer Erin Valent.
      p. cm.
   ISBN-13: 978-1-4143-2432-6 (sc)
   ISBN-10: 1-4143-2432-4 (sc)
   1. Girls—Fiction. 2. Race relations—Fiction. 3. Virginia—Fiction. 4. Domestic fiction.
I. Title.
   PS3622.A4257F57 2008
   813'.6—dc22   2008034383

Printed in the United States of America

14 13 12 11 10 09
 7 6 5 4

TO MY PARENTS, JOE & BARBARA VALENT,
for believing I could do this.

AND TO MY SAVIOR
for holding my hand every step of the way.

Acknowledgments

My sincerest appreciation goes out to Jerry Jenkins and all those with the Christian Writers Guild for their tireless dedication to those whom the Lord has called to write; to Nick Harrison, for believing in my work and keeping me in the game when I felt like giving up; to my agent, Wendy Lawton, for graciously showing a rookie the ropes; to everyone at Tyndale House for taking a leap of faith; to my editor, Sarah Mason, for her time and effort on behalf of myself and my characters; to Karen Watson and Stephanie Broene for putting their hearts into this project; to my entire family for their love and support; to my aunt, Jan Corrie, and to Rosemary Howren for being faithful prayer warriors on my behalf; to my First Readers Club—Mom, my sister Trish McGonigal, my cousin Cristi Kimmel, and Melissa Ridenhour—for being my unofficial editors; to Melanie Payton and Amy McCreight for making me laugh when I wanted to cry. And last but not least, to my nephews and niece—Josh, Ethan, Micah, and Cady—and to all the kids I've been blessed to work with over the years, for reminding me how to see life through a child's eyes.

Chapter 1

The summer I turned thirteen, I thought I'd killed a man.

That's a heavy burden for a girl to hang on to, but it didn't surprise me so much to have that trouble come in the summertime. Every bad thing that ever happened to me seemed to happen in those long months.

The summer I turned five, Granny Rose died of a heart attack during the Independence Day fireworks. The summer I turned seven, my dog Skippy ran away with a tramp who jumped the train to Baltimore. And the summer I turned eleven, a drought took the corn crop and we couldn't have any corn for my birthday, which is what I'd always done because my favorite food was corn from Daddy's field, boiled in a big pot.

To top it off, here in the South, summers are long and hot and sticky. They drag on and on, making slow things seem slower and bad things seem worse.

The fear and guilt of the summer of 1932 still clings to my memory like the wet heat of southern Virginia. That year we had unbearable temperatures, and we had trouble, just that it was trouble of a different kind. It was the beginning of a time that taught me bad things can turn into good things, even though sometimes it takes a while for the good to come out.

The day I turned thirteen was one of those summer days when the air is so thick, you can see wavy lines above the tar on the rooftops. The kind of day when the sound of cicadas vibrates in your ears and everything smells like grass.

On that day, as Momma got ready for my birthday party, I told her that I wanted nothing to do with watermelon this year.

"We have some fine ones," she told me. "Just don't eat any."

"But the boys will spit the seeds at us like they do all the time," I said. "And they'll hit me extra hard today since it's my birthday."

"I'll tell them not to," she said absentmindedly as she checked her recipe again with that squinched-up look she always got when trying to concentrate.

I knew I was only another argument or two from being scolded, but I tried again. "Those boys won't listen to you."

"Those boys will listen to me if they want to eat," she replied before muttering something about needing a cup of oleo.

"They don't even listen to Teacher at school, Momma."

That last reply had done it, and I stepped back a ways as Momma picked up her wooden spoon and peered at me angrily, her free hand on her apron-covered hip. "Jessilyn Lassiter, I won't have you arguin' with me. Now get on out of this house before your jabberin' makes me mess up my biscuits."

I knew better than to take another chance with her, and I went outside to sit on my tree swing. If God wasn't going to send us any breeze for my birthday, I was bound and determined to make my own, so I started pumping my legs to work up some speed. The breeze was slight but enough to give me a little relief.

I saw Gemma come out of the house carrying a big watermelon and a long knife, and I knew she had been sent out by her momma to cut it up. Gemma's momma helped mine with chores, and her daddy worked in the fields. Sometimes Gemma would help her momma with things, and it always made me feel guilty to see her doing chores that I should have been doing. So I dug my feet into the dry dirt below me to slow down and hopped off the swing with a long leap, puffing dust up all around me.

I wandered to the picnic table where Gemma was rolling the green melon around to find just the right spot to cut into. "I guess this is for my party."

"That's what your momma says."

"Are you comin'?"

"My momma never lets me come to your parties."

"So? Ain't never a time you can't start somethin' new. It's my party, anyways."

"It ain't proper for the help to socialize with the family's friends, Momma says."

"Your momma and daddy have been workin' here for as long as I can remember. You're as close to family as we got around here, as I see it. I ain't got no grandparents or nothin'."

Gemma scoffed at me with a sarcastic laugh. "When was the last time you saw one brown girl and one white girl in the same family?"

I shrugged and watched her slice through the watermelon, both of us backing away to avoid the squirting juices.

"Looks like a good one," Gemma said as the fragrant smell floated by on the first bit of a breeze we'd seen all day.

"All I see are seeds for the boys to hit me with."

"Why do you let them boys pick on you?"

"I don't let 'em. I always push 'em or somethin'. But they're all bigger than me. What do you want me to do? Pick a fight?"

"Guess not." A piece of the melon's flesh flopped onto the table as Gemma cut it, and she popped it into her mouth thoughtfully. "I'll never know why boys got to be so mean."

"It's part of their recipe, I guess." I helped by piling the slices on a big platter, and I strategically picked as many seeds as I could find off the pieces before I stacked them. Never mind my dirty hands. "You come by around two o'clock," I told her adamantly. "I'll get you some cake and lemonade. You're my best friend. You should be at my party."

Gemma shushed me and shoved an elbow into my ribs as her momma went walking by us.

"Gemma Teague," her momma said, "you girls gettin' your chores done?"

"Ain't got no chores of my own, Miss Opal," I told her. "I figured on helpin' Gemma instead."

"Then you two make certain you keep your minds on your work, ya hear?"

"Yes'm," we both mumbled.

Gemma's momma walked past, but she looked back at us a couple times with a funny look on her face like she figured we were planning something.

In a way we were, but I didn't see it as being a big caper or anything, so I continued by saying, "You know, I ain't seein' any sense in you not at least askin' your momma if you can come by for cake. She's usually understandin' about things."

"Every year it's the same thing from you, Jessie. She won't let me come, and besides, I'll bet your momma don't want me here no more than my momma does. It just ain't done."

"'It just ain't done'!" I huffed. "Who makes up these rules, anyhow?"

Gemma kept her eyes on her work and said nothing, but I knew her well enough to see that she didn't understand her words anymore than I did.

Momma called me from the open kitchen window, but I ignored it and kept after Gemma. "Now listen. You just

5

come on by after we've cut the cake and pretend to clean up somethin', and I'll be sure you get some."

"Ain't no way I'm gettin' in trouble for some cake and lemonade that I'll get after the party anyhow," she argued. "You're just bein' stubborn."

I sighed when Momma called me again. "She's gonna tell me to take a bath, I bet. You'd think at thirteen I'd be old enough to stop havin' my momma order me to take baths."

"You'd never take one otherwise," Gemma said. "Ain't nobody wants to smell you then."

"I hate takin' baths on days this sticky. My hair never dries."

"Takin' a bath on a hot day ain't never bad."

"It is when the water's hot as the air is."

Gemma shook her head at me like she always did when I was being hardheaded. "Water's water. Cools you off any which way."

I didn't believe her, but I headed off to the kitchen, where Momma had filled the big metal tub we'd had to take baths in ever since the bathroom faucets broke. The sheet she'd hung across the doorway into the next room flapped as the breeze I'd prayed for began to pick up.

I hopped out of my dungarees in one quick leap and crawled into the tub. "It's hot as boiled water," I complained.

"Well then, we'll have you for supper," Momma replied as she measured out flour, obviously undisturbed by my discomfort. "Your guests will start gettin' here in a half hour, so don't dawdle unless you want everyone findin' you in the tub."

"Yes'm."

"And don't forget to clean behind your ears."

"Yes'm."

Water splashed as I washed with my usual lack of grace, landing droplets about the kitchen floor. It didn't really matter since Momma always made a mess when she cooked and the floor would need cleaning after she was done. No doubt the flour and water would mix into a fine paste, though, and she'd have a few words to mutter as she tried to scrub it up. As she measured sugar, I could hear her praying, "Oh, dear Jesus, let me have enough." Momma prayed about anything anytime, anywhere.

By the time I'd scrubbed and dried, the smell of biscuits was drifting through the house and Momma was putting the oil on for the chicken. She was a good cook, no matter the mess, and she always put on quite a show for these birthday parties.

As I walked up to my room, wrapped in a ragged blue towel, I heard Momma call after me not to forget to put on my dress. Then she added, "Please, Lord, let the girl look presentable." I think Momma often wondered why, if she was to be blessed with a girl, she had to get one that mostly acted like a boy.

"No dungarees!" she added. "And put on your church shoes."

I rolled my eyes, knowing she was nowhere near me. I would never have dared to do it in front of her. I hated dressing up, but for every birthday, holiday, church day, and trip into town, I had to wear one of the three dresses that Momma had made me. She was as fine with a needle as she was with a frying pan, but I hated dresses nonetheless. Mostly because when I wore them, I had to sit all proper in my chair, and I couldn't do cartwheels, at least not without getting yelled at. But I put on the dress because I had to and buckled up my church shoes.

I could hear Daddy's footsteps coming down the hall, and I turned to smile at him as he stopped at my doorway.

"Lookin' pretty, dumplin'," Daddy said.

"That's too bad."

"Now, now. Ain't nothin' wrong with a girl lookin' like a girl."

"Who says wearin' dresses is the only way to look like a girl?"

Coming into the room, his dirty boots leaving marks that Momma would complain about later, Daddy tossed his hat onto a chair and helped me finish tying the bow on the back of the dress. "We don't make the rules; we just follow 'em."

"Well, someone had to make the rules in the first place. We should just make new ones."

"No doubt you will one day, Jessilyn," he said with a sigh. "But for now, you'd best follow your momma's instructions. She ain't one to be disobeyed."

"Are you gonna be at the party?" I asked hopefully, knowing full well that he'd been in the fields all morning and looked in need of a nap.

"Wouldn't miss it, you know that. I got the corn on

already." Daddy rubbed his tired eyes, picked up his hat, and walked out, whacking the hat against his leg to loosen the dust.

He worked hard, especially this time of year, and no matter how many men were willing to work the fields, he would always put in his fair share alongside them. I had suspected of late, however, that he was working harder more out of necessity than a sense of duty. We'd had fewer men to help than in years past, and it wasn't due to lack of interest, I was sure. I'd seen my daddy turn three men away just the day before.

Things were poor, especially in our parts, and for having a working farm and a good truck, we were fortunate. We even had some conveniences that other people envied, like a fancy icebox and a telephone, and Momma was pretty proud of that. We weren't rich like Mayor Tuttle and his wife, with their big columned house and fancy motor car, but we were thought to be well-off just the same. Momma and Daddy never talked money in front of me, and I decided not to fuss with it. It caused too many problems for adults from what I could see. What did I want to do with it?

I made my way downstairs and stepped out onto the porch, disappointed to see Buddy Pernell was the first to arrive. I didn't like Buddy very much. But then, I didn't like many kids very much. I thanked him for coming—mainly because Momma's glare told me to—and received the plate of cookies his momma handed me. In those days, we didn't give gifts at parties; it was too extravagant. But every momma felt it only proper to bring some sort of favor along.

By the time we had a full crowd, one side of the food table was filled with jars of jelly, bowls of sugared strawberries, a couple pies, and even one tub of pickled pigs' feet. I promptly removed those, but Momma stopped me cold.

"We accept all gifts with thanks, Jessilyn," she hissed in my ear as she replaced the tub on the table.

"Even pigs' feet?" I argued.

"Yes ma'am! Even pigs' feet."

It took only ten minutes before the first watermelon seed landed in my hair. All the other girls started screaming and ran for cover, but I fought back at the boys out of sheer pride. I did a little shoving, Momma did some yelling, but I got pummeled anyhow.

After we finished eating lunch, I spotted Gemma hanging laundry on the line and ran over to get her help brushing all those sticky seeds out of my hair.

"You ought to not let 'em do this to you," she said.

"I told you before," I said with my eyes shut tight to stand the pain of Gemma's brushing, "they're all bigger than me."

"I think they're too big for their britches. That's the problem."

"Maybe so, but that don't change nothin'. I still can't whip 'em."

"Well, I did the best I could." Gemma peered closely at my sun-streaked hair. "I can't see no more."

"Just wait till we go swimmin'," I told her. "I'll find some critter to stick down Buddy Pernell's knickers. He's the one leadin' the boys in the spittin'."

"You best be careful. Them boys might do somethin' to hurt you back."

"I ain't scared of them," I lied. "Besides, they got it comin'."

Gemma shook her head and grabbed a pair of Daddy's socks to hang on the line. "You're stubborn as a mule, Jessie."

I figured she was right, but I wasn't about to give her the satisfaction of hearing me say it. Instead, I rejoined the party, grabbed a piece of cake, and stood by watching the boys scuff about with each other, playing some kind of rough-house tag. The other girls stood around watching the boys, giggling over how cute this one was and how strong that one was. I couldn't figure them out.

"All that fussin' over boys," I said through a mouthful of frosting. "If you girls had any smarts, you'd be playin' tag right along with 'em."

"Why don't you?" Ginny Lee Kidrey asked.

"I'm eatin'. Ain't no reason to stuff down cake when I can play tag anytime I want."

"You're just a tomboy, Jessie Lassiter," said Dolly Watson, who always wore dresses and perfume that smelled like dead roses. "What do you know about boys?"

"Enough to know that they ain't worth wastin' time on."

The girls turned their noses up at me—all but Ginny Lee, who was the only real friend I had outside of Gemma, and even she had started to become more like the other girls of late.

The only reason I even had those other children at the party was because Momma insisted on it. She liked entertaining guests, but in our parts we didn't have much chance to entertain, and she took every chance she got. So every year I had to invite the kids from school to interrupt my summer vacation and celebrate my June birthday with a party. The only thing I ever liked about those parties was the food. I would have been satisfied to spend my birthday having boiled corn with Gemma.

Buddy Pernell stopped in front of me and tugged at my braid. "Still stuffin' your face?" he asked with a smirk. "Don't you like to do nothin' but eat?"

Knowing my short temper, all the boys loved to tease me just to see how much they could rile me. I responded to Buddy in my usual way. "I just like standin' here watchin' you boys beat each other up. And besides, ain't nothin' wrong with eatin'."

"There is if it makes you fat."

"I ain't fat!"

"You keep eatin' like that and you'll be fat as your momma."

Now, my momma wasn't fat. I knew that as well as I knew that Buddy Pernell's momma was. But it didn't matter. True or not, he'd insulted my momma, and it took me no time at all to react by shoving what was left of my cake right into Buddy's face, making extra sure to push upward so the frosting would fill his freckled nose.

Buddy wasn't so brave then. He began clawing at his face like I'd thrown acid on it, crying something fierce about not being able to breathe.

Momma ran over, hysterical, simultaneously scolding me and coddling Buddy. I responded to her by saying I'd never heard of anyone suffocating on cake before, but she didn't appreciate my rationalizing. I got a whack from her left hand and Buddy got a wipe across his face from her right.

The other boys were laughing, throwing insults at Buddy about how he'd gotten shown up by a girl, but he was too worried about not being able to breathe through his nose to hear them.

I watched with a smile as Buddy's momma grabbed a cloth and ordered him to blow his nose into it. Buddy blew like his brains needed to come out, and eventually he found that he was able to breathe right again, although his momma insisted on getting a good look up his nose to be certain that it was clear of frosting.

The boys loved the picture of Buddy having his nose inspected by his momma, and they couldn't get enough of the jokes about it.

I got hauled into the house for a scolding and a whipping. I tried telling Momma that thirteen was too old for whippings, but she said if I was acting like a child, I should be punished like one. Every time I got another whack with that wooden spoon, I thought of a new way to make Buddy pay for the walloping. After all, if he hadn't made fun of my momma, I wouldn't have made him snort up that cake.

I took my punishment without explaining because I didn't want to hurt Momma's feelings by telling her what Buddy had said, and I made my way slowly and sorely back out to the party with revenge in my mind.

Gemma saw the silent tears that I'd been biting my lip to keep from letting out, and she came over to wipe them with her apron.

I smiled at her halfway. "I'm okay. At least I will be once I get back at Buddy."

"Get back at him? He's the one who'll be wantin' to get back at you."

"Just let him try. I wouldn't have gotten that whippin' if he hadn't made fun of my momma in the first place."

"Don't you go talkin' like that. He's already got it in for you, and if you do anythin' else, he'll go and do somethin' awful."

"I ain't afraid of him!"

Gemma shook her braided head at me. "You talk tough, but you won't be so tough if Buddy Pernell hurts you bad."

I sniffed at her like she was worrying over nothing, but I knew deep down that I could have been asking for trouble by playing with Buddy. Boys with no sense can be dangerous, my momma had told me a few times, but my stubbornness didn't leave any room for being cautious. I was determined to hold a grudge against Buddy, and that was that. But I could see that Buddy was keeping his eye out for his first chance to get back at me, and I watched him with a little worry in my heart as he and the other boys stood together in whispers.

I tried to pretend I wasn't nervous, and when Gemma got called into the house, I joined the other girls, who'd gone back to twirling their hair and talking about the boys.

With the boys standing around making plans and the girls standing around watching them, my mother got irritated and told us to find something active to do. "Go on down to the swimmin' hole. Get some exercise, for land's sake."

All of us girls went to my bedroom to put on our swimming suits, but with a knot in my stomach and a lump in my throat, I changed slower than them all. Gemma had been right, I figured. I'd be paying, and good, and the perfect place for Buddy to get me would be at the secluded swimming hole.

After I'd changed, I went downstairs to find my momma. "Maybe we shouldn't go to the swimmin' hole," I told her while she was making up another batch of sweet tea.

"It's hot as hades out there. It'll do you all good."

"It's not that hot."

Momma stopped scrubbing and looked at me strangely. "Were you in the same air I've been in today? It's thick as molasses."

"But swimmin' ain't no fun."

"You love swimmin'."

"Not today, I don't."

By now, Momma was curious, and she wiped her hands

15

on her apron before placing them on her hips. "Why don't you just up and tell me what's got you so ornery?"

"I ain't ornery!"

"Don't argue with me, girl. If I say you're ornery, then you're ornery."

I looked down at my toes and sighed. I couldn't tell Momma that Buddy had called her fat, and I didn't want to show her I was afraid, anyway.

"Tell me one reason why you shouldn't go to the swimmin' hole."

I continued staring at my dusty feet and shrugged.

"You don't know, I guess you're sayin'. Well, if you ain't got a reason, you best be headin' out to that swimmin' hole. I'm too busy to wonder what's goin' on in that silly head of yours."

I could feel Momma watching me as I scuffed out of the kitchen without another word, letting the screen door slam behind me. I took several steps before glancing back at Momma through the window, where she stood humming some hymn I remembered hearing in church. I took a deep breath. In my dramatic mind, it was as if I were saying a final good-bye. Who knew if I'd come back from that swimming hole alive? Momma would feel pretty bad if I ended up dying, and she'd have to live the rest of her life knowing she'd sent me to my death.

Poor Momma.

Chapter 2

At the swimming hole, the courage I'd displayed earlier had completely faded. Gemma wasn't there for me to crow to, and the sight of those boys still whispering made me nervous. For the first fifteen minutes I wouldn't even get in the water, no more than my toes, and even those I pulled out every time a boy swam near them. I sat apart from the other girls since I didn't want to hear them squealing about how the boys looked without their shirts on and kept a watchful eye out for any trickery.

"What're you doin', Jessie?" Buddy asked, his sunburnt face painted with amusement. "Not hot enough for ya?"

Oh, it was hot enough; there was no doubt of that. Sweat poured down my forehead in little rivers and my hair had curled into frizzy ringlets, but I would let myself get to boiling point before I'd get in that murky water filled with scheming boys. "It ain't so hot," I said indignantly. "When I get hot, I'll get in."

"I don't see why you ain't gettin' in now."

"Well, when has what I do ever been any business of yours?"

I heard a footfall behind me and snapped my head around to see one of the boys sneaking up on me. That was all Buddy needed to yank me feetfirst into the swimming hole. I spluttered once I got my head back above water and kicked my feet like propellers to keep Buddy away from me. By that time, though, the other boys had come to circle around me like sharks.

"That was a rotten trick!" I cried.

"So was what you did to me," Buddy said. "I ain't gonna let a girl show me up."

"You might as well get used to it."

That was the last thing I said before Buddy dunked me underwater, holding me down by my head. I kicked my feet desperately and tried to rise to the top. I could hear the boys laughing like they were ten miles away. By the time he dragged me back up top, my chest was sore from holding my breath, and I hardly had time to breathe in before he pushed me under again.

The murky water swirled around me. I watched the boys' feet as they treaded water and tried to grab on to one of those bony legs to pull its owner down with me. But I couldn't reach. They were pushing it too far this time, keeping me underwater much longer than I could take, and I started to panic.

Finally they dragged me up again. With wide eyes, I watched the sunlight come closer to me as I rose to the top, relief filling me once I broke the surface. My breaths came in loud gasps, and I struggled to see through the water that stung my eyes. Once I caught my breath, I fought hard to free myself from Buddy's grasp, swimming away the minute I slipped from his fingers.

"She ain't gettin' away that easy," I could hear Buddy yelling behind me.

I swam as fast as I could toward the banks, where the girls stood screaming for me to hurry up. Apparently they were on the boys' side only until they tried to kill someone.

I was glad they had some conscience.

Ginny Lee, in particular, was scared enough to stand there wringing her hands and crying. "Hurry up, Jessie," she called. "Swim! Swim!"

I tried as hard as I could, but I was losing ground, I knew. After all that fighting, I was what my momma would call plumb tuckered out. My arms and legs felt like they belonged to someone else, and my head felt like it did after I'd spun in the tire swing for too long. I'd never make it to the girls, so I changed course to climb the mossy rocks that rose out of the south side of the swimming hole. Everyone knew this was the worst way to get out of there—even the boys never did it unless they were dared—but I wanted to get out too bad to care about that.

The sound of the boys' voices told me they were gaining on me, and I reached up, grabbed hold of the lowest rock, and slithered onto it as best as my rubbery arms would let me. I mounted the second rock with a little extra effort. But just as I thought I'd reached safety, a tug on my leg changed my mind, and I started to slide down the rocks. My fingernails dragged along them in a desperate attempt to hang on, but it was no use. One more tug from a cackling Buddy, and I dropped down those slippery rocks, smacking my head on the last one before I plunged into the water.

That bump on my head made everything go fuzzy, and I dropped below the surface like one of those rocks I'd slipped off of. I could hear muffled voices, and I could hear the voice in my head telling me to swim, but that was all. The rest of me felt sleepy, unable to move anything.

But while I don't remember much of those seconds in the water, I do remember what happened to get me out. I remember that as clear as a bell. Just as my foot hit the slimy bottom of the swimming hole, I felt someone grab on to the back of my swimming suit, yanking me upward so fast it was like he had a motor attached to him. Once my head popped above water, I sucked in air in a panic, making myself even dizzier.

"Calm down," said a gasping voice beside me. "Take slower breaths."

When my rescuer pulled me onto the shore, I flopped down like a dead fish, unable to move. The sunshine on my face warmed me up quick, but I was still shivering and gasping. I could faintly hear the girls crying and screaming about how I looked like I was dead, and even though I felt a bit like I was, I wanted to tell them all to shut up. Their fussing was hurting my ears.

The voice above me spoke again, this time more firmly. "I'm tellin' you, stop breathin' so fast. You got to calm down."

I didn't know who this person was, and I felt too dizzy to even open my eyes to see, but instead of making me angry like it normally would have, his scolding actually helped me relax. Within another minute, I had stopped hiccuping in air and my strength was returning.

"There you go," he said. "There's your color comin' back. You're lookin' better now."

Finally I felt like I could move again, and I opened my eyes to try to see who had saved me from what I was certain would have been a watery grave. I liked that phrase, "watery grave." At the beginning of the summer, I'd read a book about a girl whose momma had died from a drowning, and the book had said that the lady "tragically perished in a cold, watery grave." As sad as I was for the girl, I thought it was pretty dramatic to perish in a watery grave, but I had to admit I was glad I hadn't just then.

My eyelashes were stuck together with wet, and with the sun shining into my eyes, I could only see what was like little prisms with a shadowy form behind them. "I can't see. I think I went blind. Everything's sparkly."

The man above me reached down and wiped my eyes gently with the back of his hand. "There you go. You're not blind, just wet."

I shivered before looking at him more clearly . . . and then I shivered again. I had never understood those silly girls and the boy-watching they did. I was of the mind that boys were nuisances, and I'd go my whole life without one and be happy for it. But as I stared into the suntanned face dripping with the water that had almost killed me, I remembered those books I'd read with the sloppy love talk and suddenly realized what that had been all about.

He was smiling at me, sort of making fun of me for thinking I was blind, but his bright teeth and dark blue eyes kept me from caring. He could make fun of me all he wanted, I figured, and I'd never hate him like I hated those other boys.

His smile turned to a frown when Buddy asked him how I was, and I watched him with childish satisfaction as he scolded the boys for pushing me under. "What's it to you? You weren't so worried about her when you were almost drownin' her. I saw you pullin' her off those rocks, and you thought it was right funny."

"I didn't mean to hurt her."

"What'd you think you were gonna do by shovin' her underwater?"

"It was that bump on her head that made her stay under. I didn't bump her head on purpose."

He turned to look at me and asked, "What bump on your head? Where'd you hit it?"

"Right here, I think," I murmured, lifting my arm that felt like lead to touch the tender spot over my eye where my wet hair lay in a clump. The stinging pain that shot through my head told me I had the right place.

He pushed the hair away and whistled in admiration. "You've got a bump to beat the band, all right. It's bleedin' like crazy." Taking part of his wet shirt in two hands, he ripped a strip off and wrapped it around my head like a mummy.

For the first time in my life I was actually embarrassed about how I looked.

"Is she gonna die?" Ginny Lee asked when she saw the blood. "She's gonna die, ain't she? You see what you done, Buddy? You killed her!"

My rescuer picked me up in one fell swoop and started to carry me over the muddy ground away from the water. "She ain't gonna die. But just you come on and tell me where she lives. I'm takin' her home."

"Are you gonna tell her daddy what I did?" Buddy asked nervously. "He'll skin me alive."

I had found my tongue again in time for that remark, and I answered him before he even finished his question. "Ain't no way you're gettin' away with this, Buddy Pernell. My daddy will tell your daddy, and he'll wallop you good. And you thought your daddy was mad when you cut my hair last summer. You wait till he hears about this. My daddy will tell him, all right."

"Just who is your daddy, girl?" the young man asked as he walked.

"Harley Lassiter."

"The Lassiters down by Rocky Creek?"

"Yes, sir."

"Don't go callin' me sir," he said with a laugh that came out breathless from hauling me around. "You'll go makin' me feel like an old man."

"Oh, you're not an old man," I said hastily.

"You bet your life I ain't! Now, if you're a Lassiter, you best be tellin' me which one you are."

"Jessilyn," I said, using my whole name, thinking it would make me sound older.

"Well, Jessilyn, I'm Luke Talley. I expect we're somethin' of new neighbors since I just took the old cabin down the road a piece. Sorry we had to meet this way."

I wasn't sorry. Being rescued and carried off in strong arms didn't seem so bad a way to meet someone, but I wasn't going to tell him that.

In the meantime, the rest of the kids had followed us, and although they had quieted down, Buddy had a look of death on his face, no doubt knowing that my daddy would lay into him something good.

And I was looking forward to seeing it.

My momma was the first to spot us. She yelled for my daddy and came running, grabbing my bandaged head in her hands. "What happened? What's happened to my baby?"

I wanted to tell Luke Talley that I wasn't a baby, but I didn't have a chance. Once Momma got a look at my bloodied wound, she started screaming like the sky was falling. "She's bleedin'. My baby's bleedin'! Do you see this, Harley?" she asked as my daddy came running from the barn. "Your daughter's bleedin' from her head."

Miss Opal and her husband, Joe, came running out too, looking worried like I was dying or something. "What in tarnation is goin' on?" Miss Opal cried. "What's happened to Jessilyn?"

Gemma grabbed Miss Opal's hand and told her, "I'll bet those boys hurt Jessie. I knew they'd be up to somethin'."

Miss Opal ran for supplies and Mr. Joe took a close look at my cut. "I'll call for the doctor," he said. "Might need sewin' up."

I thought it was an awful lot of fuss over nothing.

Luke set me down on the outside couch, where Momma had ordered him to, and told my parents who he was. "She took a spill on them rocks by the swimmin' hole," he said. "Took in a good bit of water too."

Gemma knelt at my side, her hands shaking.

"The boys dunked me. I almost drowned," I told her before adding in almost a whisper, "He saved me."

"She almost drowned," Momma muttered as she got to dressing my wound. "Thank You, dear Jesus in heaven, for bringin' my baby home." She patted my sore head with a wet cloth, leaning close to me to inspect the wound.

"I told you not to fool with those boys," Gemma scolded. "I told you they'd dunk you, and they did, didn't they? You best listen to me from now on."

Gemma's words sparked an extra bit of anger in my

momma, and she stopped all her fussing over me to turn and glare at the boys. "Which one of you did it?" Momma asked in a shaky voice. "Which one of you roughnecks hurt my baby?"

"Momma," I whined, "I ain't no baby."

Momma ignored me and kept staring at the boys. "I'm askin' you a question. Which one of you hurt my baby girl?"

I wasn't going to say a word because I didn't want to be known for a tattletale, but it didn't matter because I knew my daddy would figure it out. He had a sixth sense about those things. And Buddy's guilty face and the hard gulp he made when Daddy fixed his eyes on him made it pretty clear to anyone that he'd done it.

"Buddy Pernell," my daddy said in his mild-mannered way, "you do this to Jessilyn?"

"He did," Ginny Lee said before Buddy had a chance to speak. "He did, and he was laughin' too."

Even though she was mad as a hornet, Momma went back to dressing my cut, leaving my daddy to take care of things like she knew he would. I watched, wincing every time Momma touched my head, and saw my daddy take Buddy by the neck almost like a new puppy and push him toward his daddy, who stood there with a hand on his belt as though he was ready to whip it off and take it to Buddy's backside any second.

Buddy Pernell was in trouble, sure and simple.

Chapter 3

The night after my near drowning I wore a dress to supper.

Dr. Mabley had come by the day before and given me a clean bill of health. "She'll have a good scar over her eye," he'd told Momma. "But that's not the worst of what could have happened from that hit on the head. A good night's sleep and a little nursin', and she'll be fine. She's a lucky girl."

But when I walked into the kitchen the next evening, Momma and Daddy looked like maybe Dr. Mabley had been wrong about my head not being hurt.

They stared at me with wide eyes, wondering at me all dolled up with my hair pulled back in a cockeyed braid. I had been too embarrassed to ask Momma to fix my hair, and I was an awful hand at it. Daddy grinned, but Momma stopped him from saying anything. She knew as well as I did that my dressing up was due to the fact that Daddy had invited Luke Talley to supper.

When I got downstairs, Luke stood up from the big green chair where he'd been sitting, polite as if I'd been a grown lady. "Well, looky there. You got yourself right cleaned up and lookin' fancy."

"Oh, this old thing?" I drawled just like I'd heard Myrna Loy say in a picture I'd seen. "It's nothin'."

Daddy snorted, but I snapped him a look good and angry, so he corrected himself by making a serious face.

At dinner, I did nothing but swoon while Luke ate pot roast and potatoes and talked shop with my daddy. I listened in rapt attention as he told us about his life. I admired him for being the man of his family after his father had died three years before; for leaving his mother and two younger sisters to come to Calloway County so he could work in the tobacco factory and send money back.

I watched in a sort of trance as his strong, calloused hand lifted the fork to his mouth with each bite and eagerly asked him at two-minute intervals if I could get him anything. "More lemonade, Luke?" I would ask sweetly. "More potatoes? More gravy?"

"Jessilyn, why don't you set on down there?" Daddy finally asked. "You're makin' me nervous."

"Daddy," I said with something of a whine, "I'm just bein' hospitable."

"Since when did hospitality get so pesky?"

That got my dander up, and I stuck my bottom lip out,

making me seem a whole lot younger than I'd been trying to let on with Luke.

"Harley," Momma warned softly, "Jessilyn ain't bein' pesky; she's bein' polite."

Poor Luke sat by uncomfortably for a second before agreeing with Momma. "It sure is nice to know a man won't go without seconds when he needs 'em. I could go for more of them snap beans, Miss Jessilyn."

I jumped up so quickly my chair squealed and almost fell over, but I tried to be as graceful as I could when I served him that extra helping of Momma's special bean salad. "You can call me Jessie," I told him. "Everybody does."

He nodded at me with a lopsided grin. "Thank you, then," he said, adding emphasis when he finished by calling me "Miss Jessie."

I pretty much floated back into my chair, barely touching my food for the rest of supper.

Later that evening as I watched Luke walk away from my house, I never let my eyes stray from his tall form. He stopped when he neared the apple tree and turned to wave a final good-bye. I pushed the screen door open and waved back with a sigh, watching him until he disappeared from sight.

"Jessilyn, you gonna stand there all night?" Daddy asked as he picked up his book and headed toward the den. "Them mosquitoes are gonna come in and have us for dessert."

Momma put down her dishcloth and came over to take my shoulders in her soapy hands. "He's a nice boy, ain't he? I owe him a lot for takin' care of you."

"He saved me from dyin'," I said, mostly to myself. "I almost drowned."

"It's a miracle straight from God Himself; that's a fact."

"Jessilyn!" my daddy called again from his seat on his old wooden rocking chair. "I just got bit by one of them bloodsuckers."

"We'd best be shuttin' the door now," Momma said quietly. "You know how cranky your daddy can be when he gets to itchin' from his bug bites."

"I'll bet Luke Talley wouldn't complain over a little bug bite," I murmured as I closed the door.

"Now, don't you go puttin' down your daddy. There ain't no man tough as he is."

I followed her into the kitchen and caught the towel she tossed at me so I could dry the dishes. "Luke Talley's tough," I responded.

"No doubt he is."

"And he's strong. He carried me the whole way home."

"I saw that." Momma started humming like she always did when she puttered in the kitchen, propping her bare right foot up on the cabinet beneath the sink—to take the strain off her back, she always said.

"Momma," I said as I dried the colander.

"Hmm?"

"How old do you think Luke is?"

Momma stopped washing the potato pot and looked thoughtful. "Oh," she said in a high voice, "maybe about nineteen, I'd say."

"That's older than me."

"Quite a few years."

"I guess he'll get married soon."

"Why do you say that? Does he have a sweetheart?"

"I don't know."

"Then what makes you think he's gettin' married soon?"

I inspected my face in a spoon and frowned at the fun house reflection I saw in it. "Well, boys that age get married, don't they? Katey Pike's brother got married when he was twenty."

"But that don't mean all boys get married at twenty. Your daddy was twenty-five when he married me." She handed me the potato pot and smiled. "You askin' for any particular reason?"

"No," I insisted uncomfortably. "I was just askin'."

She nodded at me slowly, a grin on her face, and went back to her washing and humming.

I could tell Momma guessed at my way of thinking, but I didn't take much time to care. I was too busy dreaming about Luke Talley and hoping that Momma was right.

I didn't want him getting married anytime soon.

Nobody saw much of Buddy Pernell that next week, even at the swimming hole. Rumor had it that his daddy had sent him off to military school or had locked him up in the cellar or worse, depending on whose version you heard. I asked my daddy one night if he knew what had happened to him.

"You leave Buddy to his father," Daddy told me. "He'll take care of him as he sees fit."

"But he's not gonna beat him too bad, is he? He might up and kill him," I said, feeling that it would be a shame to have someone get killed over something they did to me. I didn't want that hanging over my head.

"Buddy's daddy ain't gonna kill him," my daddy said with a laugh. "You kids all think us daddies are capable of murder."

"Sometimes you look like you want to murder someone."

"Maybe sometimes I even feel it, but I never would."

"Why not?"

"For one thing, it's against the Scriptures to take someone's life."

"That's right," I said with a nod. "It's a commandment."

"Well, there you have it. And I know Waylon Pernell enough to know he ain't gonna kill his own boy."

"But we ain't seen hide nor hair of Buddy in a week."

"Don't you think maybe he's just bein' punished? Seems a lot more likely that he'd be stuck at home doing chores for discipline."

Momma came into the room and tossed a load of sun-dried laundry onto the rickety old table. "Stop talkin' about murders, Jessilyn, and help me fold." She wiped her sweaty brow with the back of her hand and sighed. "I'm tellin' you, Harley, I can't take a full summer of this heat. Thank the

Lord, there's a breeze whippin' in. Looks like we may get a storm soon."

I grabbed a pair of britches to fold and ran to the window to look outside. I loved thunderstorms, and sure enough, the clouds that rolled in were looking big and dark, coloring the outdoors with shadowy gloom. Once I finished working out the laundry with Momma, I headed outside to the porch.

"Just look at that girl," I heard Momma say through the open window. "Headin' outside to meet a storm on purpose."

"She just likes lookin' at weather," Daddy said. "Ain't nothin' wrong with bein' interested in nature."

"There will be if the lightnin' gets her."

"You worry too much."

"And you don't worry enough. If you had your way, she'd be climbin' trees in storms."

"I didn't never tell her to climb trees durin' storms."

"You may as well have, talkin' about Ben Franklin and his kite."

"I didn't tell her to go flyin' one, now did I?" Daddy asked.

I peered through the window screen and smiled as I watched Daddy pull Momma down into his lap, teasing her about being a worrywart. The scene made me feel safe, and I curled up on the porch swing, completely content.

It was a funny thing, all Momma's talk about lightning, because that storm rolled in fast and strong, bringing fierce winds and lightning that lit the sky in jagged streaks. I watched it in fascination until a crack that shook the house resounded through the countryside, making Duke, our basset hound, start barking like crazy.

Momma ran to the door and called, "Jessilyn, you get in this house before you end up crispy."

But I was too distracted to reply because I'd seen a bright flash past the thicket at the edge of our property some two acres away, right near the house where Gemma and her parents lived.

"Jessilyn," Momma repeated, "what are you starin' at? Get in this house."

"There." I pointed into the distance. "I saw the lightnin' hit there."

"What?" Momma came through the door onto the porch, standing on her toes to see across the meadow. "Over near Gemma's house?"

"Right past the thicket."

"Harley," Momma called, "you best come out here."

"What're you doin' out here, Sadie?" Daddy asked as he joined us on the porch. "You were just yellin' about lightnin' a few minutes ago."

"Jessie says she saw lightnin' hit near the field house."

"Are you sure, Jessilyn?"

"Uh-huh."

We stood there watching for about a minute before the first wisps of smoke started creeping up above the treetops.

"Land's sake, somethin's on fire over there," Momma cried. "Harley, what do we do?"

"You two are stayin' right here," Daddy replied. "Call for help, and I'll drive over to find out what happened."

I was scared for Gemma's safety, even more scared than I'd been when I almost drowned. If Daddy had a sixth sense about when someone was lying, I had a sixth sense about bad things, especially bad things that happened in summertime. I'd thought that maybe my ordeal at the swimming hole was my bad turn for that summer, but now I was feeling numb down to my toes.

I knew something was horribly wrong.

"I'm comin' with you," I told Daddy.

"Jessilyn, you stay here."

"Daddy, wait!" I called as he walked down the steps. I was as determined to go to Gemma as I'd ever been to do anything, and I was sure my face showed it. "I'm worried for Gemma. I'm goin' too."

Daddy looked at me hard, and I could tell by his own face that he read mine perfectly. "All right, you can come," he said reluctantly. "But don't you go doin' anythin' without me sayin' you can. Understand?"

"Yes'r."

"Harley, it's too dangerous," Momma said, tears already rolling down her cheeks. "Jessilyn should stay home with me."

Daddy took Momma in his arms and quietly said, "Some things a body just has to do, and Jessie's gotta go. You can see it in her eyes. You go on now and call for help, and I promise I'll watch out for her."

Momma's face showed plain fear, and she grabbed me hard. "You be careful, Jessilyn Lassiter. You hear me? I don't want nothin' happenin' to you."

I nodded and then broke free, wanting to tell Momma that I'd be fine, but I couldn't say anything. A big lump was forming in my throat, and my heart raced, but I managed to run to the truck and jump in beside my daddy.

As we drove down the road, I inwardly willed Daddy to speed up his truck, wanting to get to Gemma's house as fast as I could. But once I reached the house, I started wishing I'd never gotten there at all.

The place was ablaze, like it had been made of kindling. At first we couldn't see anything for the flames and sparks that flew through the air on the wind. With all the storm about us, not one drop of rain had fallen, and I found myself praying that God would send some right away.

Daddy hopped out of the truck, ordering me to stay put, and went running toward the flames. I screamed at him, begging him not to go, but he either didn't hear me or didn't listen. And anyway, I knew he had to go look. If he didn't try to help, who would? In this part of the country, neighbors weren't exactly within seeing distance. It would take time for any help to get here.

I watched Daddy run from one side of the house to the other, trying to see in windows without getting burnt. All the while, I sat still and prayed hard. I prayed that God would save Gemma and her parents. I prayed that rain would come. But I didn't feel right. I had that sick feeling in the pit of my stomach, the one I'd always gotten whenever trouble was brewing.

Thankfully I saw a droplet splatter against the front window of the truck, followed by another and then another. "Thank You, Jesus," I murmured, sounding just like my momma did whenever anything good happened.

The rain began to come in buckets, but it wasn't doing much to calm the inferno that was Gemma's house. I couldn't see my daddy anymore, and I started to breathe a little harder. Scared senseless, I opened my door and stepped into the pouring rain, shielding my eyes with my hand to look around. I still couldn't see Daddy. In fact, I couldn't see much of anything. But I thought I'd seen something moving near the tractor, so I trudged through the mud, ignoring the lightning and wind, to investigate.

When I reached the tractor, I looked into the cart on the back and saw something. "Gemma? Gemma, are you in there?"

A bolt of lightning lit up the sky to show me that it was Gemma in the cart, curled up in a ball, her clothes black from soot. She was shaking all over, her eyes wide and scared, and I felt awful for her. I'd never seen anyone so afraid.

"Gemma, are you all right? Can you move?"

"Your daddy told me to get away from the house," she said softly.

"Why didn't you come to the truck?"

"I couldn't find it."

"Where's my daddy?" I asked in fear. "Is he all right?"

"I think so."

I tugged at her shirt to get her moving. "Come on. Let's get you out of the rain."

I managed to get her into the truck and wrap her with the blanket Daddy kept on the floor for Momma to cover her legs with when we went into town on cold days. "Where's your momma and daddy?" I asked her. "Were they in the house?"

Gemma just sat there shivering with the blanket clutched around her. Her face made me nervous. The feeling I had inside made me nervous too. And when I finally saw Daddy coming back to the truck, my fears were confirmed. He was wet to the bone, his face drawn longer than I'd ever seen it, and his steps were slow like his feet were too heavy to move. I stared at him while Gemma put her head down to hide it behind the blanket, and I kept staring at him until his eyes met mine. The look in his eyes said it all.

Momma must have got word out to the neighbors because trucks started pulling up to the burning house just then. As people began climbing out and yelling to each other about what to do, Daddy put his hands out toward them and shook his head sadly.

One of the men who came was Luke Talley. I remember how he walked over to Daddy and started talking, words I couldn't hear, and how his shoulders slumped after he heard what Daddy had to say. He stood there in the rain, his hat wet and droopy, shaking his head just like Daddy had done. Luke said something else and Daddy replied, nodding toward the truck as he did so.

Through my tears I could see Luke glance at me, his face looking like I felt. He stared at me for a second and then tugged at the front of his hat in a sad hello. I gave him a nod back and put my arm protectively around Gemma.

That was the day that Gemma came to live with us.

Chapter 4

That drive home after the fire was the longest of my life, with Gemma and Daddy both sitting still and quiet beside me.

Getting home wasn't much better, with Momma crying and Daddy pacing the porch. Once Momma got hold of herself, she started rushing about fixing things for Gemma, which I think she did mostly to keep her mind busy. But Gemma didn't want any apple tart or milk. She didn't want a bath or a pair of my pajamas. She didn't want anything, and she didn't *say* anything. Her silence worried me more than I'd ever been worried.

I helped Gemma out of her sooty clothes and into my best nightgown. She never said a word until I fluffed up my pillow and steered her into my bed.

"This is your bed," she mumbled to me.

"So?"

"Where will you sleep?"

"Right there beside you," I said, pointing to a makeshift bed Momma had made on the floor out of a couple sheets and blankets. It was supposed to be for Gemma, that bed on the floor, but I wouldn't have it. If anyone needed a good sleep that night, it was Gemma. "That way I'll be here if you need anythin'."

"The floor's hard," Gemma said. "You won't sleep."

"I can sleep anywhere. When the horse was sick, I slept in the barn."

She didn't argue any more after that. She was too tired to, I figured.

The next two days were a blur of phone calls and people dropping by to give their sympathies. A lot of people brought over food too, sometimes including a little something sweet for me and Gemma. But Gemma wouldn't eat barely anything. She was quiet and strange, something Momma told me probably wouldn't go away for a while. She told me I had to be patient.

I couldn't get rid of the pain in my stomach. It hurt all the time, but especially when I saw Gemma's face or thought about her poor momma and daddy. Momma told me my stomachache would go away eventually too, just like Gemma's strangeness.

The funeral was on a Tuesday. It didn't rain at all. Instead it was a beautiful day, sunny and not too warm. I'd always thought rain was more appropriate for the gloominess of a funeral. The Reverend Wright from Gemma's church said some nice words about Miss Opal and Mr. Joe and told us that we should be rejoicing because they were with Jesus. I figured that was true, but I still felt bad for Gemma. After all, she'd been left behind.

There weren't too many white people at the funeral, and those of us who were there stood on one side of the graves while the colored people stood on the other. Except, of course, that Gemma stood with us. Gemma didn't have any other family that anyone knew of, so it was only her church family who were there to tell her they were sorry. She still wasn't talking much, so my momma thanked the well-wishers for her.

Luke was one of the last people to come up to Gemma. "Your daddy helped me fix up my house. He was a fine man, and I'm glad I got to know him." He put his hand on Gemma's shoulder and then looked at me. "You're a good friend to her. You keep on takin' care of her now, ya hear?"

"I will," I reassured him. "I always will."

Some of the people at the funeral came by to have supper on our lawn, but it was the saddest supper I'd ever had, and no one ate much.

By the time things got settled down, we were all tuckered, and Gemma and I went upstairs early. After seeing her to bed, I crawled into my pajamas, but I couldn't think of sleeping yet, so I headed downstairs for some milk. My parents were on the porch, and I could hear their voices floating in through the open windows.

"You can't be thinkin' right, Harley," Momma was saying,

her voice barely above a whisper. "There ain't no way that would work. There just ain't no way."

"The girl ain't got no one else. She done lost everythin'."

"She has to have some family somewhere."

I made my way to the stool that sat in front of the den window and peeked over the sill to spy on them. I could see Momma walking back and forth in her bare feet, her arms tightly folded against the chilly evening breeze.

"She ain't got no one, I'm tellin' you," my daddy said. "I promised Joe Teague I'd look out for his girl if somethin' ever happened."

Momma stooped down in front of the chair where my daddy sat and looked up at him. "You've got to understand. There won't be no gettin' by for us if we do this. People will talk."

"I don't care about what those people say, Sadie." Daddy took my momma's hands in his and leaned forward to get his face closer to hers. "You know I ain't never cared about people's idle talk. Never have. I ain't gonna start now."

"It just . . . ain't . . . done!" Momma said almost desperately.

"Just because something ain't done don't mean it shouldn't be."

Momma stood and started to pace again. "You'd best think about your family," she said, sounding angry now. "You'd best think about your daughter."

"Jessilyn loves Gemma. She'd take her as a sister; you know that."

"But what will other children say? Buddy Pernell almost killed Jessilyn the other day. What do you think those boys might do if they find out she's got a colored girl livin' with her?" Momma whispered those last words like she knew someone was eavesdropping.

"Jessilyn can take care of herself. She's always been on Gemma's side. She won't care if she gets ribbin' from them boys."

"I ain't talkin' about ribbin'. There's violence from people about mixin' colors."

Daddy seemed like he'd had enough talking, and he sighed loudly before walking over to my momma, taking her little face in his big hands. "Sadie, I told that man I'd watch out for his daughter if anythin' happened. We're as close to family as she's got." He looked at her steadily and with a voice full of firm decision said, "The girl's stayin'."

Momma backed away from him. "Then let it be on your head what happens for it, Harley Lassiter. If unhappy times come to this family through your decision, I'll not take the blame for it."

"Sadie, I never asked you to take the blame. I ain't never asked you to take the blame for none of my decisions."

Momma stood looking at him for about a minute before she marched to the door and into the house.

I bolted up the stairs quick as a hare, making sure to jump over the creaky step near the top, just before Momma let the door slam behind her.

I didn't sleep much that night. All I could think about was

why my momma wouldn't want Gemma staying with us. Ever since the tragedy, I had assumed that she would stay and be part of our family. I'd never met another soul who claimed to be kin to her, and she'd been living on our farm for as long as I could remember. I couldn't see any reason why she should leave.

Now, I knew that there had always been certain ideas about colored people and white people mixing. Not one colored person went to my church or my school, and Phil the barber had a sign in his window that said Whites Only. I knew all about some people not wanting to be friends with other people just because of the color of their skin. My momma and daddy had told me about that when I started asking questions. But Momma had always agreed with Daddy that such talk was ridiculous and that people are people no matter what they look like or where they come from. To hear her speak to my daddy like she did made me worry and started that stomachache hurting worse.

Why would Momma not want Gemma to stay when she had told me herself that God made us all and we were to love everyone the same? I couldn't figure on it, but I knew one thing: I wanted Gemma to stay more than anything. I didn't want to send her off to live with strangers or to be put into an orphanage. I'd read books about children in orphanages, and they sounded like horrible places.

Well, Daddy had told Momma that Gemma was staying. That was settled. But I wondered about what Momma had said about violence, and I started to worry that maybe our lives were getting ready to change.

My stomach hurt for the rest of the night.

We lived in a small town where most people knew who we were, and up until that day in June, we were just the Lassiters. But after that day, we were mostly known as the people who took in the colored girl.

It wasn't only the white people who thought we were crazy; it was the colored people too. It seemed we were caught up in a game of tug-of-war.

After a while of having Gemma with us, a few of Momma's friends came by to "have a chat," as they put it. I could tell by the few words I heard that they were talking about how wrong it would be to keep Gemma. It didn't do anything to change Daddy's mind. Even our minister, Pastor Landry, came to talk to Daddy. I watched from my bedroom window and saw Daddy smiling kindly but shaking his head. I knew that look enough to know that Daddy was probably saying something like, "I understand where you're comin' from, but I know what I know, and all I can do is stick to my guns."

My daddy hadn't always seen life the way other people did, so he'd had to say things like that a lot.

He said the same kind of thing to the people from Gemma's church who came by to warn him of the trouble he'd cause by keeping her. The colored folk wouldn't like it any more than the white folk, they told him. Stirring up trouble was all that would come of it, and Gemma would suffer. Only a week passed between the time of the fire and when she officially settled in at our house, but we got a couple months' worth of complaints.

Luke was different. He came by to check on us about every other day on his way home from work at the tobacco factory, always bringing some treat for me and Gemma. Some days he'd bring flowers he'd picked in the meadow on his travels home; other days he'd bring a stick of chewing gum or a piece of penny candy. Momma said he was spoiling us, but she really knew it was his way of showing how sorry he was. Most days he would stay to supper, considering that he was on his own and had no one to cook for him.

"A man ought to have a hot meal to come home to," Momma would tell Luke when he'd say she was being too kind to him. "I ain't doin' nothin' but what any woman should." And then she would follow that proclamation by saying, "Now, you sit on down here, Luke Talley, and fill that stomach before you go weak and scrawny."

I was convinced that Luke would never be weak. To me, he was the strongest man alive, aside from Daddy of course. In the last few weeks, I'd been seeing the world a bit differently. I wasn't sure if it was because I'd turned thirteen or if it was because of what I'd been through with Gemma, but I was starting to feel different. I told Momma as much one day as I helped her hang the wash.

"That's just natural, Jessilyn," she said around the clothes-pin she was holding in her mouth. "A girl's bound to change when she gets closer to womanhood. It'd be odd if you weren't feelin' different."

"But I ain't been thirteen for even three weeks. It happens that fast?"

Momma finished hanging up my nightgown and turned to smile at me. "Daddy's always tellin' me I change my ways faster than he can keep track. A woman's just like that some-times."

"But I ain't no woman," I said almost angrily.

"You may not think so, but you're gettin' there, sure enough. I think you just don't see some things as bein' womanly changes."

"Like what?"

Momma turned away and grabbed Daddy's socks to hang before saying, "Oh, like maybe how you're feelin' about Luke Talley."

As much as I knew that Momma probably had an idea of such things, hearing her say it out loud made my cheeks flush red as a beet. "Momma!"

"I ain't sayin' nothin' you didn't already know."

"I don't think nothin' about Luke Talley," I lied. "He's a neighbor, is all."

"Uh-huh," Momma murmured.

"He ain't even close to me in age," I continued to argue, "and I ain't thinkin' about boys that way, anyhow."

"Well, you're right about that. He is older than you." She

looked at me and smiled again. "But bein' sweet on a boy ain't the same as wantin' to marry him."

"It don't matter any to me what it means, because I ain't sweet on nobody."

It was then that I heard Luke holler a hello as he turned the corner of the lane. I jumped at the sound of his voice and flushed even redder.

"It's just Luke come for supper," Momma said with a grin. "You know, he usually does come by this time of day. You shouldn't be so embarrassed to see him."

"I ain't embarrassed." I turned away from Momma slightly so I could fix my hair without her noticing, but when I turned back around, I found her hanging up my under-clothes. "Momma," I whispered, grabbing them from the line. "There ain't no call to be hangin' up my bloomers."

"There you are, Jessie girl," Luke said as he came up behind us. "I brought some stick candy for you and Gemma today."

I tucked my underthings quickly under my arm and with-out turning around said, "Thank you, Luke. I best be get-tin' inside to check on supper." I tore off toward the house without looking back at him and didn't emerge from my room until I'd changed into clean clothes and straightened my hair.

No doubt about it, I was changing.

Chapter 5

We were on our way to town in the truck, all four of us, with our dog Duke in the back, and everyone was quiet. Momma and Daddy had been that way since their big argument, and I had started wondering if things would ever get back to normal between them.

Gemma still wasn't saying a whole lot, although I had gotten her to start reading with me every night. We'd take turns reading paragraphs, and I figured if it did anything for her, it would get her voice muscles used to working again. I didn't know if they would quit working altogether, but I had always been a big talker, and I couldn't imagine a girl not talking for so long without something quitting on her.

Since everyone else was silent, I didn't say much either. Besides, I was a little worried about heading into town because I knew how the people of Calloway felt about Gemma being with us. At the back of my mind was Momma's talk of how people could get violent about mixing colors. I didn't know what to expect.

At the least, I figured on hearing some talk. Truth was, I didn't care what they said any more than my daddy did, but usually when someone in town did some careless talking, I lost my temper and gave them some words back. And that always got me into trouble with Momma.

I just had a feeling that I'd be getting a tongue-lashing after this trip.

Even Duke was quiet except for when he saw a fox run past the truck. After about ten barks, Daddy shut him up with a holler, and then the rest of the trip was as boring as the first part.

When we got into town, Daddy sent me and Gemma off to the general store with a list so we could do the shopping while Momma got her hair done and Daddy got the farming supplies.

Before we left, Daddy pulled me aside. "Don't let nobody push you around, Jessilyn. You hear? Let people say what they say. It don't mean nothin' to us; ain't that right?"

"I don't care if people say things about us." I looked over at Gemma, where she leaned against the truck. "Ain't no reason Gemma shouldn't be treated like anyone else."

"No there ain't, but that won't change the fact that we're gonna hear it from people. Now, you get on in that store, get what you need, and then walk back to the truck. If anyone gives you any trouble, start yellin' your head off for help."

"I ain't never had any trouble yellin' my head off," I replied, coaxing a grin out of him. "We'll be okay." But I felt less confident than I talked, and my heart skipped as I watched Momma and Daddy walk off.

"'Flour, sugar, cornmeal, salt' . . ." I read nervously as Gemma and I walked together. "The same old stuff. I've gotta find me some work so I can get somethin' good when we go shoppin'."

As we walked, I knew we were being stared at. We'd been stared at from the time our truck had pulled along the sidewalk. I just kept talking like nothing was different, hoping my chatter would keep Gemma from noticing the dirty looks we were getting. But my efforts didn't matter at all, I knew. She was a smart girl even if she was quiet these days, and she could sense the hostility as much as I could. Out of the corner of my eye, I saw her put her head even lower than it had been. Instinctively I grabbed her arm to support her, but she yanked it away.

"Don't do that," she told me sharply.

I did as she said and stuck my hands in my pockets. I may have been a tough nut to crack most times, but the stares were starting to get to me, making me squirm. It was a first time for me, being watched like that, and it didn't help having Gemma act so harshly.

When we reached the store, Mr. Hanley, the owner, raised an eyebrow at me. "Ain't seen much of you of late, Miss Jessie." Then, being one of the nicest men I knew, he smiled a little at Gemma and said, "Ain't seen much of you lately either, Miss Gemma. I was sure sorry to hear about your momma and daddy."

Gemma nodded, and I chipped in by telling him quietly, "Gemma ain't been much for talkin' lately. But I'm sure she appreciates you thinkin' of her."

Mr. Hanley put a hand on my shoulder and gave it a squeeze. "I understand that, no doubt. Now, do you girls have a list?"

While Mr. Hanley put together our order, Gemma stood off in a corner, and I wandered around looking at some dresses. Mr. Hanley gave me a funny look when I stood in front of the mirror, holding a blue dress up in front of me, but he didn't say anything. I felt pretty dumb doing it, but I did like the way I looked behind it.

I heard the brass bell on the door jingle and put the dress back quickly so as not to be caught looking so vain. Peering over the stack of cans in front of me, my throat tightened. Walt Blevins had come in that door, and if there was anything I knew about Walt, it was that he hated colored people. Some five years before, Walt's daddy had been found dead behind the place Daddy said wasn't fit for good people, and Walt had always said he'd been killed by Sam Dickerson, a colored man who had worked for my daddy for two years. Even though Daddy insisted that Sam wasn't capable of hurting a fly, Walt wouldn't hear of anything else.

The law hadn't seen it Walt's way, thanks to Sheriff Slater, who was a decent soul, and Walt had made it plain he meant to get whatever vengeance the law wouldn't. In the end,

Daddy had helped Sam hightail it out of town before Walt could get hold of him, and that made Walt mad enough to kill.

I well knew he'd use any opportunity to harm our family, and our having Gemma would be a perfect chance for him to stir things up. I glanced at Gemma, where she stood in the corner by the hammers and nails. She couldn't have picked a worse place to stand, I figured, seeing as how Walt was likely to want something like that. I watched from my place behind the cans, hoping Walt wouldn't see either of us.

"What can I do for you, Walt?" Mr. Hanley asked as he finished packing my order. "Need anythin' particular?"

"I'm comin' in for them traps I ordered. Can't keep them critters out of my crops for nothin'."

"Just got them in," Mr. Hanley said as he rechecked my list. I prayed hard that Mr. Hanley would help Walt before he'd finish with me, but it wasn't to be. "Here you go, Miss Jessie," he called, holding the list up in the air. "I've got your order good and filled."

I took a deep breath, and determined not to be intimidated by a big oaf like Walt, I walked around the stack of cans with my head high. "Thank you, Mr. Hanley," I said stoutly as I dug in my pocket for the money Daddy had given me.

Walt watched me for a minute like he was trying to recollect who I was. As I took my change from Mr. Hanley, Walt pointed at me and said, "You're that Lassiter girl, ain't you?"

"Depends on who's askin'," I charged.

"You sure talk like a Lassiter."

"Can't say as I noticed."

Mr. Hanley hurriedly brought my sacks around the counter, realizing that trouble could be brewing. "Jessilyn, you need any help carrying these things? I can get Dale to help you out if you need it."

"I'm okay," I told him, taking the bags from him. In truth, they were too heavy for me, and it took all my strength to carry them, but I just smiled as best I could and began walking from the store. On my way out, I caught Gemma's eye and nodded for her to get out the door fast.

But Walt was too interested in me to not see Gemma as we started out the door. "You're the Lassiter girl, all right. You're the one who took the colored girl in." He snorted and said wickedly, "Just like your daddy to go helpin' worthless niggers."

I whirled around to glare at him, my fear gone on the heels of my anger. Gemma tugged at my arm to get me out, but I was stubborn. "If my daddy were like to help someone worthless, no doubt you'd be first on his list."

"You got a smart tongue on you, girl."

He took a few steps toward me, and as much as I wanted to run, I stood still, almost challenging him. "Ain't nothin' wrong with that."

"There is if it gets you hurt."

"Are you threatenin' me?"

Mr. Hanley walked between us very cautiously. He was

a nice man but a weak one, and I knew the last thing he wanted was trouble in his store. "Jessilyn," he said, "why don't you head on out before those sacks get too heavy for you?"

"You should give them sacks to that one," Walt said, referring to Gemma like she wasn't even human. "That's all she's good for anyway."

Now, Daddy had told me time and time again that talking back to people who don't have any sense doesn't make any sense, but I had never learned that lesson. I did try to follow Daddy's advice at first. I pushed Gemma out the door and was about to leave and make my momma proud when Walt had to go and say that one more thing that plucked my last nerve.

"Just look at you go, girl," he said. "You run faster'n your daddy, and he's the biggest coward I ever done seen. He ran from me like a scared chicken."

He could make fun of me all he wanted, but picking at my daddy was taking things too far. I spun around and narrowed my eyes into slits, saying, "Any man would run from a face as ugly as yours."

Walt took that as something of an insult, I guess, even though I saw it more as truth than anything. He grabbed his package and started toward me, mumbling something about me being a rotten brat.

I dropped the bags and ran out the door like a shot, nearly crashing into Gemma on the other side. "Get out of here," I told her breathlessly. "Quick!" I caught her hand

and pulled her along, looking back to see if Walt was really following.

He was.

Everyone in the street stopped and stared as we went by, but no one interfered. I guess we must have looked a sight—the white girl dragging the colored girl, both of us being chased by the ornery white thug. But I couldn't figure why somebody didn't call him off. Since when was it okay for a grown man to chase after young girls, hoping to hurt them?

He was gaining on us fast when I ran square into my daddy, letting out a gasp of air when I hit him hard.

"Stand aside, Jessilyn," was all Daddy said. He didn't ask me what was going on or anything. He just put me and Gemma behind him and waited for Walt, who stopped about ten feet away.

"You keep that rotten girl of yours and her smart tongue away from me, Lassiter," Walt said, more winded than a man of his young age should have been. "She ain't nothin' but a troublemaker . . . just like her daddy."

"Ain't nothin' that gives you the right to threaten harm to my daughter," Daddy said. "I want you stayin' far away from her."

"Since she's spendin' her time with that colored girl, I don't guess it'll be hard for me to stay away from her."

Daddy drew a long, deep breath, took off his hat, and ran his hand through his hair before saying, "I ain't gonna argue with you, boy. It ain't worth the breath. You just stay away from my family." He started to walk away but stopped and turned back for one last thing. "And that includes Gemma."

Gemma looked up at my daddy with eyes like a scared deer's.

"Get on back to the truck, girls," Daddy said simply. "Jessilyn, did you get your momma's things?"

"Yes'r. But I left them at the store."

"You get on back to the truck, then, and I'll get the things."

I pulled Gemma by the arm, turning once to see my daddy walk past an angry Walt, the sea of onlookers parting for him as he walked to Mr. Hanley's store. They all backed up, but not one of them would look at my daddy. In fact, most of them turned away on purpose, like seeing my daddy would hurt their eyes.

For the last time that day I took a long look at Walt Blevins.

He grinned at me with hate in his eyes, pulled the traps out of his sack, and said, "See these, smart girl? Know what them is?"

I stood there without saying a word.

"Them's nigger traps," he said. "Best keep that girl locked up else she lose a leg or somethin'." Then he spat his tobacco on the road and walked away.

Much as I wanted to do something awful to that man, I did what I knew was best and followed my daddy's orders. I turned around and nearly shoved Gemma into the truck.

When we were settled inside, the fear crept back into my bones, and I started to shake.

Gemma sat there for a minute sort of hugging herself like she was cold, and then she looked at me with amazement in her eyes. "Did you hear your daddy?"

"I heard him."

"He talked like I was kin."

"Why shouldn't he?"

Gemma shook her head. "It'll get him in trouble, talkin' like that."

"Daddy ain't worried about those people."

We sat quietly for a few minutes before Gemma said, "You think he means it?"

"My daddy never says nothin' he don't mean."

Gemma curled up in the seat with her feet beside her, like Duke did when he sat in front of the fire. She didn't say anything more, but I could see a touch of a smile on her face. It had been so long since I'd seen her look anything but sad, I noticed it right off, and it made me smile too.

I'd never been so proud of my daddy.

Chapter 6

Gemma started talking a lot more after the day we went to town, but she wouldn't speak a word about her parents, wouldn't even say their names. Momma, Daddy, and I had agreed to follow suit so we didn't upset her, but it was really for our sake, too. We were all still pretty sore inside from the tragedy.

It was as if Daddy's words to Walt Blevins had reassured Gemma that we really did want her. Now, I couldn't speak for Momma any more than Daddy could, but for Gemma, knowing that Daddy accepted her meant something. Anyway, she already knew that *I* wanted her.

As for Momma, she wasn't around to hear what Daddy had said, and neither of us thought to tell her. She wasn't having the easiest time with the whole thing, and I figured why bother bringing it up to her. Momma was just having a hard time adjusting, Daddy told me one evening after I'd asked him about it.

"You got to understand, Jessilyn. Momma needs company, and not too many people in this town will keep company with someone who sees colored people the same as white people. Your momma, she don't think nothin' bad about Gemma. It's other people that make it seem that way."

"Those other people are wrong."

"Sure enough, but sayin' so don't change them none, and Momma knows she'll lose friends over this."

"Momma always told me if people don't want to be my friend, then they probably ain't worth havin' as friends."

Daddy gave me a puzzled look, like he was having one of those rare moments when he didn't know what to say. Then he answered, "When you live in a small town, pickin's are slim. You find friends where you can. Your momma already lost a friend in Gemma's momma. She don't want to lose no more."

For a minute I chewed on my fingernails, even though I knew Momma would scold me for it later, and then I said, "Why?"

"Why what?"

"Why do people hate us now?"

Daddy shook his head slowly. "People don't hate us, Jessilyn. Not all of them. There are different kinds of people in this world. It's true some of them are full of hate, but others are just scared, is all. Some of 'em don't understand us, and people can be afraid of things they don't understand. And others . . . they don't like being looked down on, so they go along with other people's thinkin' so to keep themselves from trouble."

"Trouble like we're havin'?" I asked.

"Sure enough. Trouble like that."

"Seems cowardly to me," I said, "not standin' up for somethin' or somebody."

"You can't go tryin' to figure other people, baby. People have all sorts of reasons why they are what they are. Some people are scared because life's been so hard on 'em."

"But they're still wrong."

"Don't give us the right to be hateful to 'em. They're wrong—that I can say, but I can't say I know all that goes on in their hearts, can I? So best I can do is pray for 'em. Leave 'em to God."

I was tired, and I laid my head back, looked out at the star-dotted sky, and sighed. "Sometimes I don't know what God expects us to do."

Daddy didn't say anything for a minute or so, and then he reached up and caught a firefly as it glowed beside him. "See this light?" he asked me when the firefly lit up his hand.

"Yes'r."

"That light is bright enough to light up a little speck of the night sky so a man can see it a ways away. That's what God expects us to do. We're to be lights in the dark, cold days that are this world. Like fireflies in December."

Then Daddy opened his hand, and we both sat and

watched the insect crawl around for a moment before taking off into the dimness.

"Ain't much lightin' one of them can do, Daddy," I said.

"Not by himself. But give him some company, and you'd get a good piece of light."

"Don't look to me like we got much company in this town."

He leaned over and patted my knee softly. "It's got to start somewhere, Jessilyn. It's got to start somewhere."

Down the road a piece from our farm lived an old lady most people just called Miss Cleta. She was known countywide for her baked goods, most particularly her cinnamon buns that dripped with white icing. She'd been a widow ever since I'd known her, but there were pictures of her husband, Sully, all over the house. There wasn't a room that didn't have Sully looking over it. He was the handsomest and kindest of men, Miss Cleta always said. She would show me the furniture he'd made—even though I'd seen it dozens of times—and insist I sit in his handmade rocker in the front room because it was the most comfortable chair anyone could ever rest their backside in.

Miss Cleta lived in a big two-story house with a long porch and window boxes. It was her house that inspired me to vow that someday I would have a house with window boxes. Most days that I would pass by, she'd be sitting on one of Sully's porch rockers knitting or stitching. Through her old eyes, she'd watch her hands form perfect knits and purls, her face pressed up close to her work. But she never failed to put it down and invite me up for a treat.

Miss Cleta would always invite Gemma in too, when we were together. Color didn't matter any to her. In fact, she'd told Gemma that her momma's great-grandmother had been colored, and that just showed that we're all connected somewhere, somehow. "There weren't but two people at the start of life, anyhow," she'd said. "That's about as close a relation as we can get."

Gemma and I were walking by her house one morning when Miss Cleta called, "Yoo-hoo."

"Hey there, Miss Cleta," I called back with a wave. "Nice mornin'."

"Nice as they come. Not much to make it better but a little sweet and some lemonade."

Gemma and I glanced at each other and smiled. We'd been hoping for this.

"Come on up here and set awhile," she said. "I could use the company, and I'll never finish that rhubarb pie on my own."

Gemma and I looked toward the windowsill where a golden pie rested, and Gemma put an elbow into my side.

"I know," I whispered. "Rhubarb's your favorite."

Gemma, Miss Cleta, and I sat on the porch together, warm as toast but enjoying every bit of that pie. Even Miss Cleta's lemonade was better than most with its slices of strawberries floating inside. And to make it better than anything else, she'd wet the top of the glass and dip it in sugar. Miss Cleta and Sully had never had any children, which I'd always thought a real shame. A child could have had quite a life in a house like that, I figured.

"You been entertainin' yourselves this summer?" Miss Cleta asked. "Ain't but so much to do in the heat."

"We get on all right," I said after a sip of lemonade. "Ain't much to do, you're right."

"When I was your age, I used to like pickin' berries."

"We got a good crop of blackberries up on the south hill," I told her. "Gemma and me picked some last Friday and had them with cream."

Between bites of pie, Miss Cleta and I talked on about this and that, but Gemma sat quiet the whole time. I didn't think much of it. I figured it was because she was enjoying her rhubarb pie. It was only while Miss Cleta and I were talking about fishing bait that Gemma's reason for being silent came out.

"You can find good worms in my garden," Miss Cleta said. "Come on over and dig them out if you want."

"Momma would wallop me for diggin' around your flowers."

"Not if I say you can. It won't hurt my flowers none." Miss Cleta stopped rocking her chair. "What about you, Miss Gemma? You like fishin'?"

Gemma stared at her lap for a few seconds before she finally said, "My momma and daddy died."

I swallowed my gulp of lemonade hard and looked up in disbelief.

Miss Cleta nodded several times. Then she said, "I know that, darlin'." She leaned over and put one worn hand on Gemma's knee. "I cried for you, sure enough."

Gemma hopped up with a sob and buried her face in Miss Cleta's yellow apron. That was the first time I saw Gemma cry about her momma and daddy.

"It's okay, baby," Miss Cleta said, smoothing Gemma's hair and rocking her from side to side. "You go on and cry. Ain't nothin' wrong with that."

It wasn't long before I started to taste salty tears too, but mine were quiet. I tried to take another bite of pie, but it stuck in my throat. I put my plate down on the small wicker table and wiped my eyes as secretively as I could. I hated crying, but I figured it was for a good cause. I knew that if I'd lost my momma and daddy, I'd have cried buckets, and I knew it would do Gemma some good.

Gemma and I walked home that day in silence. She spent most of her time sniffling and wiping her nose on the back of her hand. I spent my time kicking a pebble along the path in front of me.

That night at suppertime, Gemma stayed in our room, tired out from all the crying, and went to bed early. Daddy had made another bed for my room, so Gemma had a nice bed to crawl into just a few feet away from mine. I left her there after asking her a few times if she was sure she wasn't hungry.

Luke came to supper that night as he usually did, so I made sure to pretty myself up as best I could before I went downstairs. I'd taken to wearing a dress to supper on nights when Luke was coming, and I'd learned to do a much better braid.

"What went on with Gemma today?" Momma asked as she scooped peas onto her plate. "Is she sick?"

"Maybe she's sick in a sort of way," I said. I took as few peas as I could without looking like I hated them, which I did, and passed them on to Luke with a smile. "We stopped by Miss Cleta's today, and Gemma had a good cry on her."

"She had a good cry on Miss Cleta?" Daddy asked.

"Right on her apron."

"About her momma and daddy?" Luke asked.

"Uh-huh."

"Poor thing," Momma said, her voice shaky with sadness. Momma could work up tears faster than anyone I'd ever seen.

"About time," Daddy said. "Ain't right not to grieve properly."

"Well, she grieved, all right," I said. "I think she's plumb tuckered out after it. That's why she's in bed."

"Well, if she's gonna pick a person to cry on," Daddy said, "Miss Cleta's a good one for it. That's one kind soul."

"I'm worried she'll go hungry," Momma said, looking up at the ceiling like she could see Gemma through the floor. "It ain't good for a girl to go without a hot supper."

"We had rhubarb pie at Miss Cleta's," I told her. "Gemma had two pieces and two glasses of lemonade. She's had food, sure enough."

"Rhubarb pie and lemonade don't take the place of ham and collard greens."

I didn't argue with Momma. She was pretty determined about the importance of good eating, and I knew I wouldn't convince her of anything. Instead I turned my attention to Luke. "Goin' fishin' on Saturday mornin'?"

"Plan to. Early as I can get my eyes open. Barter's Lake is jumpin' with bass, so I hear."

"Usually is," Daddy said.

"I got my boat ready to go out on the water. Patched it up last night, so I'm lookin' forward to it."

I pushed my peas around my plate and sighed. "I ain't been fishin' in a while. Daddy used to take me, but we ain't gone in weeks."

"We can go fishin' if you want, Jessilyn. I just need to make me a new pole." Daddy gave Luke a hearty smile. "Last pole I had sits at the bottom of the pond. I tossed it in the water when I lost my catfish, mad as a snake."

"Don't go bringin' up your temper, Harley Lassiter," Momma said, pointing her fork at him. "You've lost more poles in that creek because of it. There must be about twenty of them in there."

"Just try bein' this close," Daddy told her, pinching two fingers almost shut, "without catchin' the biggest catfish in the South. See how long you keep your temper."

"And that's another thing. Every time I hear about this catfish that you keep losin', it gets bigger and bigger."

"It was five feet long, sure as I'm born."

"Five feet long! It started out two feet and grew to five feet in three sightin's of it."

"Maybe it ain't the same catfish. Maybe I'm seein' the whole family at different times."

Momma sputtered and got up to refill the water pitcher. "Harley Lassiter, you're more full of it than Tom Bodine's cow field!"

Luke and I shared a smile, and Daddy took one look at us and laughed in his big, loud way. "I always know how to get her goat. Don't I, Jessilyn?"

Luke smiled at me again and said, "Come on with me if you want, Jessie. You can bring Gemma too. I've got room in my boat. You'd have to get up before the sun, though."

My heart started to beat like crazy, and I looked at Momma and Daddy with pleading eyes. "Can we go? I'll still get my chores done. I promise."

Momma and Daddy exchanged a glance before Daddy said, "Well, Jessie . . . much as I hate someone takin' my place as your fishin' partner, I do have other things to do besides fishin'."

"I'll watch out for them like my own sisters," Luke reassured them.

I wasn't too happy about being likened to his sister, but I figured it was worth putting up with to go fishing with him. I just said, "So I can go?"

"You can go," Daddy said, tossing his napkin onto the table. "Providin' you don't catch my giant catfish. That's for me to do."

Momma shook her head and poured more water into Luke's glass. "It's more likely they'll catch some of your old fishin' rods, Harley."

"There likely ain't any left. The giant catfish family probably ate them."

"Enough catfish talk," Momma said.

"All right," Daddy said, winking at me while Momma wasn't looking. "No more catfish talk."

Momma said, "Good" and sat down and went back to eating the rest of her greens.

"'Course, I'll show you all someday when I catch that seven-foot catfish."

Momma must have kicked Daddy under the table just then because he let out a yelp and rubbed his shin.

I wasn't too worried about finding out what happened. I was too busy thinking about Saturday morning and my fishing trip.

Chapter 7

If there was anything I knew about the South, it was that everything in the South was slow. People ate slow, talked slow, and walked slow. Heck, people even thought slow.

For example, Mr. Poppleberry, who ran the pharmacy on Second Street, was the slowest thinker I knew. If I asked him where he kept the quinine, he'd put a finger to his chin and say, "Hmm . . ." for about a minute, and then he'd say, "Miss Jessilyn, I think it's on aisle three. No . . . no. I moved it last Friday. Or was that Wednesday? Couldn't have been Wednesday because I closed up early on Wednesday seein' as how my back was actin' up. And it couldn't have been Friday, neither, seein' as how I spent Friday afternoon talkin' to Digger Thompson about his grasshopper problem."

Finally, after I'd heard about every day, he'd figure out which day it was by saying something like, "Now, that's it,

Miss Jessilyn. It was Tuesday. So it was. And it was about three o'clock because that was when Mrs. Sykes came in for her heart pills." About five minutes in, I'd finally be shown to the quinine. And that was how it went when I wanted foot soak for Momma or bandages for Daddy's blisters or anything.

Most people in town weren't much different. It wasn't that they were stupid; it was just that they liked to take their time and not rush at anything. That sort of way didn't suit me too well. I was more of a rusher.

Momma always said she didn't understand where I got it from. "But heaven knows, Jessilyn," she'd often tell me, "if you keep rushin' around for somethin', you won't notice when you've got it."

That Friday night was one of those times when the slowness of the South was making me restless. That night just plain lasted too long.

Gemma had said she didn't want to go fishing. I'd figured she might not because she'd never really taken to it before. So she was sleeping soundly and snoring in the bed near mine.

But me? I'd close my eyes and toss and turn; then I'd hold my clock up to the moonlight to find that I'd wasted only ten minutes. I'd get up, wander the room awhile, trying not to squeak the floorboards and wake Gemma, and stick my face against the window screen for a little fresh air. Then I'd get back to bed and try again.

It was no use. I wasn't sleeping that night.

By four o'clock, I knew I couldn't take it any longer. The plan had been that I would wait outside for Luke to come by and pick me up at five o'clock, but I decided that since I was already awake, I'd head on over to Luke's and wait outside his house instead. The walk through the fields would spend a good twenty minutes of my time, and I thought it was easier to go to the lake from his house because he was closer to it than we were. Seemed to me I was doing him a favor.

When I set out at quarter past four, I had made a pretty good case to myself that I was doing the right thing. I grabbed my pole and some bait I'd gotten ready the day before and walked off through the darkened fields. I cut through the corn crop to save time. It took me about a minute to get my eyes used to the dark, but I managed to find a good path in the middle. The corn rustled and whacked my face as I went, but I ignored it, breathing in the early morning air and daydreaming about my day with Luke.

It was as still and quiet as could be once I came out on the other side of the crop, with only the crickets and frogs to interrupt, and I slowed my pace to enjoy the peace of it.

I passed Herschel Jode's house, climbed over the fallen tree that belonged to Lyle Bowman, and splashed through the creek that ran across the back section of Tyrus Blackwell's farm. Just five minutes from Luke's house, I started to think it wasn't so peaceful as it had been, and I slowed down. I knew I heard something, but I couldn't figure out what, so I stopped altogether and tilted my head to one side to get a good listen.

It seemed to me there was some sort of buzzing noise, and as I crept farther, I realized it was whispering I was hearing. Not really whispering, though, it was more like what Ginny Lee's little sister called whispering, which was really just yelling in a hoarse voice.

That's what I heard as I continued to move closer to Cole Mundy's property. I knew that property well because all of us kids used to climb on the big magnolia tree there. But when Cole bought it, he caught us playing on that tree and raised a ruckus, swinging his big rifle around and yelling at us to get off his land. I never went near it anymore, but I was feeling that curiosity Daddy had always told me would get me in big trouble one day, and I went even closer until I reached the magnolia tree. It was there that I hid, practically holding my breath as I peeked through the split in the trunk.

I could see a dozen men standing around a fire in a pit, all of them wearing white robes. I shivered the minute I caught sight of them and ducked further down behind the tree.

I knew who they were. Maybe not their true names, but I knew what my daddy had told me about those men who wore the white robes and what they did.

"They're cowards," he'd told me when I asked who they were as they held a small parade through town. "They're cowards, plain and simple. That's why they wear them hoods. They like to push around people they're afraid of, and they hide their faces to keep from lettin' on who they are."

He'd told me that they didn't like colored people or Jewish

or Catholic people, either. They only liked people like themselves. It frightened me to see them this way, standing around that fire in the dark, sparks from the flames floating on the breeze around them. One of the men was praying in a strained voice, and the others were nodding in agreement. I wanted nothing more than to get away from there fast, but I couldn't move. I was too afraid.

I studied the men, trying to figure out who they were. I knew one of them had to be Cole Mundy. After all, it was his property, and he was mean enough to be part of a group like that. And the man talking was Walt Blevins. I'd have known that gravelly voice anywhere. Hoping to get an idea of who the others were, I shifted to get a better look. To my dismay, when I moved my right foot, a stick snapped, making a loud cracking sound.

I froze, and so did the men. The talking stopped, and the hooded heads looked up. I ducked, but only enough to still be able to see them, and I really did stop breathing. I was afraid they'd hear it. I was so scared then that every move I made seemed bigger than it was. To me, that cracking stick had sounded like a gunshot.

"Who's there?" one of the men called gruffly. "Who is it?"

Of course I didn't answer. I didn't move a muscle.

The men started murmuring to one another, and one of them leaned over and seized a rifle that was set against a tree. That was all I needed to get my legs into gear, and though they felt like rubber bands, I managed to make them propel me across the property toward Luke's house. God graced me with speed that early morning, guiding me across the creek and up to Luke's door before the mournful howling of Cole's dog came within earshot. There was no need to pound on the door, as my fists were cocked to do, because Luke threw it open before I had the chance. He had fishing gear in a canvas sack that hung across his back, and his lips were poised to whistle a tune, but when he caught sight of me, he stopped dead still and dropped the sack on the ground.

"Jessie, what're you doin' here?" he demanded. "Is somethin' wrong? someone hurt over at your place or somethin'?"

I was so out of breath all I could manage was a shake of my head and a spluttering "Gotta get inside. Now!" I threw one terrified look over my shoulder before Luke picked up the sack in one fist, took my collar in the other, and hauled me inside. By the time Luke slammed and locked the door behind us, I was nearly hysterical inside, my mind reeling with all the ways I could have been hurt.

"You the reason that huntin' party's out?" he asked me pointedly.

The howling was growing louder and closer, and I felt miserable that I'd led trouble to Luke's doorstep, but all I could do was nod. I watched Luke as he peered out his curtain, one hand on his shotgun that lay propped against the wall beside the window. The howling reached a crescendo, a mournful warning that my curiosity had brought the fury of evil against us, and I peered at Luke with a grimace of regret. "I'm sorry, Luke," I managed to murmur. "It's my fault."

Luke said nothing to me. He let the curtains drop back into place and messed up his hair, pushed his suspenders down, and unbuttoned his shirt. He threw his shirt on a chair and then went behind the closet door, coming back out in nothing but sleeping pants. I suddenly felt like I needed to close my eyes.

"Get under the bed," Luke ordered. "Get under there fast and don't make a sound." I hesitated, not sure what was going on, but he whispered to me loudly, "Get under that bed now."

I crawled in with Luke pushing me from behind and squeezed back as far as I could. If I pressed my cheek flat to the floor, I could get a glimpse of the doorway, where Luke went and stood, waiting tensely.

No more than ten seconds later, someone started pounding on the door. I waited, barely breathing, to see what Luke was going to do. He grabbed the shotgun and stood by the door. It took three knocks before he finally opened it. "What in blazes . . . ?" he said drearily, like he'd just woken up. "You boys tryin' to give me a heart attack?"

"We's lookin' for someone, Luke," Cole said. "Someone was sneakin' on my property."

The men had removed their robes, and I strained to get a good look at who they were. Unfortunately there were only two, Cole and Walt, the ones I already knew of.

"I ain't figurin' on entertainin' this early in the mornin', boys," Luke said in irritation. "I tend to sleep this time of day."

Cole seemed satisfied with Luke's answer, but Walt craned his neck to look inside the cabin. "You sure you ain't seen nobody? Cole's dog done tracked somethin' to the creek."

Luke held his hands out in front of himself and asked, "Do I look like I been runnin' through creeks?"

"I ain't talkin' about you," Walt said. "I'm askin' if you seen anybody."

"I just said I ain't," Luke argued back.

Walt looked around the place again and then said, "Then if you ain't, you won't care if I take a look around."

He started to move into the house, but Luke put his arm across the doorway to stop him. "Funny thing is, I kinda do. Ain't nothin' in this here cabin you can't see from where you are. And besides," he continued, glancing down at Walt's feet, "your boots are all muddy." He flashed Walt a smile that was more a warning than a welcome. "I just mopped my floor yesterday."

Every muscle in Luke's body was primed for action, and Cole stepped away, respectful of the fact that Luke was twenty pounds heavier and ten years younger than him. "That's okay, Luke. Sorry we woke ya."

Walt only stared at Luke. Cole called for him to move along, but even when he did, Walt never stopped staring at Luke. He just backed away like Luke was a king or something, although Walt's intent wasn't to show reverence.

Luke slammed the door and locked it, peeked through the curtains for a couple minutes, and then whispered, "You can come on out, Jessilyn."

After I crawled out and straightened my clothes, I sat in a nearby chair.

He swung around to look at me, his face creased with anger. "What in the sam hill were you doin' out there? Are you tryin' to get yourself killed?"

"I didn't think I'd come to any trouble, Luke. Honest! I was just comin' to meet you. I thought it'd save you the trouble . . ."

"Fact is, Jessilyn, you brought trouble to my door instead. Now, what'd you do to get those boys on your trail?"

"All I did was see them. That's it. I was walkin' past Cole Mundy's place, and I saw them there, all dressed in them white hoods. There was a whole bunch of them."

"And you just had to investigate, is that it? Jessilyn, you beat all. Them men ain't playin' around. That ain't no game. Hear that dog? He's out huntin' for spies, not rabbits. Who taught you to sneak around in the dark like that?"

"I was comin' to meet you. I wasn't sneakin' around."

"I didn't tell you to come meet me, now did I? I told you I'd come get you." He ran a hand through his hair in a nervous way before saying, "I swear! That was the stupidest thing you could've ever done."

Luke's angry words painted a clear picture of the danger I'd been in, and I started to shake all over with the shock of everything, like I did when I had the measles.

Luke stopped ranting and looked at me with wide eyes. "What's wrong with you?"

I couldn't tell him what was wrong with me because I

didn't know myself. I just sat there and shook, and a tear ran down my face without me even knowing I was crying.

Luke's face turned pale with anxiety, and he ran to fetch a blanket. After wrapping me up tight, he stoked the fire and got me some coffee from the pot on the stove. "It's all right," he said quietly. "It's all right now, Jessie." The anger had disappeared from his face, replaced by sympathy. "I ain't mad. I really ain't. I was only scared, just like you."

I tried nodding, but my neck wouldn't move. After all, I knew why Luke was so upset. My daddy had acted angry before when he was afraid. "It's just what men do," Momma had told me. But I couldn't find a way to tell Luke that I understood. I couldn't do anything but shake.

Luke helped me take a few sips of the coffee, and I was grateful for it, even though I hated the taste of it. Anything warm was welcome then.

The whole time I took those slow, hard gulps, Luke was telling me how sorry he was for yelling. Finally my shaking started to calm, and I was able to tell him in an unsteady voice, "I'm sorry for causin' trouble. I didn't know . . ."

"'Course you didn't know," he told me. "How would you know about bad stuff like that? You weren't meanin' to get into anythin'."

"But what were they doin'? Why were they out there?"

"Ain't no knowin' why they do what they do. They were holdin' a meetin' of some sort, I guess."

"They were prayin'," I said. "To God. But what my daddy said those people do ain't God-fearin'."

Luke leaned back in his chair and sighed. "They ain't prayin' to the God they think they're prayin' to. They don't even know who God is."

We sat quietly for a few minutes before I asked, "You don't suppose they're figurin' on doin' anythin' to my family, do you? I heard they forced Becky Luter's daddy out of business 'cause he served colored people in his restaurant, and they had to up and leave town because of it. Those same people might try and hurt my daddy somehow too."

"They ain't nothin' to worry about," he said adamantly, taking my hands in his. "They ain't nothin' but a bunch of cowards, and your daddy is a fine, respectable man. Your daddy prays to the real God. He's watchin' over him."

There was a moment of silence while I was thinking things over and then I asked, "You believe in God, Luke?"

"Well sure I do," he said, giving my hands a squeeze. "I was brought up on the Scriptures."

"But do you believe in God and Jesus . . . like my momma and daddy do?"

Luke let go of my hands and leaned back in his chair. "Well now, Jessie. I expect maybe I ain't never thought about it much."

"I have," I told him. "I've thought about it a lot seein' as how I hear about it all the time at home." In my mind I saw those hooded men illuminated in firelight, and I shivered beneath the warmth of the blanket. "I don't know what I think, but it makes me wonder when I see things like this. Seems to me if there's so much evil in the world, then there

83

needs to be an awful lot of good out there somewhere to win out over it."

"You can bet there's good out there, Jessie. Don't you ever go thinkin' them men are what this world is made of. There's plenty of good people out there."

"I know it." I flashed him a smile that wobbled with my shivers. "You're proof of that."

He ruffled my hair and made his way to his closet to get dressed again, and I settled back in the chair and relaxed, warmed by his presence.

We did end up going fishing that morning just as we'd planned. Only we waited until well after sunup to go. Luke didn't want us running into Walt or anyone from our morning adventure. The fishing wasn't fun like I had been expecting, though. We were both quiet, thinking about that morning's worries, and neither of us caught one little thing. We went home empty-handed around noon, and Luke and Daddy went off into Daddy's shed to have a talk. I knew what they were talking about, and I sat down on the front steps to wait for them to finish.

When they came out, Daddy had a tight look on his face, and he stooped down in front of me. "You okay, baby?"

"Yes'r."

"Ain't no one hurt you?"

"No, Daddy. Luke took care of it."

"Well, ain't no one gonna hurt you, neither. You hear?"

"Yes'r."

That was all that was said. Daddy shook Luke's hand, said

good-bye, and went on inside, slamming the door behind him.

"He's mad," I told Luke.

"Not at you. At them." Luke walked over and tousled my hair like Daddy always did. "You be good, Jessie girl. I had a fine time fishin' with you. We'll have to do it again sometime."

I just smiled at him halfheartedly and nodded my good-bye.

The day had not gone as I'd hoped.

Chapter 8

We were in the end of June, and the summer was giving us a good taste of its heat. Some days were so still and blistering we didn't want to do anything. Gemma and I would usually head to the big oak tree on the hill because that was the best place to get out of the sun but still be outdoors where the air could move around us. Inside the house was like an oven. Even the doorknobs were hot.

I'd take a book and trudge up there with Gemma, roll my pants up as far as I could, and lie down in the grass. We were getting started on *Anne of Green Gables* one such day, and I made it through only three pages before I stopped for air. "It's so hot, talkin' ain't even fun," I complained.

For several minutes, we sat there hearing nothing but crickets, and I swore the air was so thick with wet heat, I could hear it moving, like wind. I pulled my braid out from under me to cool my neck. "This hair," I moaned. "I should cut it all off."

"Don't go talkin' about it," Gemma said. "You won't like your hair short, nohow. Last time you did it, you said to never let you do it again."

"I can't see why not."

"You said you couldn't pull it back in a tail, and all it did was hang in your ears and make your ears hot."

"Well, that don't help me none when I'm this hot. I should just shave it down."

"Don't be stupid!"

"I'll start wearin' it in a bun, like Granny Rose did."

"Only old ladies wear buns," Gemma said. "You ain't no old lady."

"That don't matter to me none. I just want to cool off."

Gemma clucked her tongue like her momma always used to do when I talked nonsense.

I plucked a buttercup from the ground, twirling it between two fingers. "There's only so much a girl can take, and I can't take much more of this heat."

"You ain't got no choice. You ain't God."

"I don't know why God likes to make us so hot."

"Maybe it's to remind us why we don't want to go to hell."

I laughed at her as much as I could manage on that sleepy day. "You do beat all, Gemma."

"I ain't kiddin'! There ain't nothin' wrong with rememberin' what's bad about hell."

"You'd best not let Momma hear you talkin' about hell. I ain't allowed to say that word."

"You just did."

"Well, not in front of Momma."

Gemma shook her head. "Don't make no sense not talkin' about hell. It's a place, anyhow, and we ought to remember how much we don't want to go there. Makes us remember how good Jesus is."

"I never said Jesus wasn't good. I just wondered why He gives us so much heat, that's all."

My sharp answer put an end to our discussion. Sweltering heat didn't make for easy friendships. Somewhere after that the two of us dozed off, and when I woke, the sky was darkened with clouds. My head felt fuzzy, and I was chilly from a cool breeze, with goose bumps popping up on my arms and legs. I sat up and rolled my pant legs back down.

"Momma's gonna kill us," I murmured.

I looked at Gemma, but she was asleep with her mouth wide open. A thought ran through my head that she was lucky a bee hadn't flown down her throat, and then I shook her, making her jump in surprise.

"What?" she asked quietly.

"I said Momma's gonna kill us. We fell asleep out here. You know how Momma hates us bein' late for supper."

Gemma sat up and rubbed her eyes. "What time is it?"

"How should I know? The sky's covered in storm clouds. We'd better get goin'."

Gemma glanced at the sky, her face turning fearful. She'd

been scared to death of storms ever since the fire, and she grabbed my book, hurriedly hopping up from the grass. "Let's go. I want to go home."

"I'm comin'," I told her harshly. "You don't need to order me around."

I followed Gemma on our way through the field at a fair pace. She was practically running, but I didn't feel like hurrying. I was still too tired. Every now and again a rumble of thunder would sound off in the distance, and Gemma would start to go even faster. I felt sorry for her because I understood her fear, but I figured she didn't need me to hurry for her sake. She obviously wasn't worried about leaving me behind.

Rain started to fall in big, sporadic drops, so I picked up my pace. But just before I reached the line of pine trees that separated me from the house, I got distracted by some voices off to my right. I was suspicious because most of the land around those parts belonged to my daddy, and I wanted to find out who was hanging around on it and why.

I edged up to a patch of brambly hedges, peering through them. On the other side was a gazebo my daddy had built for my momma a few years back, and in it were a man and a woman taking shelter from the rain. I wondered who it could be, and being as interested as I'd suddenly become in romantic things, I leaned forward, trying to get a better look.

Gemma came up behind me and grabbed a fistful of my shirt. "What're you doin'?" she asked, angry and scared. "I want to go home."

"Shh!" I scolded. "They'll hear you."

"Who?"

"Them."

Gemma stepped up beside me and peeked through the hedges, careful not to touch the prickly leaves that were mixed into the bunch of shrubs. She took a good look and said, "So?"

"So . . . I want to find out who it is."

"Ain't no right of ours to spy on someone's courtin'."

"It is if they're courtin' on Lassiter property."

"You're curiouser than a cat, Jessie. And I don't want to be killed by lightnin' just 'cause you can't mind your own business."

"Fine then! Just get on home, and I'll follow when I'm ready."

Gemma sighed and stayed next to me. It didn't matter how much we drove each other crazy. We always stuck together.

The rain started to come down harder, and my clothes were wet through within seconds, but I was bound and determined to find out the identity of the courting couple.

It wasn't too much longer after that when I wished I hadn't.

Soon enough, the lightning and thunder began to get worse, Gemma started to complain again, and the couple hadn't budged from their shelter, so I moved to get a better look. The noise of the storm was enough to keep me from hearing their voices, but it was my safeguard too since they couldn't hear my noisy approach through the bushes.

That didn't help me much, though, when a gust of wind dropped a loose branch from a tree behind me, sending Gemma to yelping that I could've been killed. She knew that branch wasn't even big enough to put a good goose egg on my head, but she was all nerves, and her screech could be heard across the property. It wasn't too much of a surprise, then, that the couple turned toward us.

I froze, ready to be humiliated for being caught peeping, but I was more mortified to find out that the man who'd been entertaining the girl so well was Luke Talley.

Now, it wasn't as though I had fooled myself about his feelings for me or that I'd thought he wouldn't be courting at his age. In fact, I knew that with him being nineteen and me being thirteen it would have been a little funny for him to want to court me. But I'd had a hidden hope that maybe he'd just stay away from girls until I was old enough to catch his fancy. And now here I was caught watching him like this, with my muddy bare feet and wet, floppy hair.

Luke squinted like he was having a hard time making me out through the rain before he called, "Jessilyn! What are you doin' out in this drenchin'?"

I didn't say anything back. I was too busy looking over his girl. She was pretty, I guessed, with her blonde hair and big blue eyes . . . if he liked that sort of thing. She was awfully short, though, I noted to myself. He'd have to bend full at the waist to give her a kiss.

Gemma called from behind, "Jessie, I want to go . . . now!"

Luke stepped out of the gazebo toward me. "Get on in under cover, Jessilyn." Then he spotted Gemma and added, "You get on in here too. You'll both catch your death."

But I was determined that the last thing I was going to do was wait out that storm with Luke's girl laughing and twirling her hair. I turned tail and bolted away from him, cutting myself in three places as I hastily climbed through the hedge and dragged Gemma along with me toward home.

I heard Luke call us once more, but we quickly put plenty of distance between him and ourselves so I couldn't hear if he called again.

By the time we reached home, the rain had stopped, but Gemma and I were soaked and out of breath. She still had enough air left to tell me, "Next time I say I want to go, you best make sure you go."

"I was just curious."

"Ain't no use findin' out what you're curious about if you get killed findin' out."

"We weren't gonna get killed, Gemma."

"Ain't no promise you won't get killed in a storm like this."

"It weren't that bad of a storm, anyhow," I shot back.

Gemma narrowed her eyes and said, "That's what my daddy said that day before it all happened."

I swallowed hard and felt my stomach sink when she said that, and I just stood without anything to say, watching her slam through the front door and run upstairs.

After about a minute, I went in and let the door slam too.

Daddy looked up from his paper and said, "Were you

outside in this weather, Jessilyn? I thought you two were upstairs."

"I best had been," I muttered. I clambered up the steps, and when I went into my room, I passed Gemma, who had changed and was lying on the bed in a ball. I didn't say a word while I put on dry clothes, but just before I left the room, I said quietly, "I'm sorry I had you scared. Ain't right of me to drag you into things like that."

Gemma shrugged. "It's okay."

"And, Gemma," I said with half of me out the bedroom door, "I'm sure sorry about your momma and daddy."

She looked at me with half-closed eyes. "You already done told me that a hundred times."

"I know," I murmured. "But I wanted you to know I was still sorry."

I waited for a few seconds until she said, "Okay," and then I closed the door behind me as quietly as I could.

I stopped in the bathroom to do some washing and combed my wet hair. The mirror reflected my slightly freckled face and made me sigh. I wasn't nearly as pretty as Luke's girl was, and I wasn't half as grown-up looking. She'd had her hair put up with wavy curls under a big hat. Mine was long and limp and had the look of Momma's dirty dishwater. I swept my hair up and held it there so I could look in the mirror and pretend I was sophisticated.

It didn't work.

I didn't know what I thought about my looks since I'd never really cared about them before, but I didn't think my face was so special. I had light brown hair with sun streaks in it, a little nose, and plain old lips just like anyone else. It was only my sort of slanted green eyes set against my suntanned face that stood out as anything different. I knew how angry my eyes could look when I got my dander up. Buddy Pernell called me Jessie the Cat because he said my eyes were like cat's eyes. I didn't know if that was a good thing or a bad one. It didn't matter any, I figured, since I couldn't change anything. If Gemma saw me worrying about my face, I was sure she'd tell me, "What's the use worryin' about what face you got? It's the one God gave you, and there ain't nothin' you can do about it."

On my way downstairs, I stopped dead on the third step down because I heard Luke's voice coming from the porch.

"I didn't even know they wasn't home," Daddy was saying when I moved closer to listen. "I sure appreciate you checkin' on them."

"They had me worried is all. I came over as soon as the rain stopped."

"Well, they're home and safe," Daddy told him.

I heard Luke clomp down the porch steps.

"Thanks again," Daddy called.

That night at dinner, I sat staring into my black-eyed peas and pushed them around with my fork.

"You're gonna wear out them peas before you get to eat them, Jessilyn," Daddy said. "I ain't much used to a girl of thirteen playin' with her supper."

"Ain't you hungry?" Momma asked. "You feelin' okay?"

I didn't say anything for a few moments, but I finally asked almost defiantly, "Did anyone else here know that Luke Talley is usin' our property for chasin' girls?"

Gemma stared at me in surprise, and Momma and Daddy exchanged confused glances.

"He's doin' what?" Daddy asked, trying not to grin.

"We saw him today, didn't we, Gemma? We saw him with some crazy girl out at the gazebo in the meadow, takin' shelter."

"Well, there ain't no reason for them to get all wet," Daddy said. "I told Luke he's welcome on our property anytime."

I dropped my fork. "You mean you knew about this? You gave Luke permission to go playin' around with girls on our property?"

"I really doubt he's playin' around. Boys court girls. It's that simple." Daddy was getting angry just like me now.

"Ain't no reason for a boy Luke's age to be goin' about with girls. And without a chaperone!" I cried in proud disgust. "Ain't fittin', sure and simple."

Daddy tossed his napkin down and seemed ready to give me a good yelling at, but Momma laid a hand on his arm before he got a chance. She gave him a look and a nod, and then she said to me, "Luke's only nineteen, Jessilyn. He ain't gettin' married anytime soon."

"I didn't say nothin' about marriage."

"No, you didn't, but I'm just sayin'. Ain't no big deal for

Luke to have a little walk-and-talk with a girl. Mercy, I had three beaus before I settled up with your daddy."

"Here we go talkin' about your beaus again," Daddy said, rolling his eyes. "I'll have you remember that I did some courtin' myself before you."

Momma smiled. "There now, see, Jessilyn? Ain't no need to worry like Luke's gettin' close to the altar."

I went back to playing with my peas. Even though I felt better after Momma's words, I didn't want anyone thinking I was jealous, so I said, "I ain't worryin' about Luke Talley gettin' married. I was just makin' sure you knew we had some trespassers."

"Luke Talley ain't a trespasser," Daddy told me. "He's welcome anytime on my property, and he knows it."

"Well," I muttered, "I was just sayin' . . ."

Momma smiled that knowing smile of hers, but Daddy shook his head in exasperation.

My stomach swirled nervously. I knew I wasn't fooling anyone.

The next day, I was outside washing laundry when Luke wandered up the back path. I was embarrassed to see him, but it was even worse that I was sweaty and wet from scrubbing dirty clothes. I used the back of one hand to push some of the frizzy hair away from my forehead and started going over ways to explain my behavior from the day before.

As it turned out, Luke didn't leave me space to give an excuse. He was the one doing all the explaining.

"Doin' a little washin'?" he asked.

It was the first time since I'd known him that he seemed nervous. I could hear it in his voice, and I found it funny that he was the one to act nervous between the two of us.

I just kept looking into the water. "Uh-huh."

He sighed and said, "Sure is a hot one today to be out workin' under this sun."

"Ain't no different from every other day this time of year."

"No. No, I suppose not."

I was scrubbing the life out of Daddy's best church shirt, but I couldn't seem to stop myself.

"You know, Miss Jessie, I was goin' to introduce you to Peggy yesterday if you'd stayed around."

"Gemma wanted to get home. She was afraid of the storm."

When all else fails, blame Gemma.

"I'm sure she was afraid. I was afraid for you too." Luke reached over and took my arm. "You best leave that shirt alone, before you rub it raw and your daddy has to wear his work shirts to church."

I got goose bumps when he touched me, and in my embarrassment I pulled away almost like he'd burnt me. I did put Daddy's shirt in the rinse water, but I didn't say anything to Luke.

"Anyway," he continued, "I didn't not want you around

or nothin'. Peggy and me, we were just havin' a stroll up the lane, and it started to rain, so we took cover. Ain't nothin' more than that. You didn't need to run away."

I finished Daddy's shirt and tossed it into the basket. "So what?" I asked, my embarrassment turning into anger. "I don't care if you take a girl for a walk."

"She's a nice girl," he said. "You'd like her."

"I doubt it," I snapped. "I don't like many girls."

"But you'd like this one. I'm sure of it."

I stood taller and put my hands on my hips like Momma always did when she was mad. "Don't tell me who I'd like, Luke Talley. It ain't for you to say. And what difference does it make if I like her, anyhow? You can court and marry anyone you want."

It was Luke's turn to get riled, and he said, "Who said anythin' about marryin'? I ain't gettin' married. I saw her twice, that's all."

"Well, what're you yellin' at? Get married. Don't get married. I'm just sayin' it don't mean nothin' to me."

"Well, fine then!"

I nodded at him firmly. "Fine!"

I expected him to charge off, but instead he folded his arms and sighed loud and long. I took my laundry basket and headed toward the line to hang up the wet clothes. He grabbed the basket from me.

"I got it," I told him.

"Ain't no time I ever stood by and watched a girl carry somethin' heavy. I ain't gonna start just because I'm mad."

Luke about threw the basket down onto the grass in front of the line before saying, "You do beat all. I came here to make sure you didn't think I didn't want you around, and you end up gettin' all fired up."

"Don't go doin' me no favors." I shook out Momma's wet apron and stuck one clothespin in my mouth before finishing, "Don't need no favors."

"I can't talk to you any which way when you're all het up. I best leave you alone before I say somethin' I'll regret." He started to walk away and kicked a stone hard enough to send it ringing against the tin roof on Daddy's shed.

"Where you goin'?" I asked, grinning because Luke had jumped when he heard that stone hit the tin.

"Gettin' outta here, like I said."

"All right." I sighed. "If you ain't wantin' supper."

Luke stopped cold like he'd forgotten all about supper, but the minute I reminded him, there was no mistaking the smell of Momma's roast. I figured he'd change his mind once he remembered the food.

Despite my being angry with him a few minutes earlier, I didn't want him to miss supper any more than he wanted to, so I said, "Best help me hang up these clothes, then. Faster we get it done, the faster we eat." I smiled at him coyly.

He shook his head and grabbed some wash and a handful of clothespins. "Like I said, you beat all. One minute you're yellin' at me, and the next minute you're invitin' me to supper. I can't figure you out."

"Maybe you best not try to, then."

Luke fumbled to pin up Daddy's work socks and dropped one of them square in the dirt. "Dangit!" he said in a loud whisper. "Now look what I done."

I laughed at him and kept on hanging the wash.

"You think it's funny, do ya? I dirtied up your daddy's sock."

"Just smack it out. Most of the dirt'll fall off. Anyway, it's just his work sock."

I watched him as he carefully picked a leaf off the sock and then smacked it against the clothesline post, and I laughed quietly so he couldn't hear.

He inspected the sock closely before shaking his head with a low whistle. "It came clean good enough."

"What're you so worried about?" I asked. "You act like gettin' that sock dirty would be your death knell."

"Maybe it would, bein' it's your daddy's sock."

"You afraid of my daddy?"

"I am, and I ain't afraid to say so. He ain't no man to fuss with."

"It ain't fussin' to dirty a man's sock by accident. Besides, Daddy ain't killed no one to my knowin' . . . yet." I raised an eyebrow at him and smiled.

We were interrupted by Momma calling for supper, and I finished pinning up Momma's dress and followed Luke inside. I suddenly didn't care about that Peggy girl anymore as I watched him open the door for me. After all, she wasn't having supper with him nearly every night, was she?

Chapter 9

I never heard much else about Peggy from Luke. I guessed he must have lost interest in her, and my sincerest wish was that I'd never hear him talk about another girl as long as I lived . . . unless it was me.

We were coming up on the Independence Day holiday, and I was anxious for the fireworks. It was the social I wasn't so sure about. Just like every year, everybody would gather at the barn on Otis Tinker's farm for some guitar playing, dancing, and plenty of food. It had always been something that I looked forward to. That was when people talked to me, though.

But Momma, she looked forward to it even more this year because she'd been craving company lately. I didn't know why she figured on it being a good time because, the way I saw it, we were bound to be treated just as coldly there. If no one wanted to come by our farm, why would they want to come by our table at the social?

Nonetheless, Momma was determined to go. It worked out that Luke was going to be there, so I decided to go along too. It couldn't be too bad if Luke was around. And I didn't want to miss out on the homemade ice cream we'd find there or the good music. Otis Tinker was one of Daddy's oldest friends, and Daddy would take his guitar to the party and join Mr. Tinker and his harmonica for a couple of songs. It made me happy to see him up there playing. He always seemed so happy when he was playing his music.

Gemma didn't want to go, and she made it clear to us at dinner the night before.

"But you'll miss the ice cream," I told her.

"I ain't never gone, and I ain't gonna start goin' now," she said, her voice very stern.

It was true, I supposed, that she had never gone. Gemma and I had always kept company in different places. She'd gone to socials with her parents, but there weren't any white people at those parties, same as there weren't any colored people at ours.

Gemma said as much in reply to Daddy's urging her to go. "Ain't never been mixin' at those socials. I done caused enough trouble here. I ain't gotta be stirrin' up more just to get some ice cream."

I tapped my foot against my chair anxiously because I hated all these discussions about color and how Gemma and I had to be separated sometimes. But I knew it to be true, no matter whether it was right, and I was trying to figure a way we could make it work.

Leave it to Luke to solve the problem.

He came in to supper late, apologizing from the time he stepped in the front door. "I can't tell you how sorry I am, Mrs. Lassiter," he said, even though Momma had told him time and again to call her Sadie, "I done got caught up at the factory again."

"Ain't no worry," she said. "If it's cold, we'll heat it."

Luke shook his head and took his usual seat across from me, giving me that beautiful grin of his when he caught my eye. "Ain't nothin' gonna be too cold for me," he told Momma. "Your food don't need heat to taste plumb perfect." Just as he was about to dig in to his shepherd's pie, Luke pointed his fork at Gemma and said, "I done run into Boaz Jones on my way home today, and he says I should tell you you're welcome to come to the social out at the church tomorrow evenin'. He'll even pick you up on their way if you want."

"Now, there you go," Daddy said with a snap of his fingers. "That'd be somethin', now, wouldn't it? What do you think about that, Gemma? Would you like to go to that social?"

Gemma's face lit up, and I imagined she was happy at the thought of doing something familiar for once since her momma and daddy died. She told Daddy she'd like to go, so we sent word to Boaz Jones that she'd be ready by seven thirty.

The next evening, all of us sat on the front porch waiting

for Boaz to pick her up. It was seven thirty on the dot when their old horse-drawn wagon drove up in a cloud of dust, and Boaz's daughter, Rena, hopped out to tell Gemma to come on.

I waved happily at her as they pulled away, but I watched her leave with a little sadness. I didn't much like the fact that we couldn't do everything together.

Momma had made me a new dress out of green fabric, and I wore it to the social that night, hoping I might look older in it. She'd even helped me put my hair up, so I thought I looked almost sixteen, and I figured that couldn't hurt me any in getting Luke's attention.

The barn was noisy by the time we got there, and I had to suck in my breath when we reached it to get used to all the cigarette smoke that filled the air. Those socials at Otis Tinker's barn weren't a thing like the church socials, and that was why Momma never let me go too far out of her sight.

"You can't never trust a drinkin' man," she told me every time we went. "Those rowdy boys can't even be trusted sober. You just stay where your daddy and me can see you."

When we walked in, the music kept going, but the chatter didn't. By the looks on people's faces you'd have thought we were ghosts. Daddy smiled and nodded at people like nothing was any different and escorted Momma and me to a table. Everyone watched us curiously, and it wasn't until they were satisfied that Gemma wasn't with us that they began to talk again, although they were probably talking *about* us, not *to* us.

It didn't take me too long to spot Luke, but I didn't much like what I saw. There he was dancing with Ginny Lee's big sister and looking as happy as a pig in slop. He waved to us and tipped his hat at me, but he didn't come over.

I nodded at him and whipped my head around sharply. How dare that boy not come over to say hello to me right off? My evening was certainly not starting out like I'd hoped. I looked for someone else to talk to, determined that if Luke Talley was going to spend his evening flirting with girls, I wasn't going to be caught dead standing alone and bored.

The problem was there weren't many people standing in line to make friendly talk with any of us. As I'd predicted, Daddy's refusal to listen to people's advice had put us in bad standing with most of Calloway, and we were getting as little attention as I'd feared we might.

I eyed several boys, wondering if anyone would get the idea to ask me to dance, but the only one who got up the nerve was my daddy. He didn't say a whole lot to me while we danced, and I could see that it hurt him to be rejected just as it hurt the rest of us. All the same, he kept a smile on his face and nodded at other couples as we passed by them, even though they didn't nod back.

About an hour and two bowls of ice cream later, I saw Ginny Lee standing by the lemonade. I wandered over to her, relieved to find someone who might think it worthwhile to talk to me. "Hey there," I said. "Ain't seen you in a while."

She smiled like she was embarrassed. "We just been busy,

I guess." Then she looked more serious and asked, "You been okay since you almost drowned? Your head heal up all right?"

"Sure. It weren't that bad." I took a sip of my lemonade to fill the silence that followed. The two of us glanced around the room trying to find something to speak about. I started to ask her how her summer was going, but I stopped when I heard her momma calling for her. Ginny Lee and I looked across the room and saw her momma waving at her urgently. "Come on over here, Ginny Lee," she called.

Ginny Lee looked at me awkwardly and shrugged. "Guess she wants me for somethin'."

"Guess she does," I replied.

What I wanted to finish with was, "Guess she wants you to stop talkin' to me," but I stayed silent. I watched unhappily as she left me behind.

When I got back to our table, Momma and Daddy weren't there, so I searched for Luke, but he was still busy with his dancing. I turned my head away quickly so I didn't have to see him enjoying life without me, but it wasn't much better to look at anyone else. Anytime I looked someone in the eye, they either turned around real fast or glared at me. The men in particular liked to glare, almost as if they thought they could read what I was thinking. At that moment, I sort of wished they *could* read what I was thinking about them because it wasn't too nice, and I figured they deserved to be told just what they were. The problem was Momma would whip me silly if she caught me saying any of it.

Upset and sick from too much ice cream, I headed out the back of the barn and breathed in the fresh, clean air. It wasn't too quiet out there, but it was better to me than being inside. People's bad feelings had spoiled the whole evening for me, much as they'd spoiled my summer so far. I much preferred the solitude of being outside.

I wandered across the Tinkers' property for a few minutes, and it wasn't until I heard footsteps behind me that I remembered Momma's warning to stay nearby. I whirled around and saw Buddy Pernell, dispelling my belief that he'd been murdered by his father. "Oh, it's just you," I said, breathing a sigh of relief. "You about scared the stuffin' out of me."

Buddy didn't say anything; he just smiled and stumbled up to me.

"What do you want?" I asked. "I'm surprised you ain't avoidin' me like everyone else is."

"Now, Jessilyn," he said in a kind of singsongy voice, "why would anyone want to avoid a girl like you?"

I rolled my eyes and turned away from him with my arms folded. "If you just come out here to give me a hard time, you best get on back inside. All I'm wantin' is a little peace and quiet."

Buddy took me by the shoulders and turned me around to face him. "Come on, now. You can share a little of your peace and quiet with me, can't you? Besides, a girl as pretty as you shouldn't be out here in the dark alone." He was standing close to me then, and I realized for the first time that he smelled just like the liquor Momma kept in the cabinet for medicinal purposes.

"You been drinkin'?" I asked, backing away.

"Drinkin'?" he repeated. "Drinkin' what?"

"Liquor! Where's a boy of fourteen get liquor, anyhow?"

"Ain't too hard to get hold of out here." Buddy laughed. Then he lowered his voice and said, "You want some? I can get it for you."

I gave him a good shove. "No, I don't want some. I'm goin' back inside."

But Buddy blocked my way, taking my right arm in his left hand. "Wait a minute. I want to talk to you."

"Ain't no one wants to talk to me," I insisted, tugging my arm out of his hand. "Ain't you heard? And don't you block my way, Buddy Pernell. I ain't one to be fiddled with!"

"It ain't fiddlin' to tell you how pretty you look," he whispered into my hair. "You're the prettiest girl in town. Ain't I ever told you that?"

Part of me was flattered since that was the first time a boy had ever said anything like that to me, but most of me was scared because I remembered Momma's warning about drunken boys. When I tried getting past him again, he got hold of my arm, this time more tightly.

"Stop it!" I said. "I done told you to leave me be. Now leave me be."

"But I want to talk to you."

"You're drunk!" I said in disgust. "And I don't want to talk to you."

I was starting to get a burning feeling on my arm where he grasped it, and I was beginning to become very afraid. I yanked hard in an attempt to get away from him, but he dragged me closer.

"You always pretend to be a little girl, Jessie," he murmured. "But lookin' at you tonight, I think you've grown up real nice."

His face was in my hair, and all I could think of was how badly I wanted to be back inside that smoky old barn. And then, just as quickly as he had come upon me, Buddy went out like a light, his body weight hanging on me like a dead animal. I hollered in pain, my knees buckling.

Fortunately, Otis Tinker came up behind Buddy and grabbed him. "Steady there, boy," he said. "He botherin' you, Jessie?"

"He was, and then he up and passed out." I straightened my dress and my hair, my hands shaking. "He's drunk!"

"I can see that." Mr. Tinker hauled him toward the barn, and Buddy was half out, mumbling things I couldn't understand. "Your daddy won't be none too happy to hear about this."

"Oh, don't tell him," I begged. "He's got enough trouble, and I don't want to spoil the party for him tonight. It was just 'cause Buddy's drunk that he acted that way, anyhow."

"Well now, I don't know that I feel right about that."

I knew that Mr. Tinker was a deputy for the sheriff, so I figured it unlikely he'd go without telling my daddy, but I tried again. "Please don't. It weren't no big deal, and I didn't get hurt or nothin'."

"I'll tell you what," he said after a moment's thought. "We'll keep it between us, okay? Just as long as you promise to stay inside for the rest of the night."

"Yes'r," I said hastily. "I promise."

Otis Tinker looked at Buddy and shook his head. "Things tend to get out of hand once people get the drink in 'em. Too bad the government can't make their own laws stick. We ought not to have any liquor at all."

"That's what my momma says, but Daddy always tells her it'll be a snowy day in hades when the men of Calloway put away their liquor."

Mr. Tinker laughed his head off and dragged Buddy through the door. I could still hear him laughing as I shakily poured myself some lemonade.

Luke found me there and took over the lemonade pouring since I was spilling most of it. "Hey there, Miss Jessie," he said. "You plannin' on gettin' any in the cup?"

"Sorry."

He handed me the lemonade and studied me sternly. "You okay? You look strange."

"That's a fine compliment!"

"I ain't meanin' nothin'. I just thought you seemed scared. You can't even hold your hands steady."

I looked down at the lemonade in my cup as it sloshed back and forth, and I quickly set the cup on the table. "I'm just tired. Ain't nobody wantin' to talk to me."

"You want to go? I'll take you home if you want."

"Fireworks are gettin' started soon. I want to stay and watch them."

"Well then, let's head on out to the lake. Everybody'll be goin' out there soon, anyhow."

Momma and Daddy were ready to go too. Neither of them seemed to have found much joy in that social. Momma had worn a weary expression most of the evening, and Daddy never once played his guitar. We found much more pleasure in the simple act of walking to the lake, just the four of us.

When we reached the lake, we took a seat amid a large crowd of white people. Across from us, on the other side of the lake, Gemma sat awkwardly amid a group of colored children. I could see even from that distance that she felt as out of place as we did.

Every year I'd seen this same scene and never thought a jot about it. I'd wave to Gemma and her parents, and they'd wave back. But this year, while we sat on one side as a family and Gemma sat on the other side as an outcast among those who found her situation as strange as many white folks did, I watched the fireworks with sadness.

Luke nudged me as the first of the fireworks lit up the night sky, casting shiny reflections on the water. "That's a real sight, ain't it?"

I nodded, but I wasn't paying much attention to the show. I was too busy mulling over all the things I'd been learning about life that summer. The way I saw it, fireworks couldn't compare to that.

Chapter 10

There's always one day each summer when the heat that you thought couldn't get any worse does. Those are the days when everyone just takes the day off, like a surrender to God. We figured if He'd made it so hot, He must have meant us to have a day of rest, because no one could work in that heat and live.

On that Sunday in July, Gemma and I lay in our beds in our underclothes, windows open, cooling ourselves with fans we'd made out of newspaper. Even the crickets were quiet. No one and nothing had the energy to do a thing.

We hadn't been to church since Gemma came to live with us. She didn't want to go to her colored church alone, and Daddy said since she was family she should come with us, anyway. So Daddy said we'd go back when Gemma was ready. In the meantime, we spent a half hour every Sunday morning listening to Daddy read the Scriptures, and Momma would finish off with a prayer.

But on this morning, Momma told us we could skip the Scripture reading since everyone was too hot to even think straight.

Every now and again, Gemma or I would lean over and take a sip of the water we had beside our beds, but we hated doing it because the water was so warm. Momma would yell at us if we didn't, though, saying we'd go and dehydrate ourselves, and she didn't want to have to cart the doctor out to our place on a day like this. So we'd drink in sips and spill some onto our necks on purpose just to feel a bit of relief.

The next time I woke up, I could tell that the sun had started to dip, so I knew it was late, and I had slept the day away. I didn't much care. If I was going to be awake at all for those sweltering twenty-four hours, I'd be better off being up during the dark ones. Rolling over, I saw a tray by my bed. The tray held fruit salad, biscuits, tomato slices, and a note in Momma's curvy handwriting. *Daddy's hankerin' for some ice cream. Gone into town. Be back by nine with a little something for you girls.*

I smiled as much as I could, being half-asleep, and called out to Gemma. "We're gettin' treats tonight. Ain't had a treat in weeks."

I didn't get an answer, so I rolled over to look at her. "Gemma!" I squinted my eyes against the shadows in the room and finally made out that she wasn't there. "Gemma?" I murmured, rubbing my sleepy eyes. "Where you at?"

I got up, stretched my arms, and wandered over to the window. I could hear Duke barking like crazy, and I stuck my head out the window to tell him to hush up. That was when I started noticing the voices. They were quiet and low, sort of grumbling to each other. The voices were coming from the front of the house, and I was in the back, so I dressed quickly and padded out of my room into the hallway.

I stood at the top of the stairway and peered down. The house was dark, and I about took a tumble when I started down the steps, but I caught myself just in time. The curtains were blowing out from a breeze that had moved in. To avoid being seen, I dropped to my knees and approached the window on all fours.

My skin prickled, and my heart raced when I saw the men whose voices I'd heard. They were the same men in white I'd seen that morning in the woods. They looked liked ghosts, wearing those hoods with slits for eyes. Duke was tied to a tree, and he was nearly hanging himself from struggling to get loose. I immediately thought of Gemma, and my fear turned into panic. What had they done to her? I wondered. Had they taken her? Were they going to hurt her?

I turned away from the window and scooted off to the side, staying low. I had to think of what I should do. Mulling over ideas in my head, all I knew was that if they had Gemma, I had to help her.

But then I saw her huddled in a corner of the den, her knees tucked under her chin. "Gemma," I whispered in relief, "I been lookin' for you." I crawled over to her as quickly as I could go and pulled her with me, both of us stooped down, into the closet under the stairs. "You should've let me know where you were," I told her once inside. "I was scared near to death."

"They would've heard me," she said in a shaky voice. "Don't make no mistake. They're here for me."

"Ain't no matter why they're here," I said, angry and defiant. I always had more courage when I had someone to defend other than myself. "They ain't got no right to trespass here."

"What're we gonna do?"

"My daddy should be back soon, shouldn't he?"

"That note said nine, and it ain't but eight fifteen."

"Maybe I can call for help."

"They done stopped the phone."

Having Gemma tell me that made my lips go numb. We were trapped, and those men were aiming to make their point, no doubt.

I sat there thinking for a few minutes before we heard a pounding at the door. "Harley Lassiter," a man called, "you best come on out and face your due now. And bring that nigger with ya."

I gripped Gemma's arm hard, as much to comfort myself as to comfort her.

"I said, come on out," the man shouted.

I heard footsteps thump around on the porch, making the floorboards creak, and then I could hear them yelling in through the open windows. "Haaaarley!" a man called, drawing out the middle of my daddy's name as if he were telling a ghost story. "You ain't afraid, are ya, Harley?"

They laughed and said some things quietly to each other. Soon they were pounding on the door again and then on the side of the house. By this time, both Gemma and I were shaking from head to toe, jumping with every bang of footstep or fist.

"He ain't got the courage to come out and face us," one of them yelled. "He's probably hidin' behind his woman."

I recognized that voice, and my stomach turned with the memory of Walt Blevins's threats.

"Yes, sir," another man said. "We'd better just smoke 'im out."

With that, I made a decision and pushed the closet door open.

"Where you goin'?" Gemma asked me nervously.

"I'm goin' to get my daddy's rifle."

"You ain't got no trainin' with that thing. Your daddy always told you to keep away from it."

"Ain't no time he thought I'd need to use it," I argued. "Ain't no time he figured on this happenin'."

She clutched my shirt and hung on tight. "I ain't lettin' you. You just stay in here with me and wait till they give up."

"How do you know they aim to give up? They're talkin' of smokin' us out; ain't you heard?"

Gemma wouldn't budge. She kept her iron grip on my shirt and said, "I ain't lettin' you leave. I'm older'n you, and I say you're stayin'."

"You ain't but two years older, and I say you ain't got no rule over me, anyhow." I tried to pull away, but she still wouldn't let me. "I'll just climb out of my shirt, if that's what it takes. But I'm goin'!"

The banging on the house got louder and more frequent, and I could hardly hear Gemma over the noise when she told me, "Over my dead and rottin' body."

"Gemma," I cried, my skin crawling from the howling and pounding the men were doing. "Your dead and rottin' body's about a sure thing just now. Either they get us or they smoke us out. You want to burn in this house like your momma and daddy?"

I knew my words must have made her sick to her soul, but I had to make her see how we had no choice. Gemma didn't say a thing, but she did let go of my shirt.

I took off out of the closet and into the kitchen like a shot. I knew Daddy kept a rifle in the pantry beside the icebox, and I reached in and grabbed the cold steel of it, shocked by its weight. I could barely lift it out, and I wondered how I'd ever be able to perch it under my chin like I'd seen Daddy do. No matter, I figured. If I could hold it up and act like I knew what I was doing, I might get them to run off. After all, like my daddy said, only cowards would go around with their faces hidden. I snatched the ammunition box, loaded the gun like I'd seen Daddy do, and stuck a few more bullets into my pocket.

Letting the gun drag beside me, I went to the front door, shivering and shaking, and said a quick prayer before flinging it open. There, right on the other side of the screen door, stood a robed man, looking evil as the devil.

"You ain't what we came for, girl," the man said. "Run and get your daddy."

I just stared at him.

"I said run and get your daddy, girl. You deaf?"

"I ain't deaf," I said. "I heard you."

"Then get them legs movin'."

I kept the gun behind me so he couldn't see it and said, "My daddy ain't here, and anyway . . . you're trespassin'."

The man threw his covered head back and laughed. "We got a smart one here," he said to the other men. "Think we got us a junior lawyer on our hands."

I looked at the other men who were on the lawn, and my heart started to race as the flickering of firelight could be seen reflecting off their white robes. "I got help comin'," I lied. "You best leave before they get here and skin you alive."

"Who you got comin'? The law?"

"That's right."

"Heck, girl, we are the law!"

Behind him, a commotion sounded, men hollering at each other in urgent voices. He turned around and swore, rushing down the steps. "Can't you boys do nothin' right?"

I took that chance to shove the door open and heave the rifle into the air. In the short moment that I had to peer at them from behind that gun before they noticed me, I got a good look at the fiery cross they had set up on our front lawn.

It had started to tip, causing the ruckus that had gotten the man to rush off our porch, and now the men were struggling to keep it erect.

Through the sparks that were singeing Momma's geraniums, one of the men pointed at me and shouted, "Looky there, will you? That girl's got herself a rifle."

Several others turned around to see, laughing at me like I was putting on a show.

"Ain't your daddy ever taught you not to go around playin' with guns?" Walt Blevins asked. "'Course your daddy's stupid, so he ain't likely taught you much."

I aimed that gun at him and said, "I know who you are, Walt Blevins. Ain't no mistakin' a sinful voice like yours. You may as well take that stupid hood off your ugly face."

"You ain't got no idea what you're sayin'," he said sharply, but I thought I detected nervousness in his tone. "You best put that thing down and get out of here before you get hurt."

"I ain't goin' nowhere. It's you who's goin'."

Walt lit a match and held it up in front of his hood, casting an eerie glow. "You wanna burn, little girl? 'Cause you keep spoutin' off, and I can make it happen."

I reached up in sheer anger and cocked the rifle, everything in me consumed by rage at these men who felt they had the right to terrorize. "It's you who'll burn in hell, Walt Blevins," I spat out even though I knew Momma would've put soap on my tongue if she'd heard me. "God won't let you get by for the things you do."

With those words, Walt flicked the match toward me. The

sudden movement made me flinch, and I pulled the trigger. The sound was deafening, and the force of the blast sent me stumbling backward into the wall of the house. When I heard Gemma scream, I realized that she had been just inside the doorway the whole time.

I blinked hard against the smoke that came from the rifle and cleared my eyes in time to see a splotch of red beginning to color the front of Walt's robe. He whipped off his hood, leaving no doubt to his identity, and started shouting and swearing, calling for the men to burn our house down.

The match he'd thrown had landed in front of the door, and Gemma stomped on it with her bare foot to squelch the small flame. Once she was out that door, a man came around the corner of the porch and yanked her away from me.

I screamed at him, but I pointed the rifle at Walt because he was closer to me. "You let her go. Don't you do nothin' to her."

"You may just as well give up," another man snarled. "Ain't nobody to help you now."

"Go on," Walt yelled to the man who was holding Gemma with one hand and covering her mouth with the other. "You teach her a little respect. We'll take care of this one."

His words filled me with rage, and I straightened, cocked the gun, and used all my strength to raise it again. I could see I hadn't killed Walt, but I was scared all the same. I didn't want to go to jail, but we had no choice. It was us or them.

Although Walt was unable to do much, two other men had

made a move to finish the job, but they stopped when they heard me cock the rifle again.

"What're you waitin' for?" Walt said in a strained voice. "Burn 'em!"

"The girl's ready to use that gun," one of the men said. "I ain't gonna be the next one shot."

The other man didn't have as much fear as the first, and he picked up a can of gasoline and walked toward the house, flinging the can back and forth to soak the flowers in Momma's beds. I could feel droplets of the gasoline landing on my pant legs.

"I ain't afraid of no little girl," he said. "She just got lucky." He put the can down and took the matches in his hand. "Ain't that right? You just got lucky. Well," he continued, striking the match, "you ain't so lucky now . . . are ya?"

When he tossed the match, it seemed like it took minutes for it to land square into Momma's best rosebush. It lit up like fireworks, crackling and popping and sending sparks every which way. Everything went crazy then, with shouts and curses and gunshots.

Gunshots . . . only part of me realized that I'd shot that gun again. I could vaguely hear Gemma scream and the men shout out in voices that were mixed with anger and fear, but all I could see were the flames that had begun to lick at the porch.

As the men started to crowd into their trucks, I gathered a bit of sense, at least enough to get out of Gemma's way. Once she'd been released from the grip of the coward who was the first to run from the fire, she'd sprung into action, grabbing the rug from the porch and smacking it over the flower beds. I could only watch her work, my legs glued in place. The gun dropped from my hands, clattering down the porch steps, but I hardly noticed. It was like I wasn't even really there.

"Get some water, Jessie," Gemma yelled. "Go quick!"

Her voice gave me enough of a jolt to send me staggering into the house for Momma's mopping pail. I filled it with water and rushed back outside to dump it on Momma's flowers. Gemma had put out most of the fire with the rug, but the flames had started to spread to the stairway on one side. On my way back up the stairway to get more water, the flames licked at my legs and I heard Gemma scream again.

"What?" I called back.

"You're on fire."

I fell onto the porch in a panic, realizing for the first time the burning that had crept up my left leg.

Gemma ran onto the porch and put the flames out by smacking me all over, even places that weren't singed. After she was done with me, she finished off the last of the fire and then came back to lean over me. "You okay? Jessie! You okay?"

"Think so," I answered slowly. I pulled my charred pant leg up and peered at my skin, which was pink and had fewer hairs than before. "Don't look too serious. There ain't no blisters or nothin'. It'll be okay."

Gemma got up and soaked a rag with water, coming back

to place it on my leg. I held the rag onto the sorest spot and laid my head on one knee.

Gemma sat on her heels and shook her head. "Don't make no sense," she muttered tearfully. "It just don't make no sense."

"What don't?"

"People! Doin' things like this . . . it don't make no sense."

"Accordin' to my daddy, all kinds of people don't make no sense. Ol' Walt Blevins . . . he's just a mean ol' cuss who don't like nobody or no thing."

"He'd have burnt down your daddy's house if you hadn't shot 'im."

My heart started to race even harder when she spoke those words, bringing back all the fear I'd had once I heard the report of that gunshot. "We'd better get out of here," I said suddenly.

"What for?"

"They'll get the law on me. I don't want to go to jail!"

"Why would they get the law on you, Jessie? They's breakin' the law by doin' what they done. Ain't no criminal gonna turn himself in to turn somebody else in."

"Ain't no tellin'," I cried, getting up quickly. Putting weight on the leg made me realize that it hurt worse than I'd thought, but I steadied myself by clutching the porch rail.

"Where you gonna go this time of night? It might be more dangerous to go runnin' about in the woods."

I didn't have a chance to argue because Daddy's truck

rolled up fast as lightning, and Momma and Daddy jumped out.

"Jessilyn," Daddy yelled when he saw me. "Jessilyn, you girls all right?"

I hugged my daddy hard when he caught up to me, and Momma gripped my shoulders from behind, crying. "Jessilyn, Jessilyn," she said over and over. "What happened here, baby?"

"It was Klan. They done burnt her," Gemma said. "They would've burnt the house down too if Jessie hadn't scared 'em off."

"Where'd they burn you? You okay? Oh, my baby . . . my baby!" Momma grabbed Daddy's arm and ordered, "You get this girl into the house. I'm callin' the doctor."

"Phone ain't workin'," Gemma told them. "They did somethin' to it."

Momma gasped and put her hands to her mouth, and Daddy's face tightened up so much I thought his jaw would pop. He scooped me up into his arms in one catlike motion. "I'll run into town and fetch him," he said in a voice I could tell he was fighting to restrain. "Won't take me long." On the way in, he stopped on the steps and looked Gemma square in the eye. "You okay?" he asked softly. "Did they hurt you?"

Gemma shook her head.

"She put out the fire, Daddy," I said. "All by herself."

"That's good thinkin', Gemma," Daddy bent over her a bit so she'd have to meet his gaze. "We're sure glad to have you with us," he said, his voice strained with emotion. "Don't you ever forget that, you hear?" Then, quick as he'd turned sentimental, he got all businesslike again and nodded toward the house. "Now, you get on inside. We'll have the doctor look at you too."

I could see Gemma was as touched by Daddy's words as a body could be. Tears stung at her eyes but she blinked them back. "I ain't hurt none."

"Well, we'll have him look at you even so."

Momma took my foot in her hand as though she had to be touching some part of me to make sure I was still alive. Her other hand was on Gemma's shoulder guiding her gently inside the house, the first touch of genuine warmth I'd seen her give Gemma since the day Daddy said she'd be staying with us.

When Daddy set me down on the couch and examined my leg, his face turned crimson. I'd never seen him so angry in my life, and I didn't want to see what he might do in a state like that.

"Sadie, you stay in here and tend to the girls while I go fetch the doc. Don't you open that door for nobody, you hear?" He took one glaring look out the big front window. "But first I'm goin' outside to take care of that sacrilegious thing in my front yard."

Daddy stormed out the front door, throwing it shut. I sat up as far as I could on the couch and stretched my neck to see out the window. I heard Daddy talking nicely to Duke as he untied him and patted him on the backside to send him away. Duke ran under the porch, where he always went to lick his wounds.

In the firelight, Daddy's face glowed with rage, and he stood still for a few moments, staring at that burning cross. Then he went to work putting out the flames. Once he was done, Daddy kicked at the smoldering cross until it fell hard and loud. He kept kicking after it was on the ground, and then he backed up and tripped over something near the steps. He leaned over and picked up the rifle, looking at it strangely.

Gemma was sitting on the floor beside me, and I lay back down on the sofa and caught her hand. "He knows. Don't you leave me."

"He knows what?"

"He knows I had that rifle. He just found it. Don't you leave me when he comes in here askin' questions."

"I ain't goin' nowhere. And anyway, he ought to be happy you saved us all."

It was nice to hear her say it that way, but I wasn't convinced that Daddy wasn't going to skin me alive. I waited with my eyes squeezed shut, praying I'd make it through the next few minutes.

Daddy came back inside, and my stomach turned somersaults, but he just walked on into the kitchen. I could hear the pantry door squeal as he opened it, and I knew he was checking to see if it was really his gun. Then he came back into the den, with Momma following, her box of supplies in hand. "Jessilyn," he said with confusion, "this my rifle that was layin' outside?"

I swallowed hard and found it impossible to say anything at first.

"Well?" he asked. "Is it?"

"Yes . . . yes'r."

"How'd it get there?"

I ducked my head and said quietly, "I used it."

Daddy got down on one knee in front of me, surprisingly calm, and asked, "You used it or you held it?"

"Used it," I whispered.

"What's she sayin'?" Momma cried. "Jessilyn, what've you done?"

"She done saved us; that's what she done," Gemma exclaimed. "They'd have burnt us with the house if she hadn't."

Daddy grabbed Momma's arm with his right hand and Gemma's with his left. "Everybody just wait," he ordered, and then he said to me, "Now you listen up good. Did you shoot somebody with this gun?"

I know my eyes must have been wide as saucers when I looked at him and said, "Yes'r."

Nobody spoke in that room for a good minute until Daddy said, "Who did you shoot?"

"Walt Blevins," I said. "He was one of 'em."

"Did you kill him?" Momma asked loudly.

"There ain't no dead body out in the yard that we could see," Gemma said. "But she hit him, sure enough."

"Where'd you hit him?" Daddy asked me.

"In the shoulder, I think. Least that's where I saw the blood on his robe."

Momma's head dropped, and she started mumbling things under her breath.

"You shoot anyone else?" Daddy asked.

"I don't know for sure."

Daddy emptied the leftover bullets, counting them aloud. "You shot three times. How'd you manage to shoot this thing three times?"

"Don't know," I said. "I just shot. I was scared they'd hurt us."

Momma was crying by this time, wailing about how the law would be on us.

"It was self-defense, Sadie," Daddy said. "The sheriff ain't gonna arrest a thirteen-year-old girl for protectin' herself." He got up and patted Gemma and me on the head. "I'll fetch the sheriff while I'm at it. You girls stay here with your momma."

I could see the shock in Gemma's face when she heard Daddy talk about my momma like she was her momma, but I was just as surprised when Momma took Gemma's hand. "I was so scared," she said to both of us. "So scared they'd hurt you girls." She wiped her wet eyes with the back of her other hand and said, "Oh, thank God you're safe. Thank You, God! Thank You, Jesus!"

That was when we all let the tears come, and the three of us huddled together on Momma's threadbare gold sofa, crying.

Sheriff Slater and Mr. Tinker, his deputy, drove up right after my daddy and Dr. Mabley. They and Daddy spent most of the first half hour talking and looking around outside. It wasn't until Dr. Mabley had dressed my leg and told us I'd gotten by pretty lucky that they came inside to talk to me and Gemma.

I did most of the talking, and I went through every bit of what I could remember about that night. Every now and again, Momma would groan about something I said, especially when I mentioned shooting the gun or repeated the awful words the men had said.

"You sayin' these men was Klan, Jessilyn?" Mr. Tinker asked. "Every one of 'em?"

"They was Klan. All of 'em. And I recognized one as Walt Blevins, like I said."

"You sure, now?" Sheriff Slater asked. "You sure that was Walt Blevins who got the first shot?"

"I knew it just by his voice, but he done took his hood off when I shot 'im. There's no doubt."

"The bullet hole in his shoulder ought to tell you somethin', Moe," Daddy told the sheriff. "Can't be too hard identifyin' a man that way."

"No . . . no, it can't be. Question will be who else might've taken a bullet. From what I hear from the girls, I can't tell if we have more injured men than we know of."

Daddy had been chewing on his pipe, but he took it and threw it hard against the fireplace, making me jump. Then he yelled, "It'd be better if they all took a bullet. It'd serve 'em right!"

"Harley!" Momma gasped.

Sheriff Slater put his hand on Daddy's shoulder and said, "Now, Harley, a man in your position has every reason to feel spittin' mad, but it won't do no good for you to go gettin' yourself into trouble by bein' rough. You just leave them boys to me and the law, you hear?"

"It'll all work out, Harley," Mr. Tinker said calmingly. "Don't you start frettin' your wife none by takin' things into your own hands."

Daddy shook his head. "Won't do much good to let the law do justice if the judge is Klan too."

The sheriff crossed his arms and nodded rapidly. "I'll watch out for it. I know who's who in this town's courts. Judge Riley's a good sort. Ain't no Klan connection with him, and he's even ruled on the side of Negroes before. I'll make sure Judge Riley gets the case, and he'll take care of Walt Blevins."

"What about the rest of 'em? You heard Jessilyn say that there was another one plannin' to burn the place down after she shot Blevins."

"Well, we may not be able to track 'em all down, but Walt's likely the ringleader. Once he's out of the picture, things'll settle down. You wait and see."

"We'll take care of 'em in court, Harley," Mr. Tinker said.

"I don't want my girls testifyin' in court," Daddy insisted. "I teach mine all about standin' up for what's right, but there ain't no way I'm makin' these girls tell their story to a jury full of Klan-sympathizin' white men who'll just let Walt walk away to do more harm. Besides that, they might start tryin' to get after Jessilyn for shootin' that gun. It ain't like we're the most popular people in town these days. Ain't unlikely they'd be happy to blame us for somethin' else." He shook his head adamantly. "No sir! It ain't gonna happen."

"But we can tell 'em–," I began.

He cut me off. "There are things you don't understand, Jessilyn. That's why you got a momma and daddy to help you make decisions, and I'm makin' this one. There ain't gonna be no testifyin' in court."

The sheriff was visibly upset, but he could see that Daddy's mind was made up and he wouldn't be changing it tonight.

Daddy and Momma showed the men out, and I lay back and closed my eyes, holding on to Gemma's hand. "They'll just let Walt go," I said in a frightened whisper. "He ain't gonna pay at all for what he done."

"Your daddy's right," Gemma muttered. "Ain't no way a white jury would convict Walt of anythin' against a white family who took in a colored girl. Folks around here think that's a mortal sin. They'd figure we all got what we deserved." She looked down at her skirt and let two tears drip down and soak into it. "Seems I ain't done nothin' but bring trouble around here."

"Don't you go sayin' that!" I said, sitting upright in a hurry. "Don't you never go sayin' that. You heard my daddy tellin' you we're glad to have you here, and there ain't nobody–no

Walt Blevins, no hooded men—nobody who's goin' to change that. It's what we think that matters, and what we think is that you belong with us. And with us is where you'll stay." Gemma had her face turned aside, and I grabbed it, forcing her to look at me. "You hear, Gemma Teague? It's here you're stayin'."

She nodded slowly, her tears making tracks from her eyelashes to her chin, and then she threw her arms around me. We clung to each other for a while, and I could tell Momma purposefully puttered around the kitchen longer than she needed to so Gemma and I could have our time alone.

"Gemma?" I whispered after a few minutes of silence.

"Huh?"

"Thanks for savin' my leg."

"Thanks for savin' our lives," she whispered back.

She set her head down on the sofa beside me, and I rolled my head over so our foreheads were touching. It felt special, that bond between the two of us. We'd faced death together, and I figured we couldn't have had anything happen that would have made us see each other as any more important.

We couldn't have been closer if we'd been blood sisters.

Chapter 11

As it turned out, Walt Blevins was wanted in Coopersville for an assault, and by good fortune he was arrested there just a day after our ordeal. Daddy told me and Gemma that he and Sheriff Slater had agreed to keep the shooting a secret.

"We agree it'd do no good for it to get out if it don't have to, all this trouble," Daddy said. "If Walt's goin' to jail anyhow, ain't no need for anyone else to know what's gone on here, you see?"

"But won't people hear about it?" I asked. "This town ain't good at keepin' secrets."

"There ain't no one more used to keepin' secrets than them Klan boys," Daddy answered. "Them cowards don't want no one knowin' who they are. We'll tell Luke, but he'll be the only one, you hear? The doc's agreed to keep his peace, and Sheriff Slater and Mr. Tinker are the only other ones who'll know anythin'."

It all seemed to be tied up with a bow. Walt was gone, the Klansmen were quiet not wanting to incriminate themselves, and we Lassiters kept our traps shut. We agreed that if anyone asked, we'd say I burnt my leg on the tractor, but I figured it unlikely anyone would ask, anyway.

The evening after the incident, I was sitting on the porch when Luke came by for supper. I had my injured leg propped up on the railing, and I watched him over the bandages as he flew across our driveway. "What're you doin'?" I called. "Dinner ain't even ready yet and you're runnin' like a jackrabbit."

He skidded to a stop right in front of the porch and whipped his hat off. "Don't no one think I ought to know about things when they happen?"

"What're you yellin' about?"

"That," he said, pointing at my leg. Then he looked at the singed grass in our yard and waved his arm at it, saying, "And that! You just about get your place burnt to ash, and you girls about get killed, and you don't say nothin' to me?"

Daddy came out of the house then and said, "Now, Luke, I was gonna tell ya—"

"It's a little late. I had to go and find out from Sheriff Slater. Ran into him at the pharmacy, and he says, 'Well then, Luke, what do you think of all that trouble out at the Lassiter place?' And I'm left sayin', 'What trouble?' like I'm some sort of stranger or somethin'."

"We're all fine and good," Daddy said. "Everyone's alive and well, and Jessie'll be back on both feet in no time."

"I knew that boy was trouble. I knew it!" Luke walked

one way across the yard and then another, like a nervous squirrel, before he turned back to us and said, "Animals like Walt Blevins ain't fit to live; you know that? They ain't fit to live."

"Seein' as how I figured you might feel that way, I thought I'd let you know after things had calmed down a bit," Daddy told him. "We don't need you goin' and gettin' yourself in trouble by causin' violence. The sheriff had to tell me the same thing last night."

Luke put his head down and took a long, deep breath.

Daddy rested a hand on his shoulder. "Son, I appreciate you carin' for my girls. I just don't want you gettin' in trouble over it, you hear?"

Daddy headed inside the house, and Luke came up onto the porch to sit in the rocking chair next to me. He rocked back and forth for a couple minutes before he nodded at my leg and asked, "It hurt?"

"A little."

Then he rocked some more before saying, "Gemma okay?"

"Suppose so. She's helpin' Momma with supper."

That was the way all our conversation went that night. No one said much more than five words at a time. No one ate much either, even Luke, who could usually eat more than me, Momma, and Gemma combined. It was like the events of the day before had soured everyone's stomachs.

For me, it had started to change the way I saw life and the people in it. I'd known that some of the colored people in town had been harassed by white men who didn't think colored people should be treated the same as white people. Gemma had a friend who didn't have a daddy, and she had once told me that he'd been hanged for talking back to a white man. But now it was happening to me, and I had no choice but to look the evil of it full in the face. Some people were full of hate, and I was going to have to accept that for what it was.

Once I'd told my momma that I hated Buddy Pernell, and she'd taken a switch to my backside, saying, "There ain't no worse thing to say about a body than that you hate them. It's like tellin' them to go to the devil."

When I was nine, that didn't mean much to me, because sending a mean boy to the devil didn't seem anything but good. But once I saw the hate in Walt Blevins's eyes and heard it in the voices of those men, I started to realize the point of Momma's words a little more. I didn't like the way it felt to be hated, and if being attacked by those men was anything like being sent to the devil, I didn't want any part of that either.

A few days after that devastating night, Gemma and I were out for a walk through the backwoods on our property, the one place we knew had shelter from the scorching sun, when Buddy Pernell leapt out at us from behind a tree. We jumped a mile and screamed, setting him into a chorus of laughter.

I flashed him a sore look. He was one of the last people on earth I wanted to see, and all I could think of was his drunken breath on my neck on Independence Day.

"You think you're so funny, Buddy Pernell," I said angrily.

"I swear you girls looked like you'd seen a ghost."

"We don't believe in ghosts," I shot back.

"You'd best have if you're goin' walkin' through these woods. This here's Cy Fuller's property you're on now."

"No, it ain't. It's my daddy's."

"Not if you cross over the creek there. You do that and you're on Cy Fuller's property. Can't never tell when you'll run across his ghost takin' a stroll through these here dark woods."

"What're you talkin' about Mr. Fuller's ghost?" Gemma asked. "Man's got to be dead before you can start makin' up ghost stories about him."

"Ain't you heard?" He looked around as though he was making sure no one was listening, and then he gave us a wide, mischievous grin. "He *is* dead."

"Buddy Pernell, you tell the dumbest stories a girl ever heard," I argued.

"You think I'm lyin'? Go ask the sheriff. Better yet, head on over to Cy's meadow and take a look at the search party they got goin' on over there."

Cy Fuller spent most of his time on the bottle and owned about fifteen dogs that loved to holler at night and wake me up. I didn't like him one bit, but he had a nice little girl named Missy, who was as shy as a mouse and never said much. I suppose that's why I thought she was nice, because I talked so much that anyone who would listen to me made me happy. I didn't much like the idea of her losing her daddy, even if I didn't like the man.

"You're lyin'," I argued. "Cy Fuller ain't dead."

"You ask anyone. They done found blood all over his back property, and ain't no one seen 'im since Sunday."

It was the mention of Sunday that got my heart racing and made my hairs stand on end. Ever since that night I'd wondered about what might have happened in the chaos that had followed those last two gunshots. In the dark, with the smoke and shouting, I couldn't see a thing, and all I could hear was a ringing in my ears. There was no telling what I'd done. For all I knew, I was a murderer.

Daddy had scolded me when I'd mentioned that to him. "You ain't killed no one, Jessilyn. Don't you worry none about things like that. You did what you had to do, and you scared 'em off. Ain't nothin' more to it than that."

But I hadn't been so sure, and now, hearing about Cy Fuller, my fears started to flood back. I had no doubt that Cy Fuller could have been one of those hooded men, as I had no doubt that I could have killed him with my daddy's rifle without knowing it. I figured it was possible that he'd struggled home from our place only to meet his death just a piece from his house.

The first thing I wanted to do was go right over to the

Fullers' property. Gemma squeezed my hand to stop me, saying, "You can't go there. What if someone sees you?"

"I ain't gonna do nothin' to be seen. I just want to prove Buddy wrong, is all." I gulped twice and kept my face turned toward Gemma so Buddy couldn't see how scared I really was.

"What's to see?"

"More'n you think," Buddy said. "I'm tellin' you, the man's dead."

I stared hard at Gemma and told her without words just how much I needed to go see that place for myself. She returned my gaze for several seconds before dropping her head with a sigh. "Fine," she agreed. "But if there's trouble, you got to promise me we'll hightail it good and quick."

I promised her, and the two of us followed Buddy through the woods, ducking under the brush and branches he let snap back in our faces. Gemma had a grip on my hand, and I knew if I failed to keep my promise to run from trouble she'd find some way to haul me off bodily.

When we got there, we found the place crowded with the sheriff, some of his men, and townsfolk who had volunteered to search the property.

"Told you so," Buddy whispered, his face buried in a pine bough.

"You said he was dead," Gemma told him. "But that looks like a searchin' party."

"Well, they ain't found him yet, but you can bet he's good enough dead. They'll turn him up soon." We stood in the woods, hoping for some information, but didn't see much outside of a lot of men walking back and forth with their arms locked together, shouting things at each other across the fields. As boring as it was, we watched with wide eyes, barely moving.

After an hour Buddy gave up watching. "I got better things to do," he said with a yawn. "You girls stay if you want to, but I'm tellin' you, the man's gonna turn up dead." He leaned down and put his lips to my ear. "They say the dead like walkin' best at sundown," he said in an eerie voice. "Best be gettin' home before too long or Cy Fuller will get ya."

I shoved at him with one hand and kept my eyes glued to the ordeal past the tree line.

"Let's go too, Jessie," Gemma begged when Buddy left us behind. "There ain't nothin' to see."

But I ignored her. I was transfixed by the fear that those men would any minute prove me a murderer.

Gemma kept complaining at me about every five minutes until I finally gave up wearily. "Fine. Let's go. But I ain't never gonna be able to sleep again till I find out if I killed Cy Fuller."

"Jessie, you ain't *killed* Cy Fuller," Gemma said, whispering that terrible word.

"How do you know?"

"I know 'cause I know." She stood there staring at me with her hands on her hips like my momma would do, and I could tell she expected that her words should be the end of my worrying.

I nodded to make her think I agreed, but I didn't. And as we walked back home, I figured she knew I didn't, but she didn't say anything. Neither of us said a word that whole time, and I went straight to my room and stayed there. I'd told Gemma to tell Momma I wasn't feeling good, and when she told me she wasn't going to lie for me, I said, "It ain't lyin'. I feel sick in my gut."

"Luke's gonna be here," she tried. "Ain't that a reason to come on down?"

"I can't look at him now. He ain't never gonna love a murderer."

Gemma marched out of the room in a huff. I had an awful feeling I wouldn't be eating for a while.

The days that followed were a misery. Rumors were all around town about what happened to Cy Fuller, and everyone had their own theory about it. Some people were saying he'd been shot over his moonshine business; others said he'd been beat up over some gambling debts. The method of death changed with each story, but the idea that he was dead never changed. Everyone assumed the same thing—that he'd been killed and dragged away to a hasty grave somewhere in the acres of woods around his house.

Because of that, Cy's property continued to swarm with men and dogs, a sort of makeshift hunting party, except they were hunting for a corpse. Sheriff Slater had his team out there for four days before he gave up. He stopped by our place at the end of his search and had a talk with Daddy. I watched them from my bedroom window, unable to hear a word, but I had a pretty good idea what they were saying.

The feeling around our house was that we were thinking the same thing, but no one wanted to say a word about it. I knew I didn't want to. I moped around feeling like the loneliest person in the world. After all, I was the only person I knew of who thought she might have killed a man.

That week, Daddy hired a new hand, figuring that he needed to be around the house more to keep an eye on things. Jeb Carter seemed a good sort, kind of quiet and shy, and he mostly kept to himself. I liked him a lot from the start. Just the way he smiled at me made me trust him. We had some other farmhands, but none of them paid much attention to the family. They only worked for us. But Jeb . . . he was different. He and I seemed to have something that made us like each other.

"What're you doin'?" I asked him on his second day as he sat on a tree stump taking a midday break. "Whittlin'?"

"Makin' me a bird call."

"What for?"

"Like watchin' birds."

"Oh." I sat down on the grass and picked a leftover dandelion, blowing the white tufts into the breeze. I looked at Jeb with one eyebrow cocked, wondering at his short way with words. He never seemed to speak full sentences. "Which birds you like?"

"All kinds."

I blew another dandelion and asked, "You like workin' the farm?"

"Just like workin'. Don't matter what kind."

"You like workin'?" I asked in surprise. "What kind of person likes workin'? Most people only do it 'cause they have to."

"Workin' keeps the mind busy."

"So you like keepin' your mind busy?"

"A busy mind," he said with a short nod, "quiets bad memories."

I wanted more than anything to ask him what his bad memories were, but I could see by his face that he didn't want to talk anymore, so I just sat there watching him whittle. After several minutes of silence, I got up and brushed the dried grass from my backside. "Guess I'll see you later."

Jeb reached his dirty hand out and handed me the bird call.

"Want me to keep it for you till you're done workin'?" I asked.

"Want you to keep it for good."

"Keep it? I thought you were makin' it for yourself 'cause you like birds."

"I'll make another one."

I studied it for a minute before asking, "You sure?"

"I'm sure." Then he walked off without another word, grabbing his gloves on his way.

I called after him, "Thank you!" but he kept walking without turning around.

Those were the kinds of things Jeb did all the time, I would find. He liked helping people, but he didn't like getting attention for it. So I'd always just accept his kindness, give him a quiet thank-you, and leave.

I especially enjoyed my visits with Jeb because we didn't have many visitors anymore, and life on the farm was getting good and boring. Daddy told us it would last for only a little while longer. He thought once some time had passed, people would get used to us having Gemma, and life would get easier. But from what I'd seen recently, it seemed that hard hearts had long memories.

For the first time in my life, I wasn't so sure my daddy was right.

Luke didn't trust Jeb from the start, I could tell. After our trouble with the Klan, he started hanging around our house every day after work, and he'd watch Jeb from the porch with a suspicious eye.

"What you got against Jeb?" I asked him one day.

"Ain't got nothin' against him."

I hopped onto the porch rail and tucked my knees under

my chin. "You're lyin'. You watch him like Duke watches a squirrel."

"You imagine things," Luke told me around the piece of tall grass he was chewing thoughtfully, but his eyes never left Jeb.

"Then how come you can't look at me instead of Jeb?"

He just kept rocking in his chair, stewing.

"I said why can't you stop watchin' Jeb? You listenin' to me?"

Luke stopped rocking, pulled the grass from his mouth, and looked at me with extra-wide eyes. "There! I'm lookin' at you. You happy now?"

I rolled my eyes and hopped down from the rail.

"Where you goin'?" Luke asked as I walked down the steps.

"To talk to Jeb."

"What for?"

"'Cause I like him, that's what for. What're you so worked up about?" I asked wryly, my eyes squinted to avoid the late afternoon sun. "You ain't got nothin' against him, remember?"

Luke sighed loudly enough for the neighbors to hear and got out of the rickety rocking chair so hard it slid back against the house.

"Where you goin'?" I asked.

"With you."

"I ain't goin' into town or nothin'. I'm just walkin' over to the meadow."

"So?"

"So you don't need to follow me everywhere." I watched as his mouth curved down into a frown, and I hoped my argument didn't really change his mind. I may have talked like he was being ridiculous, but I wanted him to come with me all the same. I wanted him going everywhere with me.

To my pleasure, he threw the piece of grass to the ground and said, "Ain't no law against a man walkin' through meadows, is there?"

I shrugged like I didn't care, but there was a mile-wide smile on my face when I turned back around.

Jeb was busy sharpening some tools when we came upon him, but he stopped and looked up at us. "Hey there, Miss Jessilyn. . . . Talley," he said to Luke with a nod. "Doin' fine?"

"Gettin' by," Luke replied curtly.

"I'm doin' just fine too," I said quickly to talk over Luke's harsh tone. "You look hot there, Jeb. You need some lemonade or somethin'?"

"Naw, I done got me a big old jug of water over there by the shed. That'll do me just fine."

Luke sauntered around the shed, studying the area like a detective, taking time now and again to peer sideways at Jeb.

Jeb watched him for a minute until I asked him, "Ain't you 'bout done with work today? It's gettin' late."

"I wanted to get these tools taken care of tonight so I can use them in the mornin'. Like to get started right off tomorrow." He wiped his hands on an old rag and then wiped his forehead with it too. "Guess I'm through now."

I glanced over my shoulder as a shadow came up behind me and saw Luke strutting toward us with his hands on his hips. "You been rummagin' in that shed there?" he asked Jeb.

"Just gettin' out the tools I needed to work on."

"Uh-huh." Luke eyed those tools and kept nodding methodically. "You know anythin' about that hole under the shed, Jeb?"

"Hole?" I asked. "What hole?"

"There's a big ol' hole there," he said, pointing toward the far end of the shed.

I went over and stuck my right foot down into it, wiggling my toes around. "Must've been Duke lookin' for somethin' again."

"Don't know," Luke said. "Maybe a person's been diggin' there."

"Diggin' for what?" I spluttered. "Last I heard we ain't got treasure buried on Lassiter property."

"I ain't talkin' treasure. Maybe someone dug there to get into the shed. Your daddy locks it every evenin', you know."

I shoved my foot in as deep as it could go. "Luke, you know any midgets in these here parts that want to go breakin' into people's toolsheds? I can only just get my whole foot in that hole."

"You got big feet," Luke said. "Everyone knows that."

"They ain't big as a person," I shouted, pulling my foot from the hole. "You ain't got to tease me about my feet, anyhow. You can tease me about most things, but you ain't got call to tease me about my big feet or my freckles, you hear?"

"I don't think you got big feet, Miss Jessilyn," Jeb said. "They fit you just fine."

I bit my bottom lip and stared at Luke before saying, "Thank you, Jeb. Least someone round here knows how to say polite things to girls."

"I wasn't settin' out to tease you," Luke said without much sincerity. "I was tryin' to figure out why that hole's there." He came over to me and peered into the hole again. "Maybe someone's been tryin' to bury somethin' there."

"Like Duke," I said. "Dogs do things like that, ya know."

"Y'all never tie him up over here," he argued.

"We let him run around free durin' the day, Luke. He ain't never tied up till night so's he don't go chasin' raccoons."

He shook his head and then said to Jeb, "You sure you don't know nothin' about this here hole?"

"Nope. Ain't even noticed it." He got up and grabbed the shovel that was leaning against the shed. "I can fill it in for ya."

"No, no!" Luke fairly shouted. "No, I want Mr. Lassiter to see it first."

"What for?" I asked.

"'Cause I want to make sure it's safe."

"What could be unsafe about a hole under the shed?" I argued. "You lost your marbles?"

"Jessilyn, I know danger. I done got a sixth sense about such things. What if someone was tryin' to bury weapons or somethin'?"

"Weapons?" I repeated. "Weapons?" I started laughing. "We ain't at war. Ain't you been keepin' up with the papers?"

"I ain't talkin' about war spies. I'm talkin' about Klan." He studied Jeb. "You know anythin' about the Klan?"

Jeb set the shovel down and brushed his hands against his dirty dungarees. "Can't say as I know more than most. I tend to stay clear of men like that."

"Do you now?"

"That I do."

The two of them stood there staring at one another like they were in a duel, and I threw my hands up in disgust. "This is the dumbest thing I've ever seen." I went over and picked up the shovel and started digging in the hole.

"Jessie, put that down," Luke shouted when he finally tore his eyes away from Jeb to check on me. "That might be dangerous!"

But by that time, I'd gotten enough dirt out to hit something hard with a clang. I dropped to my knees and reached into the hole with Luke yelling at me to stay away. "You want some explosives to blow your arm off?" he asked when he reached me. He tugged at my shoulders, and I fell backward onto my backside in a puff of dust. "How do you know there wasn't somethin' down there that would hurt you?"

I held my hand above my head and said, "Like this old coffee can?"

Luke looked at the can for a minute. Then he took it from my hand, inspecting it. "Well, I'll be . . ."

"You'll be an idiot," I said. "Ain't nothin' but Duke buryin' like I done told ya."

"What's he buryin' coffee cans for?" Luke asked angrily, his pride hurting.

"Momma used to keep his biscuits in that can till it disappeared one day. I suppose he done run off with the biscuits and decided to bury the evidence." I got up and dusted my britches before handing the shovel to Jeb. "Think you wouldn't mind fillin' in that hole after all? Seems Luke's done a right fine job solvin' the mystery of the missin' dog biscuits."

Jeb nodded at me with a smile, and I set off toward the house, laughing.

Luke followed, and when I turned around to look at him, I could see that his face was bright red. I laughed at him again.

"Ain't so funny as you think," he retorted, but I just kept on laughing.

Once we reached the steps, we could hear Momma calling us from the kitchen.

"There's supper," I said to Luke. "You gonna taste my

food too? I mean, if someone's tryin' to kill me, they may just as well poison me as blow me up."

Luke opened the screen door for me but kept his gaze pointed toward the ceiling, and when he followed me in, the door slammed much louder than usual.

Daddy stopped dead in the hallway and looked at us strangely. "You tryin' to break my door off its hinges, son?"

"No, sir."

Daddy studied Luke for a second. "You sure you ain't sick or somethin'? You're red as a beet."

"Don't worry 'bout Luke none, Daddy," I said on my way to the kitchen. "He knows when there's danger about. He's got a sixth sense about such things."

Chapter 12

All I could hear was the constant patter of raindrops against the tin roof as I lay there on the sofa, reading the same paragraph of my book over and over again.

"Quit chewin' your nails," Gemma said from her place on the floor where she was working on her needlepoint. "It's a nasty habit."

"I'm nervous," I whispered.

"So am I, but that don't mean you should nibble your nails down to the nubs."

"But what if the sheriff came to arrest me?"

"He ain't gonna arrest you," Gemma said, exasperated. "He came here to talk to your daddy about Walt's trial, that's all. You heard 'im."

I tried reading the paragraph again, but I gave up and slammed the book shut.

Gemma startled at the noise. "Don't do that. You near about made me stick myself with this needle."

"Sorry," I muttered. "I can't sit here waitin' to see what's bein' said, is all. I'm too nervous!"

Gemma sighed and tossed her needlepoint into her basket. "I don't know why we're arguin' over this. You know you're gonna eavesdrop on your daddy, anyhow. Might as well get it done with."

I grinned. "Ain't as though you don't want to find out too," I told her, jumping up and grabbing her arm. "Come on!"

We didn't have a chance to eavesdrop, though, since we ran square into Daddy as he came back into the house. "Whoa! Where are you girls runnin' off to?"

"Nowhere," I lied. "We were just headin' into the kitchen."

"Uh-huh," he said, nodding slowly. "You weren't headin' to the porch to listen in or anythin'?"

Being pretty bad liars, Gemma and I just stood there without a word.

Daddy smiled at us. "Weren't much to hear in an eavesdroppin'. All's he was here to say was that Walt's gonna be on trial startin' tomorrow for assaultin' a man and that I could come witness it if I like."

"You gonna go?" I asked.

"Don't know yet."

"I want to."

"Jessilyn, ain't nothin' but borin' stuff in a courtroom. You wouldn't want to sit still an' listen to all that. It ain't got nothin' to do with you, anyhow."

"Maybe not the assault, but Walt does. And if he don't go to jail, he might come back and try to hurt us again."

He took my shoulders in his calloused hands. "Ain't no one gonna hurt you again if I have any say in it. And I do. So you ain't got to worry none about Walt Blevins. You head on upstairs now and forget all about it. It's gettin' late."

I obeyed him reluctantly, with Gemma following me upstairs, but I couldn't get Walt's face out of my head. I didn't sleep a wink that night, and I was awake and dressed at dawn.

Around six thirty, Gemma rolled over and sleepily peered at me. "What're you doin'?"

"Nothin'."

"It's barely mornin', and you're sittin' there all dressed up and starin' out the window." Then she sat up like a shot and said, "Oh no you don't! You ain't doin' it!"

"I ain't doin' nothin'. Go back to sleep."

"You're plannin' to sneak off to that trial, ain't you?" She sat and stared at me, but I didn't say a word. "Well . . . ain't you?"

I hopped off the stool I was sitting on and smacked my head against the sloped ceiling. "Now see what you made me do?" I hissed at her with a grimace. "I done gone and given myself a concussion."

"That would make sense since you're actin' like you got a bad head."

"I already told you I ain't goin' nowhere."

"You're sittin' there just waitin' for your daddy to leave, and I know it. Don't you go tryin' to fool me. You ain't never fooled me before, and you ain't gonna start now."

I hesitated before saying, "So what if I am plannin' to go? Ain't no reason for me not to. I ain't no little girl no more."

"I'll give you a good reason not to. Your daddy done told you not to, and your daddy ain't one to be crossed."

"Well, Daddy ain't got no reason to know about it unless you tell him." I watched her for a minute and tapped a finger against one of my front teeth. "You ain't gonna tell him, are you?"

I could see Gemma's thoughts run across her face until finally she got out of bed and started getting dressed.

"What're you doin'?" I asked. "You gonna tell my daddy?"

"You're gonna go no matter what I say, so I'm gonna go with you." I smiled at her, but she frowned back at me and said, "Don't you go gettin' happy about this. I ain't doin' it for no reason other than to watch out for you."

She was mumbling all sorts of things under her breath while she dressed, saying things about how I was as stubborn as a mule and how my daddy was liable to tan my hide for sneaking out like this. I figured she was right about all of it, but it was the very stubbornness she was talking about that kept me from changing my mind.

Gemma and I crept downstairs, grabbed some corn muffins for breakfast, and went off to wait behind the aspen tree that Daddy parked his truck under.

Come seven o'clock, Daddy came walking out the front door, being careful not to let it slam too loudly and wake us. I felt bad at that moment for being so sneaky with him when he was trying to be nice to us, but it didn't do much to change my mind. Once he got into the truck and pulled the squeaky door shut, Gemma and I jumped into the bed under the tarp and hunkered down for the forty-minute ride into Coopersville.

As we drove along that early morning, Gemma and I tried to keep the tarp propped up so some air could get in, but we could do only so much without it threatening to puff up and block Daddy's back view. I had a good idea that if Daddy caught sight of that tarp billowing out, he'd get pretty suspicious, and every time I thought about Daddy finding us, my heart started to do cartwheels and somersaults at the same time. I knew his reaction wouldn't be good.

As far as my momma, I guessed she wouldn't suspect a thing because I had mentioned the night before that Gemma and I should head out early to do some berry picking before it got so hot. There was no telling what time we'd be back from Coopersville, but I was certain that Gemma and I would have to get some blackberries good and quick so as not to get Momma wondering. No doubt if we did, Momma would set right off to baking a pie and wouldn't bother asking us a single question about why we'd been so long at picking berries.

That ride was the worst of our lives. We didn't say a word to each other, but I could tell by her face that Gemma felt as bad as I did. The air was sweltering already that morning, which didn't surprise me much because it had never gotten a bit comfortable the night before. Sitting under that tarp was like sitting in a wet oven. The tarp kept the heat and humidity trapped around us, and every breath we took felt heavy and damp. All I could think was that it must be a glimpse into what hell was like.

By the time we got to that courthouse, sweat was pouring down my face and onto my blue dress. Gemma and I had worn our going-into-town clothes so as not to look conspicuous, but we didn't look too normal after almost an hour crumpled up under a sweaty tarp. Once we heard Daddy leave, we hopped out and stared at each other for a minute. Then Gemma said, "This is the dumbest thing you ever got us to do."

"I didn't make you come."

"You may as well have. You know I always watch out for you no matter how stupid you're bein'. The stupider you're bein', the more I have to watch out for you."

"In case you didn't know," I said defensively, "you ain't my momma."

Gemma held her dark brown hand up against my pale white one and said, "You ain't kiddin'!"

I rolled my eyes at her sarcasm and reached out to smack some dirt off her shoulder. "You look a sight."

"You ain't lookin' much better. Your momma's gonna cuss you for messin' up your blue dress."

I looked at myself in the window of Daddy's truck and sighed. I did look a sight, plain and simple. Gemma started brushing me off, grumbling at my foolishness, and I tried to straighten my braid out. There were dirty smudges across my nose and cheeks, and I used the underneath of my skirt to polish them away.

"Put your skirt down," Gemma hissed.

"Oh, hush! Ain't no one around to see my bloomers."

"There is too. There's people comin' for the trial."

I glanced around and saw that there were quite a few people coming, all dressed in their finest.

Gemma caught my arm and said, "We best go in the back way or someone will spot us."

"Ain't no one gonna know us here."

"Your daddy's here, ain't he? Besides, we're nothin' but children, and they might not let us in without an adult. We'll go in the back."

Her declaration didn't leave me much room to say anything, so I went with her around the building. We turned the corner, arm in arm, and found a stairway leading to the courthouse, but we weren't the only ones about to use that entrance. There was a group of colored people filing in quietly.

"Mornin', children," the oldest woman said to us.

Gemma and I looked at her only halfway, since we felt like fugitives that morning, and said, "Mornin', ma'am."

The other women smiled at us, two older men nodded, and the children climbed the stairs with their heads swiveled around, staring at us like we were ghosts.

One of the young men snorted and said, "Looks like the little white girl brought her slave along for the show."

"She ain't my slave," I shot back.

"Jody," the older woman yelled, "you watch that mouth of yours!"

"I ain't sayin' nothin', Gran," the young man said smartly. "I just ain't never seen white girls and their slaves holdin' hands before. Ain't no white girl that'd hold a colored girl's hand unless she was makin' sure not to let her run away."

Gemma's jaw tightened, and she walked forward, dragging me with her. "You see these hands?" she asked with vehemence. "One's dark and one's light, but they ain't shackled together."

"Jody," the grandmother yelled again, "I said shut that mouth of yours, and I mean shut it! You ain't got no right to go talkin' to those girls like that."

"Ain't got no right? It's white folks that done got my brother near killed, and I ain't gotta like seein' my own kind bound to a white girl."

The older woman walked back down the steps and seized her grandson by the ear, setting him to howling. "Your brother got hurt by a man, no matter his color, and just 'cause that one man is bad, it don't mean the rest of his kind is. You hear?" She shoved him with a force that belied her age and shouted, "Now, you get on in there. I said, get on in. You heard me!"

The grandmother stayed behind and took one of my hands and one of Gemma's. "Don't you pay no mind to that boy," she told us sweetly. "Mercy's sake! What's an old woman to do with a disrespectful boy like that? I'm bound to meet my Maker someday soon with that boy stirrin' things up all the time."

Her voice began to shake, and tears welled up in her eyes. "Jody, he's the one who always makes trouble. But his brother, Elijah. Now, he's the good one. It's him that was beat near to death by that Walt Blevins. He done near took the life right out of that boy." She took a handkerchief from her handbag, but she didn't use it. She just twisted it tight.

One of the older men came down the stairs, taking the woman by the shoulders. "Momma, don't go gettin' yourself upset again. Let's go in and set on down now."

She let him lead her in, but she was sniffling all the way.

Gemma and I didn't say a word as we watched her disappear into the courthouse. I don't think there were any words for that moment, anyway. We waited about a minute and then started into the building ourselves.

By the time we got inside, it was a packed house, both in the white section and in the colored section.

"Where we gonna sit?" Gemma wondered aloud. "Ain't no chairs left."

"We could sit on the floor somewhere."

Gemma took a long look around. "Then which section are we gonna sit on the floor in? The white or the colored? We ain't even, you and me."

"We'll sit in the white section, 'course."

"I'll be the only colored face in the crowd," Gemma

argued. "It'll stir up trouble, and your daddy would spot us, sure enough."

"Well, we can't sit with the coloreds. I'll stand out like a porcupine in a henhouse."

Gemma grabbed my hand and pulled me back outside to an alcove where a brick wall beneath a window housed rows of dahlias. "We can sit here. No one will spot us, but we'll be able to hear everything."

"I can't sit on a wall all through the trial," I snapped. "That rough brick will eat into my backside."

I could see Gemma didn't much care what I was worrying about, so I sat next to her on the bricks, puffing out a long sigh to make sure she knew I wasn't happy about it. Once I got myself organized, I realized we had one of the best seats in the house. The window was just off to the side of the jury box and covered by tipped-open shutters, providing a perfect view between the slats while keeping our curious faces obscured.

But I wasn't going to tell Gemma she'd been right after all.

There was no way for me to adequately arrange myself with that dress on, and I looked unladylike enough that Momma would have tanned my hide had she seen me. But I could better afford to be unladylike than miss the trial.

Walt Blevins sat at the very front looking as evil as ever, an arrogant grin pasted across his stubbly face. When I caught sight of him, the whole feeling of that night came back to me, and I felt like an army of ants was crawling down my spine. My hands were clasped tightly on my lap, and every time

I swallowed, I made a gulping noise, so by ten minutes in, I had started to swallow only when I began to drool.

Once the judge called the court to order, the first thing we heard about was exactly what had happened to Elijah Joel Baker. He had been beaten, kicked, and tied to a wagon and dragged. The doctors didn't even know if he would ever walk again. When the prosecutor held up photographs of Elijah after the assault, I was glad I couldn't see from where I was. Those who could see gasped and hid their eyes, men and women alike. It was a horrible thing what had been done to that boy, just like his gran had said, and by the time we'd heard the whole story, Gemma and I were in tears like most others in the courtroom.

From that point on, Daddy's words about trials being boring mostly came true. There was a lot of stuff being said that I didn't understand. I supposed I wasn't the only one who felt that way since I could hear snoring somewhere in the building, and the man sitting behind Daddy kept bobbing his head up and down like he was trying his hardest to keep from nodding off.

As for me, I was busy counting the dots on my blue dress. It was only when Walt Blevins took the stand and put his grimy hand on the sacred Bible that I popped my head back up. I thought it was a shame that a man like Walt should ever swear on anything that had to do with God, and I knew he'd lie even if he swore on his own momma's grave. I figured that a man who didn't know who God was wouldn't care so much breaking an oath to Him.

"Mr. Blevins," the prosecutor said, "do you recall the events of June fifteenth, nineteen hundred and thirty-two?"

Walt leaned back in his chair, rubbing his chin like he was hard in thought. "Well now, that was more'n a month back. Maybe you'd better narrow it down for me."

The prosecutor sighed and looked at Walt over the glasses he had perched on his nose. "Let's start with seven thirty that evenin', shall we?"

"Seven thirty," Walt muttered. "Let me see . . . that was a long time ago. Can't say as I recall what I was up to. Seven thirty . . . I was probably gettin' me some supper over at Ed's grill."

"That's what you've said before," the prosecutor said while studying a stack of papers. "Thing is, no one at Ed's remembers seein' you that night until nine o'clock. Not even old Ed himself." He faced the jury of white men and said, "Now, you boys know Ed. He knows every face that comes in and out of that grill of his." Then he turned back to Walt to say, "And Ed don't remember seein' hide nor hair of you till nine o'clock."

Walt shrugged. "Can't say as I hold much stock in people's memories."

"Yes, but the courts do, Mr. Blevins. It's called witness testimony, and we have quite a few of those who recall seein' you that night after nine. In contrast, we have absolutely no witnesses who can account for you bein' there at seven thirty."

"Maybe I don't stand out in a crowd," Walt replied. "You got somethin' else to talk to me about?"

"As a matter of fact," the prosecutor said, "I do. Would you mind tellin' the court why you were even in Coopersville that night? Because my records show that you've been a resident of Calloway for over fifteen years. Isn't that so?"

"That's right."

"So then, why were you in Coopersville?"

"Seein' friends is all. There a law against seein' friends? Do I need to get a permit or somethin'?"

"And these friends of yours . . . who were they?"

"Mr. Frank Beauman and his son, Frank Jr. They'll tell you I was here to visit them."

"That they have. No doubt. Problem is, they don't seem to know much about that night either. Seems like they lost their memories too. But then, Mr. Beauman and his son were seen, along with yourself, crossing the railroad tracks over Beaver Creek just before seven thirty on June 15. So are you sayin' that you don't remember bein' at the tracks on Beaver Creek?"

"Didn't even know there was tracks over Beaver Creek. Heck, I didn't even know there was a Beaver Creek!"

Laughter filled the courtroom, but the prosecutor went on. "Are you also sayin' that it makes sense for you and Frank and Frank Jr. to all forget what you were up to on the evening of June 15?"

"Well, old Frank . . . he's known for takin' some of that homemade whiskey of his," Walt said with a laugh, tilting his head back like he was taking a gulp of something.

The people in the courtroom laughed again at his words, but I couldn't manage to smile over anything Walt said.

169

"And Frank Jr.," he continued, "he ain't never been the brightest bulb in the closet. They's probably not the best ones to ask about . . . what'd you call it . . . witness testimony?"

The prosecutor scratched his head dramatically. "Well now, that's a funny thing about this case. For one reason or another, not one person remembers where you were at seven thirty that night." He paused, laying a finger across his pursed lips. "Except . . . ," he said, holding that same finger up in the air, "except for one man. Mr. Elijah Joel Baker. This man," the prosecutor declared, raising a photograph of a wounded Elijah. "This man knows who did this to him. He knows who beat him and kicked him, who instructed two other men to tie him up and drag him behind a horse-led wagon. He clearly remembers that face because he stared at it through swollen eyes while he was being tied to a tree in front of his grandmother's home, leaving her to find him battered and bloodied, unable to move and barely able to breathe."

My heart raced faster as that man's voice rose. It was like a preacher's hellfire-and-brimstone sermon, with him standing on his toes the way he was. I was mesmerized by his speech.

But the judge stopped him suddenly with a rap of his gavel after Walt's attorney stood to object. "That's enough," the judge said. "If you have a question, Counselor, please get to it."

The prosecutor tossed his papers onto the table behind him. "I don't have any more questions for this man, Your Honor. There's no point in asking questions of a man who seems to have so conveniently lost his memory."

The judge asked Walt's attorney if he had any questions for Walt.

The man stood stiffly. "Yes, Your Honor. In fact, I do."

I disliked the man instinctively as I watched him stand in front of the big oak table. He was dressed in an ugly brown suit with a tie that wasn't done up right, what little hair he had left combed crookedly to one side.

"Mr. Blevins," the attorney said, "did you assault Elijah Joel Baker on June 15 of this year?"

"No, sir," Walt said lazily. "I did not."

The attorney smiled arrogantly and sat back down. "No further questions."

I sat there with my hands squeezed so tightly together they were numb, and I couldn't believe that was all that would be asked of Walt.

The trial continued for another two hours or so, and by the time the judge handed things over to the jury, I was sure Walt would be found guilty. With testimonies and mounds of evidence, including a signed statement from Elijah Baker, the prosecutor had put forth a very convincing case.

About half the people swarmed out of the courtroom once court recessed, and Gemma and I went off quickly to avoid seeing my daddy. We sat under a sprawling oak and munched on some leftover corn bread and a couple of apples a colored woman had kindly offered us.

"Gemma," I said thoughtfully, "think he'll pay for what he done?"

A colored woman nearby answered for her. "Ain't no way he'll pay," she said with a sniff.

I turned around and leaned my chin on my shoulder. "Why do you say that?"

"You take a good look at that jury?" she asked.

"'Course I did."

"What'd you see they have in common?"

I stared at her, puzzled. "What do you mean?"

"Didn't they all look alike to you?"

"They's just a bunch of men," I said. "So?"

"She's tryin' to tell you that a jury of white men won't never condemn a white man for hurtin' a colored one." Gemma shook her head. "But there ain't no reason to bunch all white people in together."

"Girl," the lady behind us said, "you done fooled yourself if you think white people ain't all alike. Just 'cause your little friend here's white, don't you start thinkin' you'll be seen any different. White's white and colored's colored. The two just don't mix."

"That's 'cause people won't let them. It's people's thinkin' that's the trouble, not their color." Gemma took my hand in hers and tugged at me. "Don't you listen none to her. Maybe justice'll be done; maybe it won't. But I ain't gonna lump everyone in together. You and me . . . we'll just wait and see what happens for ourselves."

I turned around, but it didn't keep me from hearing the lady behind me say, "Ain't no one got to wait for this verdict. They probably already got the newspaper report printed up."

Gemma and I didn't say much for the next hour. The lady didn't bother us anymore, but we could hear her and others around her talking in the same way she'd talked to us.

I was scared to death, worrying about what would happen if Walt didn't go to jail. "He'll come back for us," I whispered to Gemma. "If they let him go, he'll come back. And what if he knows something about Cy Fuller?" I sent my voice even lower so I could barely be heard and said, "If he knows I killed Cy, he might tell."

"You ain't killed him," she said angrily.

"But what if I did?"

"You didn't!"

"Gemma! If I did and Walt knows it, he might tell."

"What good would it do for him to tell anything about that night?" she asked. "It wouldn't do him no good to go stirrin' up trouble and tellin' tales on himself. You best quit worryin'. Ain't no good worryin' about things you can't do nothin' about. Only God knows what happened to Cy Fuller, and only God knows how to handle a man like Walt Blevins. It ain't for you to worry about."

But I was worried all the same. I tapped my feet and squirmed. Gemma tried to get me to eat the rest of the corn bread, but I could barely sit still, and I hopped up like a scared rabbit as soon as someone called out that the jury was back. I could barely get my wobbly legs to crawl onto the wall, and when I took my seat again, I had the worst feeling in the pit of my stomach. My head told me that there was no way Walt Blevins would walk out of that courtroom a free man, but my famous instincts told me differently.

As the jury filed back into their seats, I grabbed Gemma's hand. I could feel it shaking, and it made me ten times more nervous knowing that Gemma was scared too. The buzzing of chatter faded away as the judge returned, and barely a sound could be heard in the entire room.

Every now and again in life there are those moments when time actually seems to stand still. Those are the times when sounds echo in your ears, and people look like they're moving too slowly.

That was one of those times.

I wanted to look around the courtroom, but I couldn't. My eyes were stuck in one spot, staring straight ahead at the judge through wisps of smoke that curled up from the jury box. Throughout the trial, several men in the room had smoked cigarettes and cigars, the smoke floating out the window to tickle our noses. It wasn't until that moment, when my nerves were so raw, that I even noticed it, and I began to feel choked and breathless. My eyes watered, and I swallowed hard several times to keep from coughing.

The chairs of those in the sweltering room let out vague squeals as the people nervously shifted in them. Finally getting my eyes unlocked, I let them wander over to where Elijah's family sat, and I saw his grandmother rocking back and forth, her arms wrapped around her middle, whispered prayers coming from her lips. The tears that streamed down her face made my throat feel tight, and I flashed my eyes toward the front, afraid to watch her anymore.

Then the judge rendered the verdict. I couldn't hear him over the whooshing noise in my ears, so I leaned forward, but it didn't help. It felt like my ears had stopped working. I leaned forward even farther, almost falling into the window.

I never heard the verdict. . . . I saw it.

I saw my daddy's head drop, his shoulders slump. I saw Gemma's grip on my hand loosen and fall away. I saw Elijah's family collapse onto one another in anguish, shedding painful tears.

And I saw Walt Blevins's self-satisfied expression.

My stomach ached horribly, and my teeth chattered even though it was about a hundred degrees outside in the sun.

"We better get back to the truck before your daddy," I vaguely heard Gemma whisper. I let her haul me up, but then I stopped cold.

Walt Blevins got out of his chair, took a deep breath, and gazed out the window. I could have sworn he was staring straight at me. I had thought my daddy was the last person in the world I wanted to have see me at that trial, but Walt Blevins was far worse.

"Jessie," Gemma said, "what're you doin'?"

"He's starin' at me," I whispered, my voice breaking.

"Who? Your daddy?"

I shook my head slowly. "Walt."

"Don't be stupid! Ain't no one's gonna see us through them shutters."

"Then he can feel me. I swear his eyes are burnin' into my skull."

Gemma followed my gaze and then pulled at my arm good and hard. "Come on." When I hesitated, she cried, "I said come on!"

Gemma steered me toward the truck, through people moaning and crying, yelling and arguing. I tripped on a gnarled tree root and skinned my right knee on it, but she yanked me back up by my arm like Daddy did when I was little.

In the end, all that dragging did us no good, because we took the same route back to the truck as we'd taken into the courthouse, right past the front steps. Just as we rounded the corner, Walt Blevins came sauntering out ahead of a group of his supporters, and we nearly ran right into him.

He looked down at us with a sneer, lifting a hand almost as if he meant to swat us out of the way like pesky flies, but he stopped midway and stared. It took several seconds of quizzical inspection before it finally dawned on him who I was. "What're you doin' here, girl?" he snarled at me quietly. Then he looked over his shoulder as if checking for eavesdroppers and hissed, "You aimin' to stir up trouble?"

I remained quiet, but I didn't move even though Gemma was tugging at my sleeve desperately.

"I done asked you a question. You and this girl o' yours plannin' on doin' some cryin' to the law? 'Cause I'm a free man today, girl, and I won't be takin' kindly to any trouble-maker gettin' the law on me again."

The lawyer behind Walt put a hand on his shoulder and said, "We're in front of a courthouse. Don't you go startin' up trouble."

Walt slapped the man's hand from his shoulder. "Ain't got to tell me what to do no more, lawyer man. You done your job." Then he put one meaty finger under my chin and said, "Now you just let me go on and do mine."

The simple nearness of him made my skin crawl, but I couldn't move a muscle. It was as if my entire body was as afraid of Walt as my mind was.

Gemma didn't share my paralysis, though, and she smacked his hand away. "You get your filthy hands off her!"

That was all it took for Walt to send her flying with a backhand that was so quick I could barely see it coming. I found my voice and let out a shriek, but when I tried to run to Gemma, Walt grabbed my arm and twisted it behind me. Pain coursed through my shoulder, but within seconds I could hear a scuffle in front of me, people yelling and cursing. The grip on my arm suddenly released, and I fell to the ground, nauseated.

Without glancing up, I crawled over to where Gemma was lying, her dress covered in dirt, her mouth bloody. I tried to call her name, but it only came out in a loud whisper. "Gemma, are you awake? Say somethin'!" I shook her a couple times and screamed, "Gemma! Gemma!" before she finally rolled over slowly and moaned.

All I could do was lay my head down on her stomach and cry. What had developed around us was what my daddy called a riot. Through my tears I could see nothing but flying fists, tangled bodies, and sweat. The fists were colored as well as white, and they landed soundly with each punch. For once, though, I saw colored winning out over white. The anger over the injustice inside the courtroom had spilled out in violence, and the colored men swung their arms wildly, leaving Walt battered and bruised.

There was such chaos, you couldn't tell one person from the next, but I saw someone wade through that commotion, and I could tell him apart from first glance. My daddy came through that pile like he was cutting his way through a jungle, and besides the fact that I knew he'd be furious to find me there, I was more grateful to see him then than I ever had been.

He swooped down between the two of us and picked us both up at the same time, nearly dragging us to the truck. He didn't say a word. Instead he looked us over, inspecting us for injury, and when he was satisfied that our wounds were not severe, he ran back to the fight. "Break it up. Come on, now. Break it up!" He grabbed at any appendage he could get to, but I noticed that the only ones he tried to get hold of were colored. Finally one of the men stopped and looked at Daddy, and Daddy told him, "They're gonna get extra law here in no time. You want to go to jail?"

By that time, most of the white men involved had fallen to the ground, incapacitated, and several of the colored men gave my daddy their attention as they paused to wipe the sweat from their foreheads.

"We done got a right to get justice," one man said breathlessly. "Ain't no justice for us unless we make it ourselves."

"Ain't gonna be no justice for you in them courtrooms, neither," Daddy told him flatly. "You understand that? Just as easy as they let Walt go free, they'll lock you in irons for life. Or worse. Make no mistake!" He waved a hand wildly toward the road. "Now you best hightail it outta here before you catch trouble, ya hear? Scatter! All of you!"

Like usual, my daddy made enough sense to convince them, and they all started back to their women, who had been screaming after them the whole time.

I don't remember much of what happened after that. Once Daddy got back to the truck, Gemma and I about passed out in a daze. The only thing I do remember is that my daddy never mentioned it to us again. It seemed to me that he believed by rights he should punish us for sneaking around like that but didn't want to, so he thought if he never mentioned it we could just pretend it never happened. He must have gotten to Momma, because she never said a word either, and that just wasn't like Momma. Left on her own, she would have babied us until we were better and then laid into us until we wished we were sick again.

Even Luke never said a word, but he was more of a presence than he'd ever been before. From then on, when he wasn't working, he was like my shadow. To me, it couldn't get any better, but Gemma kept muttering things about how "that man should take up a hobby or somethin'." When she was with me, he was her shadow too, and she'd always go around telling him we didn't need him tagging along at our heels all the time.

I shushed her every time because I didn't want him getting ideas.

If Luke Talley was going to have a hobby, I figured following me around was the best he could get.

Chapter 13

Otis Tinker came by early the morning after the trial, toting a sack over his broad shoulder.

I ran out to meet him, happy to see a visitor to our forbidden farm. "Hey there, Mr. Otis. You comin' to see Daddy?"

"Well now, I might like that. But I actually came to see you, Miss Jessie." He set the bag down on the ground and pulled out a tiny gray kitten. "You know our cat, Tawny? She done gone and had herself a litter."

"Sure enough?"

"Sure enough, and we thought maybe you might like this one for yourself, if your momma and daddy don't mind." My face must have lit up with the excitement of having that kitten, because Mr. Tinker laughed at my expression. "I'm guessin' you'd like to have it."

"Unless Duke decides to make it supper," Daddy said as he came walking up behind me. He took his hat off and tossed it onto a nearby fence post. "How come your pets are always havin' babies, Otis? You got the most romantic property in Calloway."

"Can't keep an eye on 'em all the time, Harley."

The two men laughed, but once Daddy caught my expectant gaze, he turned serious. "You plan on takin' care of this here kitten?"

"Yes'r."

"Like you took care of the puppy that ran away?"

"He was too rowdy," I said in my defense. "And he liked chasin' after skunks. I wasn't gonna track him down when he was trackin' a skunk."

"What about the rabbit?"

"I didn't know those berries would make her sick."

"And the duck?"

"Daddy!"

Daddy smiled at me and asked, "Otis, why in the world do you keep bringin' them animals over here when my girl lets 'em run off or just up and kills 'em altogether?"

"Better'n havin' the missus tearin' into me because our place is crawlin' with animals."

"I see. So you think it best to fill my place instead."

Mr. Tinker grinned and patted the kitten on its fuzzy gray head. "You 'bout summed it up. Now, can the girl keep the old thing or do I have to drown it in the creek?"

"Daddy," I cried, "we can't let him drown the poor thing!"

Daddy shook his head. "Now you done it. You sure know how to put me in a bind, tellin' the girl you're gonna drown it and all."

"Well, I ain't gonna feed it. I got enough mouths to feed as it is."

"Like there ain't another family in all of Calloway that's in the market for a cat," Daddy muttered. But he took a good long look at me and said, "Well, if you promise to take good care of it . . ."

I jumped up and down happily and laid a kiss on Daddy's cheek. "Thank you, Daddy! Thank you, Mr. Otis!"

I ran off right away to show Gemma. "What d'ya think I should name him?" I asked her as I sat stroking the kitten's fur.

"Don't ask me. You're the creative one, always comin' up with nicknames and stories and such."

"What about Spot?"

"What in the world would you call it Spot for?"

"It's got spots, stupid!"

"So's near every other cat or dog in the world. And they's all called Spot. Can't you come up with somethin' new?"

I shot her a sharp look, but it did seem she was right. No kitten of mine should have a boring name. "How 'bout Paws?"

"How 'bout somethin' that don't have to do with how it looks?" Gemma chided.

"All right! And here I thought you didn't care none what I called it."

"You asked my opinion," she shot back, "so I gave it."

"Fine. Why don't we call it George."

"George?" she spluttered. Even the kitten looked annoyed by that choice, his ears pricking up like he'd been startled. "Who in God's green earth ever called a kitten George?"

"My granddaddy's name was George," I said defensively.

Gemma playfully dug her elbow into my rib. "You may as well just name the thing Luke."

"Can't name a kitten after Luke. What girl wants to name an animal after the man she's gonna marry? I go and do that, I'll feel all funny someday callin' my husband after my cat."

"Oh, go on. Talkin' of marryin' Luke again," Gemma said with a shake of her dark curls. "Like he sees you any different than his sister. And besides, I was just funnin' about namin' the cat Luke."

"Luke ain't nothin' to fun about," I said. "And it ain't for you to be decidin' who'll marry who, anyhow."

By this time, Gemma had gotten fed up with the entire kitten-naming process, so she lay back against a tree trunk and sighed, her arms folded over her chest like a corpse. I could see she was annoyed with me, and when she got like that, she stayed that way until she was good and ready to talk to me again. I knew it was no use fooling with her, so I wandered back to the fields where I'd seen Jeb in the tomatoes.

"Hey there, Miss Jessilyn," he said as I approached him with my new kitten.

"Hey there, Jeb."

"Whatcha got there?"

"New kitten. Mr. Otis gave him to me."

Jeb set his hoe down and leaned a sweaty arm on it, pushing the hoe into the dirt as the earth gave way under his weight. "You say Mr. Tinker's here?"

"Yes'r."

He nodded and said, "He bring you this here kitten?"

"Yes'r," I answered again.

Jeb stared at the kitten for a few seconds, and then he just said, "Huh" and went back to his hoeing.

I ignored his odd response and asked him if he had any good ideas for the kitten's name that didn't have to do with how the kitten looked and that weren't after a family member.

He didn't seem to quite understand me, and it was a good full minute of silence before he finally said, "Ain't never had me no pets. I figure a child what's got one is pretty lucky."

"S'pose so," I murmured, holding the cat up to my face so I could inspect him. His little pink tongue flashed out and caught the tip of my nose three times before I could move him away. "I suppose I am lucky." I looked at the cat and said, "I guess Lucky's as good a name for you as any. What do you think, Jeb?"

But Jeb had gone. He had the strangest way of slipping away without a body knowing, like a ghost. One minute he was there in front of you and then . . . *whoosh*! He was just gone. That was one more thing about Jeb that kept Luke from trusting him. He said that any man who was as stealthy as that had to have learned it from years of being sneaky. In Luke's mind, poor Jeb had been everything from a spy to a thief to a convict on the lam.

For my part, I didn't know what I thought Jeb was, but I trusted him nonetheless. I just had that gut feeling about him, and Daddy always told me to put stock in those gut feelings.

Daddy and I headed into town on a Wednesday in August, loaded with chores to take care of. These days we went into town so little, we had plenty of errands when we did. Gemma had a headache and Momma didn't want to go into town to put up with people's nonsense, so it was just the two of us, and I was happy. It gave me a chance to have all of Daddy's attention, even if we were in the truck for only ten minutes each way.

The ride seemed particularly bumpy, and as I listened to Daddy talk about the presidential election and how Mr. Roosevelt was a lock to win, I tried to not think about how my stomach had started to hurt. By the time we parked along the sidewalk, my head was swimming.

"You okay?" Daddy asked when we got out of the truck.

"The bumpy ride made me feel queasy. I'll be okay."

He took my face in both of his hands and looked at me closely. "You look a little green."

"I'm fine. I just need some air, so I'll go get the mail, all right? The walk will do me good."

I walked slowly, breathing in long, rhythmic breaths, and within a few minutes, the dizziness started to ease. I passed by Mr. Dane reading his paper on the bench behind Mr. Poe, who was studying a crack in the sidewalk. "Mornin', Mr. Dane," I said brightly.

Mr. Dane lowered his paper slightly, squinted at me, and said, "That you, Jessilyn Lassiter?"

"Yes'r."

He looked at me for a few seconds before putting his paper back up without saying another word. He'd never been the friendliest of men, but I felt his frigid response keenly.

I turned my attention to Mr. Poe instead, knowing he was the one person in town who would talk to me. He was an odd man, Mr. Poe, and it wasn't just his speech. He was what Momma called "a little simpleminded." He didn't talk too much, but he would talk to anyone, no matter their race or creed. Knowing that, I felt particularly comfortable in his presence right then. "You lose somethin', Mr. Poe?" I asked, eager to interact with someone.

"Lost muh change," he replied, speaking in a fast mumble as he always did.

"Your change?"

"Muh penny. Had me a good ol' Injun penny."

"Penny, you say?" I asked, hoping to clarify his jumbled words.

"Indian penny, he says," Mr. Dane replied from behind

his paper. "The old man here thinks he's lost an Indian penny."

I smiled at Mr. Dane's smart tongue, but I wasn't sure a man of seventy should be calling a man of sixty-five "old man." I bent at the waist and examined the crack, trying to help Mr. Poe find his lost penny.

Simplemindedness aside, I'd always liked Mr. Poe. His daddy had been a well-respected judge while he lived, and after his passing, Mr. Poe had lived alone with his mother until she passed on a year ago. Some days I would go over to Mr. Poe's house to take corn and snaps. On those days, he would show me his collections. They were all over the house in cigar boxes. Things like matchsticks, spent shotgun cartridges, and soda caps. And now, apparently, Indian pennies.

"Don't see nothin' shiny," I said.

"T'weren't shiny."

"An unshiny penny?" I asked.

"Yep. T'weren't shiny."

I heard Mr. Dane shake his paper three times and clear his throat as though our search was putting a damper on his paper-reading efforts.

I ignored him and continued my hunt for one dull Indian penny. If nothing else, the search had given me a diversion from my whirling stomach, and I quickly forgot the queasiness that had struck me on our trip. "Pretty important to you, that penny, Mr. Poe?" I asked.

"Got me a collection," he mumbled, the gap from his two

missing teeth making his *t*'s sound like *s*'s. Those whistles were like guideposts in Mr. Poe's clipped conversation, giving me the necessary hints as to what he was saying. "Found this one in the diner. Wanted tuh add it."

I shuffled around to change my position, hoping a different viewpoint might help me find the penny, but I had no luck. The whole time we looked, Mr. Poe muttered things I didn't understand, but I could tell by his tone he didn't mean for me to. Every now and again he'd stop and cluck his tongue a few times thoughtfully and say, "I'll be . . ."

It was after the fourth "I'll be" that Mr. Dane threw his paper down in disgust and stood. "For the love of all that's holy, ain't a man got a right to sit here and read the paper without havin' to hear crazy talk?" He dug in his trouser pocket, pulled out a handful of about twenty coins, and fished through them with his middle finger. "Dime, dime, quarter, nickel, dime . . . Aha! There!" He handed a nice, shiny penny to Mr. Poe. "Take the stupid thing and be done with it. I ain't got but an hour to read the paper before the sun gets too high, and I want to do it in peace."

Mr. Poe tipped the penny toward the sun to get a good look. "T'ain't my penny," he determined at length. He pocketed the new penny without another word and went back to studying the crack.

Mr. Dane's face turned stormy, his lips pursed together like he meant to say something angry, but he just turned away and left us behind.

Mr. Poe continued to look for his penny, and I sat on the

bench to watch. About two minutes after Mr. Dane ran off, Mr. Poe found that penny and then sat down beside me, triumphant. "Ain't seen you much," he said after a few more minutes.

"That's true."

"Been sick?"

"No, just busy." I figured it best to avoid the particulars with Mr. Poe since he likely didn't know much about our current troubles. "Farm gets busy this time of year."

"Sure 'nough." He tapped the penny against his knee. "How's yer diddy?"

"My daddy?" I repeated. "He's fine. Just now, he's gettin' some supplies and things. I was headin' to the post office myself, till I saw you and Mr. Dane."

"Town's been busy too," Mr. Poe said.

"Usually is."

"More'n usual, what with all that Cy Fuller business."

My skin turned to pins and needles, and Mr. Poe's words hung in the humid air. I finally loosened my tongue enough to say, "Cy Fuller?"

"Yep. Cy's done turned up dead."

I stared at my knees, hoping my loose hair hid my anxious face. My sweaty hands gripped the slats in the bench like vises, and that whooshing sound started to deafen my ears again.

Mr. Poe seemed oblivious to my discomfort as he sighed and said, "Yep, they done found 'im on the edge of his prop'ty just s'mornin'."

"How?" I asked in a whisper.

"How what?"

"How'd he . . . how'd he die?"

"Shot clean through. Bled out, they's guessin'. Happened a while ago, so they say."

I stood quickly, rocking the bench with a loud rattle.

"You goin'?" Mr. Poe asked.

"Gotta get the letters," I murmured as I rushed off rudely.

I wandered through my errands that morning without even realizing I was doing them. My mind was far too preoccupied with Cy Fuller, and the town added plenty of fuel to the fire. Cy's death was the number one topic of conversation, and everyone had an idea of what had happened.

"Likely got himself shot over those gamblin' debts of his," Mrs. Tott said to Mrs. Crumley. "His wife was always worryin' about that."

Mrs. Crumley nodded. "Be sure your sins will find you out."

Mr. Will Calhoun thought it was an accident. "Fuller was a sight with that gun of his," he said to Wink Burns. "Always told 'im he'd shoot his foot off one day." He shook his head and chewed thoughtfully on his pipe. "Didn't think he'd up and kill hisself, though."

The theories abounded. Some believed Mrs. Fuller had shot her wicked husband in a rage, unable to take him anymore. Others felt Cy had been killed by a thief whose caper was interrupted.

I was the only one who thought I'd done it. The way I saw it, not one other person in Calloway had that blood on their hands. The stifling heat was nothing compared to the burden of guilt I carried around that day, and I felt sure that my face must have shown it. People looked at me oddly everywhere I walked, and though it was likely only due to my circumstances with Gemma, in my mind I was sure they suspected me of having a hand in Cy's death. I was plagued by fear and shame.

Daddy didn't say much to me on the way home, a sure sign that his mind was bent on something particular, and I was sure of what that was. He knew as well as I did that there was a real possibility I was a murderer, but neither of us was willing to say it out loud.

When we reached home, we got out of the truck silently, but on my way inside, I stopped and looked at him desperately. He stared at me long and hard, and then, reaching out to ruffle my hair, he said, "It's all right. It'll all be all right."

Up to that point in my life, hearing those words from my daddy would always make things seem better. It had always been like my daddy held the controls to everything, and as long as he said it would be fine, I could trust that he'd make sure it was. But times were changing and too fast for my comfort. I was getting older, and I realized I had entered a place where Daddy couldn't fix everything anymore.

I think that brewed more fear in me than Cy Fuller.

Chapter 14

In the long days after my trip into town, I couldn't think of much besides Cy, so I did anything I could to take my mind off him. I did as many chores as Momma could offer—laundry, washing floors and dishes—all the things I'd always hated. But of late I'd found myself not minding those things too much. I'd tie a handkerchief around my head like Gemma did and hum like Momma and hope it would keep me from thinking of gunshot blasts, bloodstains, and dying men.

Every now and then I'd feel Momma watching me, likely thinking I must have been sick or something to be doing my chores without complaint. One day I even went so far as to wax the floor so much that the woven rug sitting in front of the kitchen door wouldn't stay put. Both Daddy and Luke slid on it like they were on skates, making the icebox shake and clatter as they grabbed it to steady themselves.

When I wasn't working, I spent my time reading in the hammock, burying my worries in fictional adventures. The problem was I was running out of books, and the only way to cure that was to make the long hike out to the library. It was a good three miles there, and unless Daddy planned a trip into town, Gemma and I would have to walk the whole way. In one-hundred-degree heat, those six miles seemed like twenty. In other summers, we'd hitch a ride with one of our neighbors, but we weren't so welcome to do that anymore. It didn't make any sense to me, because people had always given me and Gemma rides together. It was only different to them now that she was living with us like part of our family. But whether it made any sense or not didn't matter one bit. It was still as hot as hades, we still didn't have a ride into town, and I still didn't have any new books to read.

I got a break when we finally had a day with a touch of coolness in it.

"Might rain," Gemma said in reply to my suggestion that we walk into town. She looked into the sky and held a hand out at shoulder level. "Feels like rain."

"No, it don't," I argued, knowing full well that I was right. "When rain's comin', you can smell it; you know that. The air's as dry as toast."

"Jessilyn, the air's good and damp."

"It's just humid. There ain't no rain in it."

"You been talkin' to God or somethin'?" Gemma asked smartly.

"No, I've lived here thirteen years, and I know when it's

gonna rain in Calloway and when it ain't, and it ain't. You just don't want to walk into town."

Gemma yanked the last sock from the clothesline and tossed it into the basket. "I've been tired all mornin'. Ain't slept well in two nights."

"How come?"

"The air's been thicker'n molasses all week. You know I can't sleep right in this heat." The wind blew slightly and tossed one of Gemma's braids into her face. She blew at it to shoo it away. "All's I've been wantin' to do since sunup is get my chores done and take a nap."

I sighed and pouted, but I knew I couldn't make Gemma walk to town if she was worn thin. One look at her face told me she wasn't exaggerating. Her eyes were droopy and bloodshot like they always got when she was tuckered. She needed a good rest, and anyway, I liked Gemma best when she was well rested.

So I left Gemma behind and headed into town alone, kicking stones along the way. Every now and again I would tilt my head skyward and study the clouds. Gemma had put a little doubt in my mind about my weather predictions, and I didn't want any part of walking home in a rainstorm.

When I passed Miss Cleta's, she hollered at me from her screen door. She liked to stand there on most days and watch what little there was of Calloway go by. "You headin' somewhere in particular?"

"Library," I said with a nod. "I up and ran out of readin'."

She opened the door and peered out. "You come on in here and look at my books, then."

I tucked my hands deep in my pockets and stared at her. I couldn't imagine Miss Cleta having any books that I would enjoy. Mostly I figured she read only the morning paper and cookbooks. But with the hope of finding something sweet inside, I scuffed into the house.

The usual smell of mothballs and baked goods welcomed me as I entered, and I followed her down the hallway. She led me to a room I'd never seen before. "Sully's study," she told me in response to my wondering glance. "He read everything there was to read."

The room was like a shrine with pictures of Sully and Miss Cleta lining the paneled walls and covering the heavy, ornate desk. Old papers lay on the desk in such a way that I imagined they had been left that way by Sully on his last day on earth. I was in awe at the bookshelves that made up an entire wall and held scores of books bound in leather.

I studied them for several seconds before Miss Cleta finally said, "Well, go on. You can touch 'em."

"You sure? They look expensive."

"Piffle! Ain't no one gonna be readin' them things now. Lord knows my eyes ain't good enough for those small words." She snatched two of them from a shelf and held them out to me. "They do nothin' but collect dust for me to clean off, anyway. You just help yourself. I'll go fix us up a snack, and you can join me when you're done makin' your choices."

It took me a full thirty minutes to do that. I couldn't believe I'd never known Miss Cleta had anything so splendid in her house. Having never known him, I figured Sully must have been just about as incredible as Miss Cleta made him out to be, and I quietly thanked his picture on the way out of the room.

"I didn't know how many I could take," I told her when I reached the kitchen, carrying a stack of six books.

"Well, how about you take those, and when you're done, you can come again and exchange them for more. Sound good?"

"Yes, ma'am!"

"And then we can have a snack together when you come. It will be fun to have some more company." Miss Cleta motioned to me to take a seat and then put a mound of sugared strawberries atop my slice of pound cake and topped them with fluffy whipped cream. "How come Gemma's not with you today?"

"She's wore out," I said with a sigh. "She can't never sleep good when it's this hot and sticky."

"Honey, neither can I," she grumbled, dropping into a chair across from me. She fanned herself with her napkin and patted her piled-up hair. "Lord knows this weather is enough to sap a woman's strength. And my hair! Child, my hair won't do a thing."

"Why not?"

"The humidity makes it frizzy. Don't you know that?"

"I don't pay much attention to hair and stuff."

"Well, you're gettin' to be quite the young woman, you know. Best be startin' to think about hair and stuff." Miss Cleta got up and retrieved a magazine from her living room. "See this?" she asked, pointing to a picture of a woman all done up and fancy. "This is what girls start to do when they become women. You're somewhere in between, but you should start practicin'."

"I hate fussin' with things like that."

"You have to fuss with them crooked old braids of yours, don't you?"

"Well . . ."

I had just scooped the last piece of pound cake into my mouth when Miss Cleta tossed the magazine down. "Come on," she said firmly. "You come with me."

And that's how I managed to leave Miss Cleta's house over an hour later in a creamy-colored dress, shoes with the smallest of heels, and my hair tucked up in a perfect twist. I wobbled my way down the steps and glanced uncertainly at Miss Cleta.

"You made it. That's what counts." She waved to me with one of her shaky hands. "You come back next week, now, and tell me what your momma says about your new look."

"Yes, ma'am," I called. I walked down the sidewalk, almost dragging the canvas bag we had piled my clothes and borrowed books into, but I only made it about twenty unsteady steps before a beat-up old truck squeaked down the road behind me. I turned to look at it and stopped dead in my tracks.

"Looky here," the driver drawled as he slowly passed me. "You headin' off to a party or somethin'?"

I stared ahead of me rather than at Walt Blevins's stubbled face and said, "I ain't supposed to talk to strange people."

"Who you kiddin'? You do more talkin' than any girl I ever seen. Don't seem to matter who you're talkin' to."

I continued to walk, but he pulled the truck up a little more to keep with me. "If you're headin' on home, you may as well hop in. I'm goin' that way. Maybe I'll stop in to see your daddy."

"You ain't got no business with my daddy," I said angrily. "You ain't got no business with none of us."

"Found your tongue there, didn't ya?"

I looked at him in staunch defiance and said, "You just stay away from my family."

Walt threw back his head and laughed, his alcohol-induced belly jiggling; then he flung the truck door open with a grinding squeal, and in three quick steps he was smack in front of me. He smelled like sweat and corn whiskey, and I backed away, loath to be near him.

"Now you listen to me," he said, backing me up so that I ran into his truck and became pinned between it and him. "I don't take orders from no little girl." Then he looked at me in a way that I instinctively knew wasn't right and said, "Or maybe you ain't so much of a little girl after all."

His face came closer to mine, and every breath he took made me cringe from the odor. I turned my head and closed my eyes as though not seeing him would keep me from knowing he was there. "Leave me alone," I whispered, my voice as weak as my knees.

"You ain't so tough when you ain't holdin' a rifle, are you?"

My mouth was as dry as cotton, and it took me three hard swallows, but I managed to rasp, "I should have killed you."

"Like you killed Cy Fuller?" he asked with humor in his voice. I whipped my head up to look into his sinister face, knowing my eyes must have betrayed my shock. "I know all," he said with a laugh. "Didn't you know that, girl? I know all about you."

I closed my eyes to avoid seeing his face and focused my attention on just breathing. It took real effort to inhale without making hiccuping noises. And then I heard the unmistakable sound of someone readying a rifle to fire. My eyelids flew open, and I gaped toward Miss Cleta's porch.

There she stood, clad in her demure green dress and pearls, pointing a rifle at Walt's back, her left eye squinted. "You best be movin' on outta here, Walt. Right now!"

Walt kept his right hand on the truck beside me and turned his head, a wild smirk on his round face. "Ain't no one told you it ain't polite for little ol' ladies to go pointin' guns at law-abidin' folk?"

"Ain't no law-abidin' folk I'm aimin' at. Now move on."

"Well now, ma'am, I was just havin' a chat with this here girl, and I ain't quite done with my chattin'."

"You are now."

Walt turned fully around to face her. "When I'm ready!"

I took that opportunity to slip away from him, and the very second I got away, the report from the rifle echoed off the truck in a deafening clang.

Dust blew up off the road, and Walt jumped further than I knew a man that fat could jump. "Are you crazy, old woman?" he shouted, sweat pouring down his face. "You almost shot me."

"Two more inches and I would have," she hollered. "I don't miss by accident. Now you just get on outta here like I said. Right now!"

Once I had gotten my senses about me, I scrambled up to Miss Cleta's porch, cowering behind her and her trusty rifle. I watched from the safety of her bent-over frame as Walt climbed into his truck, cursing and spitting. He turned and drove away in the direction he'd come from, his tires squealing and digging ruts in the old road.

Miss Cleta ushered me into the house, locking the door behind me.

I slumped into one of Sully's high-backed chairs and rubbed the ankle I'd twisted on my run up to the porch, my hands shaking all the while. I could see that Miss Cleta was a nervous wreck, but she talked calmly to help ease my nerves.

"Well, you can't be walkin' home today," she said, putting her rifle back into a nearby cabinet.

With the state I was in, I didn't want to make a lonely trek home either. But I knew Miss Cleta didn't have a telephone or a car, so I couldn't quite figure how I'd get home if I didn't walk. We eventually settled on sending me home with Luke, who passed Miss Cleta's house at five fifteen every day on his way from the factory to our house.

For the next three and a half hours we did everything from playing cards to baking muffins. I could tell Miss Cleta was trying her best to keep my mind off what had happened. She taught me how to play gin—"So long as your momma wouldn't mind you playin' with cards." I thought she just might, but these were special circumstances, so I decided that I could stretch the truth this once. I beat Miss Cleta twice, which she said was evidence that I had natural abilities, and I won ten jelly beans and five licorice drops from her.

I found out that she had a mouth full of sweet teeth. She didn't only make baked goods every day of her life; she also kept a cupboard full of candy and gum. Her house became even more of a haven to me that day.

At ten minutes after five o'clock, the two of us went out to sit on the porch rockers. Still clad in Miss Cleta's old dress, I sat straighter, my knees together and my ankles crossed beneath the chair, just like she was sitting. My heart started to beat more quickly as I wondered what Luke would think of my new mature look. I fiddled restlessly with the strap on the canvas bag and nearly jumped from my seat when I heard Luke whistling in the distance.

"Sounds like he's comin'," Miss Cleta said. "I'll get him some pound cake to take with him."

She disappeared inside the house just as Luke came into

view. I waited until he neared the sidewalk and then called out his name.

He squinted in my direction. "Hey there, Jessie. Doin' some visitin'?"

"That's right." I stood and watched him amble with a wide gait up the sidewalk. He mounted the stairway to the porch in one large step. I stood there fingering my collar nervously, the canvas bag swinging slowly in my shaky right hand.

Luke stopped and did a double take. "Jessie . . . well, just look at you."

"Miss Cleta did it," I said quickly.

"She did, did she?" He smiled one of his charming little smiles and said, "Well, she did a mighty fine job. You look a real lady now. Sure enough."

My nervousness went away but was replaced by self-consciousness, and I stared at my feet. I thanked him quietly, happy that Miss Cleta found her way back out to the porch just then. She handed Luke his cake and sent us on our way, charging me to tell him about my run-in on our walk home.

"What run-in?" he asked sharply.

"Jessilyn will tell you all about it," Miss Cleta promised. "You best set off for home before her parents get to wor-ryin'."

We hadn't hit the road before Luke started badgering me. I told him only the basics, leaving out Walt's leering advances. I was too embarrassed to tell him or anyone what he'd said and how he'd looked at me.

Luke was spitting mad by the time I finished telling him the short version, and I had to make an extra effort to keep up with his long, livid strides on the last leg of our trip. "Don't you go walkin' on your own no more," he ordered. "It ain't safe."

"But I can't act like a prisoner or nothin'. I ain't done nothin' wrong."

"I know it, but that don't matter none. Walt's no good. He's capable of anythin'."

"I ain't gonna not go places no more. He could be in Calloway for the rest of his life. You expect me to sit around and knit for the next fifty years?"

He sighed and ran his hand through his hair. "You just don't understand. That boy ain't no good."

"I think I know that better'n most, but I ain't gonna let him make me afraid. I can't be afraid all the time."

Luke didn't say any more. I guessed there wasn't much he could say. We weren't in a simple situation with an easy answer. Walt Blevins was a danger to me; we both knew that. But we also knew that I couldn't stay indoors with a guard every day of my life. There just was no easy solution . . . if there was any solution at all.

Daddy had a good holler about it when we told him, just about giving Momma a heart attack with the things he was saying. I could only imagine what he might have done if he'd known the whole truth. Then he charged off, saying he was going to call the sheriff.

"Daddy, no!" I shouted.

"What are you jabberin' about?" Daddy asked.

"I don't want you callin' the sheriff on this. I don't want the law brought in."

"Ain't got no choice, Jessilyn," Luke argued. "There's no reasonin' with a man like Walt. That boy should rot in jail."

"But he won't," I countered. "We've already seen that in Walt's trial over in Coopersville. He ain't gonna pay, and I don't want to stir him up by gettin' the law on him."

"Ain't no man gonna get away with harassin' my girl," Daddy argued. "I tell you, he ain't gettin' away with it."

"Daddy, no sheriff! I don't want it!" I was desperate to convince him, and my shaking voice showed it.

Momma came over to me and put her hands on my shoulders. She calmly said, "Jessilyn ain't no girl no more, Harley. She's got a right to have a say."

Daddy paced the faded spot he'd worn on the rug through the years. He'd paced it a lot this summer. Then he stopped and looked at me determinedly. "I'm tellin' Otis. Bein' a deputy, he can keep an extra eye on things. We won't take it any further than that . . . for now."

Luke slapped his hat against his leg. "It ain't right, Mr. Lassiter. It ain't right for him to get away with this."

"But it's what I want," I retorted.

"Don't mean you're right."

"As I see it, you ain't got any say, anyhow."

"Now listen here," Luke said, leaning down so his face was closer to mine. "As far as I'm concerned, if I've gotta follow you around lookin' after you, I ought to have some say."

I stomped a foot against the splintered wooden floor. "No one made you follow me around. My daddy ain't payin' you to be no bodyguard."

That's when Daddy stepped between the two of us, a surprising smile gracing his face. "All right, that's enough now. If you two don't beat all . . ."

"But, Daddy, he thinks he can tell me what to do all the time," I cried.

"You want me to leave you alone," Luke said, "then fine. I'll leave you good and alone."

"Fine!"

"I said that's enough," Daddy warned. "Last I checked, this is still my house, so when I say that's enough, then that's enough."

In the end, Luke scowled his way out the door, and Daddy went to call Otis Tinker.

Momma was wringing her hands, but instead of talking about the whole thing any further, she just ran her hand softly over my hair. "What'd you get all fancied up for?" she asked with a grin. "You look all tidied up. Like a present under the Christmas tree."

"Miss Cleta did it," I murmured, looking down at my dress.

Momma walked around me a couple times and nodded. "Sure enough, you look right nice. Now, don't you feel good bein' in girl stuff?"

In truth, I liked feeling grown-up, but I didn't want to act too much like Momma had been right for pushing me to wear dresses. I just said, "It's okay, I guess."

"Okay! It's lovely! You know, I could fix you up a couple new dresses in no time flat," she told me excitedly. "I've got some nice cloth upstairs, and we could fix somethin' that don't have any of those little girl bows at the waist and things, you know?"

By this time, Momma was measuring me with an invisible measuring tape, likely conjuring up all sorts of ideas in her dressmaking mind, but I didn't want her going overboard. "I didn't say I wanted to start wearin' dresses all the time, Momma."

"Well, no one said you did. But if you start wearin' them more, you're gonna need some. Besides, your dresses are for a girl, not a young lady." Momma tapped her chin a few times and then said, "I'm gonna go dig out that cloth and see if it's still fit for sewin'."

My heart was heavy as I watched her go. The events of the day had frightened me more than I'd admitted to anyone, and keeping the secret of Walt's advances made me feel more alone than I ever had. But I couldn't tell anyone. I didn't want them all hovering over me, keeping me locked in like a hostage. I'd already lost enough of my freedom as it was.

Chapter 15

I wasn't sleeping much at night. I was living in a nightmare where things seemed about as bad as they could be, and waking up in the morning didn't make them any better. The rising of the sun didn't erase my fears that I was a murderer, and I was plagued by guilt every minute. I walked around bleary-eyed and short-tempered, my nerves on edge. Dark patches underlined my eyes, my skin was pale even with my summer tan, and I walked at a snail's pace. At first I didn't care a bit. But after having Luke, Momma, Gemma, and Miss Cleta all ask me why I looked a sight, I decided I'd best fix up, even if it was just to keep them from bothering me.

When Gemma found me primping in front of the bathroom mirror, she looked at me like I was crazy. But then, she always looked at me like that. "Are you puttin' curls in your hair?" she asked me. I tried to kick the door shut, but she put her weight into it. "What in tarnation are you doin'? You fixin' to go courtin' or somethin'? You know your daddy ain't lettin' you court yet." She kept talking without giving me a chance to say anything. "And I hope you ain't thinkin' of Luke, 'cause he's too old for you, plain and simple. Your daddy'd kill him if he acted sweet on you."

"Would you shut up?" I finally snapped. "I ain't doin' nothin' but puttin' curls in my hair. There a law that says a girl can't put curls in her hair just 'cause she feels like it?"

Gemma put her hands on her hips and studied my face in the mirror. "Well, if you're gonna do it at all, you ought to do it right. Here," she said, grabbing Momma's hot iron from me. "You're gettin' the curls all uneven."

Gemma fixed my hair better than I ever could have, and I headed down the hall with a confident smile on my face, the first real smile I'd worn in days. I popped into Momma and Daddy's bedroom and went to Momma's dressing table to finger some of the little bottles and pots that rested there. By the time I left the room, I smelled like lavender and had glossy lips. I figured Momma wouldn't mind since she'd been after me for years to be more of a girl.

It was Daddy who noticed first, though. He was resting comfortably in his chair, and all I could see of him were his legs and the wisps of pipe smoke that floated up from behind a wrinkled newspaper. Shortly after I walked into the room, I saw his left hand go behind the paper and come out with the pipe in it. Then Daddy sniffed the air. "You plannin' on goin' somewheres, Sadie?"

I knew what he was thinking, but I played innocent. "What, Daddy?"

He pulled the paper down so he could see over it. "Jessilyn?" he asked oddly. "Thought you was your momma."

"Why's that?"

Daddy shrugged. "Thought I smelled her. She always smells nice when she's goin' out."

"Don't I ever smell nice?"

"Not as I can recall."

"Daddy!"

He furrowed his brow at me and took a quick puff on his pipe. "Now don't go gettin' your feelin's hurt, Jessilyn. I didn't mean nothin' by it. It's just you never wear no scents."

I folded my arms tightly and said, "So that means I smell bad?"

Momma walked in, and Daddy looked at her pleadingly. "Sadie, would you help me out here?"

"What on earth is goin' on?"

"Daddy thinks I smell bad," I declared.

"Harley," Momma said softly, drawing his name out long, "why would you . . . ?"

"I didn't! I just thought I smelled you come into the room, with your perfume and all, and it turned out to be Jessilyn."

"So he figured it couldn't be me, because I don't never smell good!"

"Harley, you've no call to make fun of her." Momma took me by the shoulders and put her face in my hair. "You smell sweet as a daisy, Jessilyn. And look at your pretty hair. Did Gemma do it for you?"

"Yes'm."

"Well, I declare, it's pretty as a picture." She looked disapprovingly at Daddy. "Ain't no call to be teasin' a pretty young lady."

"I didn't . . ." But Daddy stopped himself from talking at all, likely assuming he was safer that way, and slumped behind his newspaper, mumbling something I couldn't hear.

"I was gonna ask you to come and help fix supper," Momma commented to me. "But I don't want you gettin' your pretty dress spotted with potato peel."

"Oh, I can do it," I said. "Ain't got no one to impress round here anyways."

I heard Daddy sigh from behind the paper.

"I was just experimentin'," I said as I followed Momma to the kitchen.

"Every girl's gotta do a little of that." Momma started tapping her foot to a tune she had in her head, humming lightly. "I probably got some leftover scent upstairs. You know how your daddy likes that lavender one, so it's the only one I use these days. You can have the others."

"That'd be nice." I tied a towel around my waist and started cutting the peel off a potato in one long circular strip. "Momma?"

"Hmm?"

"Got school startin' up soon."

"I know. These summers . . . they fly by so fast anymore. I can't keep track."

"Could be different this year."

"What? School? Well, I imagine it will be, with you movin' up into another class and all. That's just the size of it, though, this growin'-up time. You got lots of changes in store for you."

"Yes'm, but that ain't what I'm talkin' about." I cleared my throat and looked around to make sure Gemma wasn't nearby before I quietly said, "I'm talkin' about it bein' different with the other kids, with all our trouble we've had round here of late."

Momma gazed out the window, staring hard at nothing. "Oh, I been thinkin' 'bout that," she said, and I could hear in her voice that she was trying to pretend it was no big deal. "I'm sure things will be just fine. You know how people get. They get all fired up over somethin' till they're bored with it, and then after a while they find somethin' else to squawk about. Come schooltime, I'm sure it'll be old news."

I didn't rightly agree with that, seeing as how school started in just under two weeks, but I pretended to believe the same words she pretended to believe. I suppose we both decided it was better to pretend a little while since the truth would be found out on my first day at school anyway. Why bother suffering before as well as during?

To change the subject, Momma went over to the icebox and pulled out some ham salad. "Why don't you run off to Jeb before he leaves and see if he'd like to take this salad with him. That poor man's so skinny, I swear he don't eat nights."

Jeb was working in the upper fields today, so I took the gravel path in his direction, careful to keep my skirt from catching on any of the wild bushes that grew alongside it. I saw Lucky curled up under a low evergreen and clucked my tongue at him. "Come on with me, boy. You don't need to be lazin' around all day."

He stood slowly and stretched his legs before following me with short, rapid steps. I squinted into the dipping sun and put a hand over my eyes like an awning, hoping to spot Jeb. I could fairly make out his form in the distance, but he didn't look like anything more than a shadow with the bright sun at his back.

I spotted another dark form across from him, and I stopped myself from calling out until I determined who it was he was talking to. I slowed my pace, but Lucky kept going, so I hurried after him and scooped him up with my free hand. "Wait a minute, boy," I whispered.

I didn't know why I was so cautious. I guessed that Luke's worrying had started to get to me, but in the end it really came down to the fact that recent events had put my nerves on their very edges. I was anxious about everything, and the dark form with Jeb was no exception. I had never seen Jeb talking to anyone but the other fieldhands since he'd come to work for us, and I was sure that the other hands had already left for the day.

The only way for me to get a real glimpse was to get

around to the other side of the field where the sun wouldn't be in my eyes, so I started around the perimeter, ducking behind bushes and short trees. Once I reached the big oak where Gemma and I carved a record of our heights every summer, I put Lucky down and lifted myself onto the high, gnarled root to get a better look.

But as quickly as I found out who Jeb was talking to, I wished I hadn't.

Walt Blevins looked as messy and unshaven as he always did, his dirty, floppy hat tipped back from his forehead.

I could see right off that Jeb's face was expressionless like it always was. "You better just lay off," Jeb told Walt. "You want to go makin' people suspicious?"

Walt laughed slyly. "You think there's a body in this town that ain't suspicious of me? Ain't nothin' I can do to make myself more suspicious than I already is."

"Maybe, but you start messin' round with a little girl, and people'll set on you quicker'n a wink."

"I'm just playin' with her mind. Givin' her a good scare is all. I ain't gonna do nothin' to her."

I could see Jeb didn't believe his words any more than I did. Walt meant to hurt me. That was plain for anyone to see.

"All the same," Jeb replied, "I say leave her alone. You ain't got no call to go messin' with her, and if you don't keep your hands off her, I'll set on you, you hear?"

"Yes, sir," Walt said with facetious respect. "Anythin' else, *sir*?"

"You just stop doin' things that'll interfere with our plans. I ain't worked this hard and long to have you mess it all up."

Walt didn't say another word. He stared at Jeb for a few seconds, and then he tipped his hat at him with a smirk and trudged off through the trees.

I sank down behind the oak, my head swimming. Luke had been right. Jeb was not to be trusted. He had plans for us, I could see now. That must have been why he came to us for work. He was here to watch us. I was starting to feel weak and shaky, my lips going numb. I was beginning to wonder about everyone in my life. I didn't know who I could trust, and that made me certain that I couldn't tell anyone about anything. I was alone in this trouble, and I was determined to find out for myself exactly what Jeb's plans were.

For starters, though, I was well aware that I would have to give that ham salad to Jeb, or Momma would find out he never got it and start asking me questions. I gave myself about five more minutes, and then I made my way back around to the gravel path and approached Jeb like I'd just wandered up. "Hey there," I tried to say matter-of-factly, but I could tell my voice was tight and strained. "Momma wanted me to bring you this ham salad."

"Well, don't that sound nice." He wiped his hands on his dirty britches before taking the bowl from me. "Your momma's the best cook in the county, you ask me."

"She's right fine." I turned my back to him and started toward the house, nearly tripping over Lucky. I yanked him up quickly and hollered, "See ya later, Jeb."

"Miss Jessie?" he called. "You all right?"

I stopped and looked over my shoulder at him for a few seconds. "I'm okay. Gotta help Momma in the kitchen is all." I headed home in what was more a run than a walk, and by the time I reached the back door, my shins were tight and sore.

At supper that night, I was particularly quiet and solemn. A few times I noticed Momma and Daddy glancing at each other in confusion, but I didn't say a word to them about Jeb.

When we had gone to bed, I asked Gemma about him without letting her know what I'd overheard. "You like Jeb?"

She rolled over on her bed and looked at me sleepily. "Sure, I like Jeb. Don't you?"

I didn't answer her. I just said, "Luke don't. He thinks he's suspicious."

Gemma snorted. "Luke's just worryin'. Jeb ain't done nothin' to him."

"Guess not."

"Sick of bein' hot!" Gemma rolled onto her back and kicked her sheet off. "What brought up Jeb, anyhow?"

"Nothin'. Just thinkin'."

"You been doin' an awful lot of that thinkin' lately. Every time I look at you, you look like you're thinkin' about somethin'. Don't look like good things you're thinkin' about, neither."

It was my turn to roll over, but I put my back to her so she couldn't read my face in the moonlight. "Just those growin'-up changes Momma's been talkin' about, I guess."

"I was thirteen only two years ago," Gemma said, "and I don't remember sulkin' around like you do."

"So what?" I snapped. "Everybody gotta act like you?"

"Shoo-wee!" Gemma exclaimed. "Girl, whatever you got, you got a bad case of it."

I didn't feel so wrong for talking to Gemma that way. I was in too bad a state to care much about other people's feelings, and I figured with all the trouble I was having, I had the right to be ornery now and again. I shut up and didn't say another word, but, as usual, I didn't sleep much. I tossed and turned, and every time I began to doze, snippets of frightening dreams would wake me suddenly.

Sleeplessness had become far too normal to me.

Chapter 16

On Wednesday, Momma decided to go to the monthly sewing guild meeting at the invitation of Mrs. Tinker.

"Alice Tinker's gonna give me a ride, and she says most everyone's forgotten their bitterness by now, anyhow. Besides, I've got some dresses to make," she said as she measured me. "Sure enough, I'd like to do my work with some chatter. Would do me a world of good." She talked on and on like she was trying to convince me that everything would be all right, but I felt that she was trying to convince herself more than anything.

From what little I'd seen of people lately, things hadn't changed so much. I didn't much believe her theory that people had forgotten, but I didn't want to make her feel bad, so I didn't say a word.

Momma must have misread my silence for something else.

"You won't be bored while I'm gone. Mr. Tinker's goin' to stay tonight to help Daddy fix his truck, so you and Gemma can watch the boys for him."

I rolled my eyes and whined, "Momma!"

"It'll give you somethin' to do. You like children."

"Not those boys. They're rowdy little things."

Her head was bent over to measure my waist, but I could hear the smile in her voice when she said, "Luke's comin' by too," as though that would change my attitude completely.

I suppose she was right, because it did.

That evening Momma smelled like lavender, her hair tucked up perfectly except for a few of her forehead-framing curls that she couldn't avoid in the humid air. She hadn't stopped smiling all day, but my daddy had walked around brooding. More than once I'd heard him gently attempt to talk her out of going, but Momma's mind was set. She couldn't wait to have an evening out.

About seven o'clock the Tinkers drove up in their truck, and Momma rushed down the stairs with her big sewing bag. "Take good care of those boys," she told me and Gemma. "Y'all can have some of the custard I made if you want." She kissed us both on the cheek. "Just make sure to keep them out of my dinin' room. I don't want them rattlin' my cabinet."

Gemma flashed me a shocked look at Momma's display of affection.

I raised my eyebrows in return. I'd never seen Momma so excited over a little sewing meeting, but I realized that she'd been without friends all summer. I smiled at Momma on the way out, silently praying she wouldn't come home disappointed.

Thankfully Mr. Tinker's boys had spent the day at the swimming hole and were good and worn-out, but the evening wasn't so special as Momma had suggested. Luke was busy working on the truck with Daddy and Mr. Tinker, and the only time I saw him was when he came in to get some sweet tea. I helped him fix the drinks for the three of them, but outside of an initial "Your hair looks real nice, Jessie," he talked about nothing but carburetors and spark plugs.

By nine o'clock, the Tinker boys had dozed off on the couch listening to the radio, and Gemma and I were sitting on the floor with our chins on our knees, bored to tears.

"Jessilyn," Daddy called, "where you at?"

"Right here," I replied with a sigh. "Sittin' here doin' nothin'."

"Well, I got somethin' for you. We need some of that strong tape I keep in the field shed."

"I'll go get it," I volunteered quickly. "Ain't got nothin' else to do."

"That'd be a big help. You want someone to go with you? It's dark."

"It's just out to the field shed."

Gemma stayed with the boys, and I grabbed a flashlight and trudged out the back door, following the path to the shed. The toads and crickets were particularly raucous, a symphony of night noises that drowned out my footsteps.

There was very little moon, and it crossed my mind that even with the lanterns Daddy had lit up, those men still must have been struggling to see. The overwhelming darkness began to close in on me halfway through my journey, giving me shivers despite the warm air.

I hated that I had to feel frightened walking on my own land, and I started to wish I'd told Daddy to send someone with me after all. I'd never felt uncomfortable on Lassiter property before, but now . . . now, life was different. In one summer, the innocence of my youth had fled away, fear creeping in to take its place.

A soft breeze rattled the bare branches of a dying tree to my right, and I leapt to the side, the rapid beat of my heart joining in with the toads and crickets.

I had that feeling of being watched, that feeling that any space outside my line of sight contained evil waiting for the perfect time to pounce. I had made this journey a thousand times, all times of day and night, and I'd never known fear of this sort. But fear of all sorts had become my constant companion of late, and I had not easily come to accept that fact. I fought it the whole way, determined that no one had the right to steal my peace of mind. In principle I may have been right, but in fact, I was always frightened, and those moments on the path were no different.

To my left, a bush rustled. To my right, an owl hooted. It was as though the entirety of nature had conspired with Walt Blevins to drive me into a panic. I walked on briskly but would not allow myself to run because I felt running would be giving in to fear.

By the time I reached the shed, I was feeling certain I was being followed, but my head kept saying I was crazy. There was no doubt that my imagination had jumped its boundaries that summer, and I told myself twenty times while I was entering the shed that I was only imagining things.

The old wooden door creaked loud and long, and I tossed the light over the shed's contents before entering. I did that quickly, however, figuring that there was less likelihood of someone being inside the shed than out. Once I was sure no one had taken up residence in our shed, I went in and slammed the door behind me, pushing a wooden crate against the door since it would only stay closed if locked from the outside.

A light breeze whistled through the broken glass in one of the tiny windows, a ghostly sort of whine. The beam of the flashlight cast awkward shadows about the place, making wrenches look like knives and hubcaps like the distorted faces of Halloween masks.

Knowing exactly where the tape was, I scurried over to get it, sticking it inside the pocket of my dress to keep one hand free to combat any attackers. But then I froze, certain now that I'd heard footsteps outside the shed. Hoping desperately that it was just Daddy or Luke come to fetch me, I called out, "Hello?"

No answer came.

"Anybody there?" I asked again.

For several moments, I stood as still as I could, holding my breath and hoping to hear something positive in reply. But I heard nothing.

I decided I had two choices. I could either sit in the shed until one of the men noticed I was missing and came looking for me, or I could brave the trip back. The former seemed appealing to me, except for the sheer humiliation of being found cowering in the shed, maybe even by Luke. I couldn't have that. I was being irrational, anyway, I decided. And the sooner I started back, the quicker I could be curled up on the cool wooden floor of the den being bored with Gemma.

With renewed determination, I stepped forward and grabbed a hammer for a weapon just in case, then walked to the door. My yank on the handle was met with stubbornness, and with a long sigh of irritation at myself, I remembered I had yet to remove the crate from in front of it.

I slid the crate loudly across the gritty dirt floor, but the door did not drift open as I expected it to. Grasping the worn handle, I pulled, but the door didn't budge.

"C'mon," I muttered. "Open up!"

But the door was locked in place, only moving enough to rattle on its hinges. The level of my panic reached new heights as I realized I had been followed. Someone had come behind me and slipped that hook into place. I had no idea as to why anyone would want me locked in there, but it didn't matter much to me what the reason was. I only wanted to be back in my house, out of the stifling darkness, with the security of my daddy's voice drifting in through the front windows.

Fearing that the same person who had locked the door would return and try to get inside to me, I pushed the crate against the door again and stacked another on top of it for insurance. Then I crossed to the back of the shed and crawled beneath the worktable to sit in the dirt, the flashlight pointed directly at the door, the hammer in my hand poised for action.

Surely one of the men would notice I'd not come back, and then they'd come looking for me. They would get impatient waiting for the tape and wonder. Or maybe Gemma would ask after me, realizing I'd been gone longer than necessary. Whatever the reason for searching, I sat there and hoped they would do it. Through the involuntary shakes in my hands and the tears of fright I couldn't blink away from my eyes, I hoped and prayed.

"Sweet Jesus," I whispered like I'd heard Momma do time and again when worried about something. "Sweet Jesus, help me. Help me, Jesus."

I murmured that over and over again without thinking. Those were the only words that would come to my head, so I just kept saying them like they were magic words. I'd never paid too much attention in church. My Bible was as dusty as boxes in the attic. But I'd been raised by my momma, and my momma knew what it was to be on personal terms with God.

Daddy knew the Lord, but he had a quiet way of worship,

and he asked me only once in a while if I remembered how important it was to know the Lord. But Momma, she was different. Faith came easily to her most of the time, and she'd talk to God at the drop of a hat, out loud, no matter who was around or what we were doing.

Once, when times were particularly thin, we had been buying flour and sugar from the grocery, and Dale Watts said, "Mrs. Lassiter, you're two dimes short."

I was so embarrassed when my momma put her hand on my head and said, "Dear Jesus, I need two dimes to feed my baby girl. Help me get them dimes." It was bad enough that I'd been called "baby girl" in public even though I was ten, but it was even worse that my momma had invoked a miracle right in the middle of the produce.

Momma got those dimes, though, when Bart Tatum placed them in Dale's hand and said, "Faith like that should be rewarded."

Momma thanked him a million times and with a "Thank You, Jesus" picked up our bag and walked me from the store.

As we walked to the truck, I told Momma that it was no miracle we'd gotten those dimes. "Mr. Tatum felt sorry for us, was all."

"Miss Jessilyn," she told me, "with the stubborn way human hearts can be, it's a miracle when we give kindnesses away with no benefit to ourselves. Yes ma'am. That Mr. Tatum would give of himself is miracle enough for me."

From anyone else, I would have thought that prayer a

smart way of using guilt to get someone to pay a bill, but that wasn't my momma. She never connived at anything. She simply believed in a God of miracles, even if I couldn't understand any of it.

Watching Momma was good enough to teach me that there was a God and a Savior. It was just that I'd never seen much need for a Savior over the past thirteen years, and despite Momma asking me every Sunday if I'd reconsidered, I'd yet to do anything about asking Jesus to save me.

But even as I sat in that dimly lit shed, I wasn't asking for salvation of my soul. I was asking for salvation of my body. I didn't want anyone hurting me, and I figured if my momma loved Jesus so much, maybe He'd have pity on me and save me for her sake, even if I was a wretch like the church song said.

It seemed like an eternity of waiting there, but it was actually only about ten minutes before I heard footsteps, and this time I was sure that was what I was hearing. But they did nothing to ease my fears because I couldn't figure any reason why Daddy or anyone good coming to find me would walk so quiet and slow. I gripped the hammer so tightly, I nearly stopped the blood from flowing to my fingers. I flipped the flashlight off, assuming I'd be better off if any intruder had a hard time finding me in the dark.

My teeth began to chatter when I heard the latch being lifted from the metal loop on the outside of the shed. I watched as best I could as the door creaked open slightly before smacking against the crates. Someone spoke softly, and the door started slamming back and forth against the doorframe and then against the crates, over and over again.

I shut my eyes against the terrifying noise and continued praying for a miracle through lips that moved without sound. Finally the crates slid far enough to allow a man to enter, and footsteps slowly scuffed across the floor.

Making my way farther toward the corner of the shed, I curled up into a ball so small, I was half my usual size. The intruder was breathing heavily from the strain of breaking past the crates, and he was muttering every time he ran into another object that was cloaked in darkness.

I could tell by the clanking of tools that he was feeling along the wall where hooks and nails harbored wrenches, hammers, and saws. Then the noise stopped, and I heard a rattling sound, like something being shaken. I knew that sound.

I froze when I remembered the flashlight Daddy kept on the shelf near the tools, the stubborn one that only worked now and again. Whoever it was that had locked me in was trying to get that light to work, and if he succeeded, I was doomed. My eyes having adjusted to the darkness, I could see the outline of the door, and I decided that my only recourse was to make a run for it, hopefully catching the man off guard, so he would be unable to stop me.

A couple more smacks on the flashlight sounded before I got up the nerve. At the count of three, I bolted for the door, smacking my foot on something metal on the way. Pain shot through my foot, but I didn't hesitate. I had just reached the doorway when a hand gripped my wrist, jerking me to a stop.

My screams pierced the air over and over again. I was hysterical, shrieking in short, loud gasps, flailing against the grasp of my captor.

That was when the flashlight decided to click on, but I had my eyes clamped shut, and it wasn't until I heard my name that I paused to identify the voice that said it.

"Miss Jessilyn," he was saying, "what's wrong with you?"

It was Jeb, and his presence there with me in the dark did nothing to relieve my fears. But I knew that my screams would have alerted half the county by then, and in sheer weariness, I collapsed to the ground in a heap.

"Heaven's sake," he said, stooping down in front of me. "You're in a state!"

By the time he got me back outside, Daddy and Luke were flying up the path in horror. "Jessilyn! Jessilyn, you hurt?" Daddy demanded. "What happened?"

"Don't rightly know what happened," Jeb said. "I found the shed locked and barred by somethin', and then she tried to run out past me, so I grabbed her arm and she just went off like a banshee."

I stayed on the ground to get my composure, and Daddy and Luke both bent down in front of me.

Mr. Tinker came running up last. "What in tarnation is goin' on here?"

"Someone locked me in," I said breathlessly. "I couldn't get out."

"What do you mean someone locked you in?" Daddy asked.

"I mean just that. I went to get out of the door, and I couldn't get it open."

"Maybe it was just stuck," Mr. Tinker said. "You know the humidity does that to the doors."

I shook my head. "No, sir! That door was locked. It wiggled but it wouldn't open."

Daddy sat back on his heels and tipped his hat off his head, thinking.

"It was locked when I got to it, Harley," Jeb said. "She's right about that. And there were some crates in front of the door on the inside. I had a heck of a time gettin' in."

"Crates in front of the door?" Luke asked.

"I did that to keep anyone out," I said. "Someone locked me in, and there was no telling if they'd come back for me."

"Now, honey, I just can't believe anyone locked you in," Daddy murmured unconvincingly. "Most likely that lock fell into place when you shut the door, is all. Stranger things have happened."

His denial of the reality of my experience angered me, but I held my tongue, realizing that he didn't know how fully I'd been threatened of late. Luke looked suspiciously at Jeb and came over to help me up. I gratefully let him, but even the touch of Luke's rough hands couldn't ease my spirits.

I saw Mr. Tinker exchange a meaningful glance with my daddy, but they didn't voice their worries in front of me. I thought it was pretty stupid for them to think they shouldn't talk about it in front of me. After all, I knew better than anyone how much trouble I was in. But I just kept silent knowing that saying such things to my daddy would have been the stupidest thing of all.

As we walked back to the house, Daddy offered all sorts of different ways that the door could have locked by itself. "Could've been the breeze. Or the force of the door closin'. Did you slam it, Jessie? That's probably all it was. Or maybe it really was swollen stuck. You know how old that shed is. Maybe the hinges are rustin'."

It was unlike Daddy to come up with so many guesses. He liked facts, not speculation, and I saw his eagerness to make excuses as evidence that he was worried but didn't want to let on that he was.

Jeb walked as far as the house with us, and then he tipped his hat in our direction. "Sorry you got so scared, Miss Jessie. S'pose I'll say good night now."

Luke stared at Jeb, his head cocked to one side. "Now, how is it you're on this property this time of night?"

"I was stayin' in the lean-to, since I had extra work to be done this evenin'."

Luke looked at my daddy for confirmation of Jeb's story.

"You know I let him stay there on late days, Luke. There ain't nothin' wrong with Jeb." Daddy said those words very determinedly, as though he were vowing Jeb's innocence in

231

his simple words. I couldn't be as sure as he was, though. The way I saw it, Daddy didn't know all there was to know about Jeb Carter. "Thanks for helpin' my girl, Jeb," Daddy said. "We'll be seein' you tomorrow."

I watched Jeb walk off, my mind full of suspicions. The lean-to was attached to the very shed where I'd been stuck, and there wasn't a single soul who had been better able to lock me in than Jeb had been.

While Mr. Tinker went back to fixing the truck, Daddy and Luke got me settled inside the house with Gemma, who we found in front of one of the windows, her face pressed closely to the glass. "Land's sake!" she shouted when we came in, sounding like her momma. "I was nearly faintin' in here wonderin' what happened! What was all the screamin' about? Jessilyn, you okay?"

"I'm okay, Gemma. Just got scared, is all."

"Scared by what? You see a snake or somethin'?"

I glared at her. "I ain't afraid of no snakes!"

"Well then, what?"

"She'll explain it to you in a minute, Gemma," Daddy said. "Let's get her settled down first."

Gemma obeyed and went to get me some cold water. She came back with a glass mostly full of ice with a little water in it. "Cold helps you calm down," she told me. "Crunch some ice."

I did as she said, and loath to be the center of attention again as I had been so often that summer, I told Daddy they should get back to fixing the truck. "Ain't no reason to hang around starin' at me," I said, pulling the tape from my pocket and handing it to him. "Gemma's with me."

"Truck can wait. But Otis wants to borrow my good saw, and I'd better get it for him before he goes. He was searchin' for it in the barn when you started screamin', and he more'n likely forgot all about it himself. You sure you'll be okay, Jessilyn?" Daddy asked, clearly concerned.

"Yes'r. I'm fine."

"Maybe I should stay with her," Luke said. "If I'm in here, then you can finish up on the truck. You boys could do it without my help."

"You'll just be outside," I said, trying not to be too convincing. "But if you want to, Luke . . ."

Gemma put a hand over her mouth to keep from laughing at me, but I figured if I was going to have such a trying night, I may as well get something out of it.

"Fine idea," Daddy said. "That would ease my mind a bit if you stayed inside, Luke."

So Luke, Gemma, and I sat in the den sipping on tall glasses of sweet tea, the Tinker boys' snoring as our background music. I told Gemma the short version of what had happened, and I could tell that she believed I'd been locked in. She hadn't been oblivious to the spite I'd received, and I think she suspected there was even more to it than what she'd noticed. But she didn't say anything about it. She just took my hand in hers and held it. Maybe she thought if she held on to me tightly enough nothing bad could happen to me.

Gemma had turned the radio off when she heard my

screaming, so Luke turned it back on, and the three of us sat there listening. I put my head on a pillow and listened to the music and the rhythmic tapping of Luke's boot on the floor.

Peace had begun to flood back into my spirit until the front door opened and Momma entered all flustered.

Daddy followed her. "Sadie. Now, Sadie, darlin'," he was saying, "tell me what happened."

Momma rushed up the stairs without answering. I could hear her breath coming in hiccups, and I knew she was crying but trying not to let it show. Daddy went after her, taking the steps two at a time.

Luke, Gemma, and I exchanged glances. I laid my head back down and closed my eyes, my heart sinking.

I didn't need to hear Mrs. Tinker's quiet and quick explanation to us as she gathered the boys' things to know what had upset Momma. "Seems people have longer memories than I thought. And we'd made it through the first bit of the night so well too. . . ." She noticed my unhappy face and said, "Oh, your momma'll be fine after a while. She's just feelin' people's smallness, is all. Thank you for takin' care of the boys."

Mr. Tinker piled both sleeping boys into his arms and nodded at us, and the family left us just that quickly.

Luke said nothing, but he smacked his knee so hard I figured it had to have stung something fierce. Gemma squeezed my hand more tightly, and we sat in silence, no doubt wondering how long life could go on like this. Or for that matter, how long *we* could go on like this.

Chapter 17

Momma wasn't too talkative about that night of the sewing meeting. "People can be strange" was all she said to me the next morning when I questioned her. "Ain't no accountin' for it." She put her hand lightly on my cheek and said, "Ain't nothin' I can't take care of. Don't you worry your pretty little head about me." And that was the end of the discussion; I could see it on her face.

I sat down at the table next to Gemma and swirled my eggs around with my fork. The clock chimed halfway, announcing six thirty. "Daddy already in the fields?"

"Got a lot of work to do today. He was out before sunup." Momma sat at the table with us and urged me to stop playing with my food and eat. "Growin' girls need food for energy."

I nodded and picked up a piece of bacon, crunching it without enjoying it.

"Daddy tells me you had a mishap at the shed last night, Jessilyn," Momma said in between blows to cool her tea. "Said you got locked in."

"Yes'm, I did. No big deal," I told her, not wanting to make things harder for her than they already were. I could see her eyes were puffy and bloodshot, and I figured she'd cried herself to sleep last night. I didn't want to upset her more.

"Sure it's no big deal? He said you were pretty scared."

"It was just dark, is all. I couldn't see nothin'. Makes a body scared."

Momma added some more sugar to her tea and stirred it, clanging the spoon from side to side. "Got you scared too, no doubt, Gemma. Hearin' that screamin' and all."

"Yes'm," Gemma replied. "Did my heart good to see them comin' back to the house."

"Well, I must say I'm glad I wasn't home," Momma told us. "I'd have been takin' a stroke hearin' that kind of screamin' from my girl like that. I don't know how I would have made it through."

"Weren't nothin'," I assured her. "Like I said, no big deal."

After breakfast, Momma sent me down to the fields with some iced tea for Daddy, but I found Jeb instead. I was uneasy the moment I came upon him. "Oh, it's you. I was lookin' for Daddy. I'll just go find him."

"He's gone to town quicklike, Miss Jessie. Seems he ran out of somethin' he needed to fix the back fence."

"I'll see him when he gets back, then," I said and turned away.

Jeb caught my arm. "Hold up. I gotta talk to you for a second."

I jumped away from him, wrenching my arm free.

My movements made Jeb turn worried, and he held his hands up in front of him. "Now, I ain't gonna hurt ya, Miss Jessie," he said in what seemed to be grave sincerity. "Honest. Just need to talk to you for a second."

I stood still, my shaky hand sloshing tea over the side of the glass. Despite my suspicions, and Luke's for that matter, I still found it hard to mistrust Jeb. I instinctively wanted to know what it was he needed to say. I looked around anxiously and said, "All right, but I ain't got long."

I stayed well away from him, and Jeb didn't try to get closer when he talked. "You know last night, when you got stuck in the shed?"

I nodded.

"Well, that was me that done it." He lowered his voice and glanced over his shoulder. "But you got to believe me. I did it for your own good."

Remembering the terror I'd felt in that shed, I had a hard time feeling anything but anger over what he was saying. "You? But why?" I asked, not sure I really wanted to know the answer.

Jeb rubbed the back of his sunburnt neck and said, "I can't rightly tell you that. You just got to trust me that I did it for your own good."

"I can't trust no one no more," I told him wearily. "Ain't a single soul I can trust."

"That's a frightful way for a body to think," he scolded gently. "You got your momma and daddy and Luke and Gemma . . . you got lots of people you can trust. And I think if you ask your daddy, he'd tell you that you can trust me too."

I gave his words a few moments thought, and then I backed away slowly. "No, sir. No, sir. Ain't nobody to trust, and that means you, too." I spilled the sweet tea onto the ground and ran, ignoring Jeb's calls to me.

When I got back to the house, I made sure to put on a brave face so no one would ask me what was wrong. It was a dull, still morning, and I found Gemma rocking listlessly on the tree swing.

"I'm bored," she told me. "Where you been? You ain't supposed to go off alone."

"I ain't alone in my own fields," I said. "Anyhow, Momma sent me to take some tea to Daddy, but he's gone to town."

"Well, we'd best find somethin' to do, else this'll be one fine, borin' day. Your momma says we ain't got any chores to be done today, and it's a day for bein' lazy."

"I don't feel like bein' lazy," I said.

"Neither do I, but what'll we do?"

After long thought, Gemma and I decided we would head over to Miss Cleta's. Since I'd been sleeping very little at night, I had read through her books in just a few days, and I wanted to exchange them for others. Knowing Walt had come upon me last time I ventured out alone, Gemma was determined I shouldn't stray far without her, so we walked through the ninety-degree heat together.

Miss Cleta was pleased as punch to see us, and we were glad we hadn't come too early to catch some fresh-baked goods. "About ready to get some popovers from the oven," she told us. "Hope you brought your sweet tooth with you."

No doubt we had, and we spent the next hour gathering books and eating sweets and milk. Around ten thirty, Miss Cleta clapped as though she'd come up with a fine idea. "This is my goin'-into-town day. Why don't you girls go home and get dressed on up, and we'll go in and have lunch together? How would you like that?"

"I don't know," I said, already nervous at the idea of meeting more ornery people in town. "Momma might not want us to."

"Oh, your momma's an understandin' woman. I'll bet she'll say yes."

"Well, Jessie may be able to go," Gemma told her adamantly, "but I got busy work to do."

I glanced at Gemma, who had told me barely an hour earlier that we had a lazy day ahead of us.

Miss Cleta took a long swig of milk, wiped her mouth daintily with her napkin, and stared hard at Gemma and then at me. "Just what is it you girls are really sayin'? You think I shouldn't take you to town for some reason?"

Gemma and I looked at each other.

"Well, is that it?" Miss Cleta tossed her napkin onto the table. "You think just because some people say white and colored don't mix, I have to listen? There any law that says that if most people believe somethin', it must be true? Is there? Because to my knowledge, there ain't no law in this country that says I can't do as I darn well please. And I darn well please to go into town with my two friends. The white one *and* the colored one."

"But there's bunches of trouble aimed at us these days," I exclaimed. "You don't know the half of it. You're liable to get in trouble yourself. We know what we got comin', but we don't want you gettin' hurt."

"Nonsense. I can take care of myself against the rabble in this town."

"I'd worry about it, Miss Cleta," Gemma said. "Ain't no way for me to have fun in town with you if I got to worry all the time about causin' you trouble."

"Now listen here. I ain't lived on this earth for seventy-five years to sit in my house cowerin' from human ignorance. I've certainly earned my right to do as I please around here within the law. And havin' lunch with you girls is within the law." Miss Cleta sat back and crossed her arms. "You girls think you're wrong for bein' friends?"

"No, ma'am!" we both shouted.

"You think colored people are less than white people?"

"No, ma'am!"

"Well then, enough talkin' about me. I'll be fine. The question is, do you girls have the nerve to go into town with me and stand up to all those people?"

"Me?" I asked, sitting up good and tall. "I got plenty of nerve. You ask my momma."

"Well then, prove it. You too, missy," Miss Cleta said to Gemma. "You two girls want to say you got nerve to stand up to people, then you got to prove it. Ain't no way to change the world for the better if you can't stand up for what's right when everyone else is wrong."

Gemma and I watched her ferocity with amazement, not uttering another word.

And that's how one o'clock in the afternoon found us stepping from Mr. Lionel Stokes' taxi cab in the center of town. Being a colored man himself, Mr. Stokes had done plenty of talking to Miss Cleta on our way into town, trying to persuade her to change her mind. As we exited his taxi, he shook his head. "Uh . . . uh . . . uh," we heard him grunt slowly. "Just askin' for trouble. That she is."

He hadn't helped calm our nerves any, but Miss Cleta seemed as serene as ever as we marched toward the Calloway Inn, where she planned to have us dine. We drew plenty of stares on that short journey. Men peered from behind their newspapers. Ladies whispered behind gloved hands. I trained my eyes on Miss Cleta's flower-covered blouse and walked ahead stoically.

"Miss Cleta," the hostess cried with a clap of her lily-white hands, "we ain't seen you here in an age. What a delight!" She stopped dead when she saw me and Gemma. It was like the smile just melted off her face like hot wax. "My, my," she gasped, stricken.

"I'd like a table for myself and my two friends," Miss Cleta said politely.

"Why, I'm so sorry to say, but . . . well . . . I believe we are full today."

"Full? On a Thursday?"

"Yes, ma'am. You know, we get some workin' folks in here durin' the week."

Miss Cleta eyed her for a second and then walked past her to peer into the dining area. She returned and put both hands on her hips. "Looks to me that you got a total of five people in that dinin' room. You tellin' me the rest all had to visit the restrooms at the same time?"

"Miss Cleta, please. Do be discreet!"

"And I would say the same to you, young lady. Do be discreet and show your customers to a table."

The hostess came forward and covered her mouth like we wouldn't hear her when she whispered loudly, "Miss Cleta, we don't have coloreds in our restaurant."

"Do you have a sign in your window?" Miss Cleta asked.

"Well, no, ma'am, but it's just understood. . . ."

"I understand nothin'. All I know is I'm good and hungry, and I want to eat."

The hostess just stood there, a menu in her hand, stumbling over words that only came out as random syllables.

"Oh, heaven's sake, just give me that," Miss Cleta said, snatching the menu from her hand. "I'll do it myself while you get your tongue back in your head." She grabbed our arms and ushered us to a table square in the middle of the restaurant.

The five diners turned with gasps and blatant stares, and

within moments the manager appeared, whispering apologies to his current patrons before hurrying over to us.

"I'm sorry, Miss Cleta," he said with forced politeness, "but I'll have to ask you to leave."

"Do you still make food here?" Miss Cleta asked.

"Why, yes, ma'am."

"And do you still take American money?"

"Yes, ma'am."

"Well then, I see no reason why you cannot allow me and my friends to eat here."

"Miss Cleta," he said, tugging at his tight collar, "please don't make me be blunt."

"Why not? I am."

His cheeks turned red. "Very well, then. We do not have coloreds in here, ma'am. It offends our customers."

She looked at me. "You offended, Jessilyn, by our Gemma here?"

"No, ma'am."

"Well, neither am I," Miss Cleta said to the manager. "So that makes two of your customers that aren't offended."

By this time the manager was becoming very anxious, and he leaned closer to say, "Miss Cleta, I'm gonna lose business if you stay. Now, either you leave politely, or I'll call the sheriff."

Gemma looked near to tears, and with a glance at her, Miss Cleta said, "Very well. We'll leave. But let me assure you that I will never set foot in this establishment again, nor will I recommend it to my friends."

The manager backed away from the table as we rose, his arms folded in determination. The other patrons watched us as we walked away, and Miss Cleta stopped as we passed one of their tables. "Don't eat the shrimp," she said loudly. "I got the diarrhea from them once." The women gasped as Miss Cleta turned with a smile of satisfaction and led us out of the restaurant. "That ought to fix their appetites," she said with a hoot once we were outside. "Well now. Where should we go next?"

We stood on the sidewalk for a second thinking up our next move when Hobie Decker came out of his diner across the street. He lit up a cigarette and leaned against the wall before catching sight of our odd little trio.

"Hey there, Miss Cleta." He put out his cigarette in a show of respect and tipped his head at me and Gemma. "Ladies," he added. "You out for a day on the town?"

"Yes'r," Miss Cleta called back. "We figured on gettin' a bite, but it seems this here inn ain't too obligin' about servin' all God's creatures."

"Well, you're welcome to have a bite in my place anytime you want."

"Why, Hobie Decker," Miss Cleta exclaimed, "I can't think of anythin' better."

Gemma and I smiled at him, just thankful at the prospect of actual food.

When we entered the diner, two men were sitting at the bar, and a family of three sat at a table in the corner. The family smiled at us, something so rare it shocked me to see.

But one of the men at the bar looked less than enthusiastic. He started to speak, but Mr. Decker put a hand on his arm, eyeing him sharply. The man reached into his pocket, plunked some change onto the counter, and stormed out. The other man at the bar just turned around and continued his lunch.

We dined on the greasiest fried chicken I'd ever had and cherry cola with two cherries floating inside. It tasted heavenly to us. When we'd had more than our fill, Miss Cleta paid Mr. Decker a fine tip, and the three of us headed off to complete her errand list. We visited the grocer, the pharmacy, and the candy store, while all along the way Mr. Stokes followed in his taxi, piling all her purchases into the car.

Miss Cleta kept her head held high wherever we went, a pleasant smile on her face, one hand on my arm, one hand on Gemma's. We followed her lead and said hello to everyone we passed. In all, we had two smiles and hellos in return, but mostly we were met with disdain or simple disinterest. Miss Cleta's stout confidence gave me and Gemma a much-needed lift, and by the time we headed for home, we felt more restored than battered.

"You done caused a commotion, sure enough," Mr. Stokes said as we got into the car. "Sure enough, you done caused a commotion. I can see it with my own two eyes."

"Sure enough we did," Miss Cleta said as we drove off down the road.

"You don't want to be startin' things up, Miss Cleta. No, ma'am, you don't."

"Mr. Stokes, ain't nothin' bad ever changed to good without startin' a little commotion," she replied. "Long as we keep a good Christian attitude with people, a little commotion can change a lot of hearts."

"Was it a good Christian attitude to warn those ladies about the shrimp?" I asked with a twinkle in my eye.

"Well . . . ," she said with a sly smile. "We should have a good Christian attitude at least *most* of the time."

I looked at Miss Cleta fondly, proud to have her as my friend and ally. We were in great need of them in those days, and I was fast discovering that the quality of her friendship was higher than most.

Chapter 18

Miss Cleta had Mr. Stokes carry me and Gemma home in his taxi, and we stepped out onto our gravel driveway like queens departing a carriage.

Momma stood on the porch, one hand holding a dish towel, the other shading her eyes from the sun. "Well, look at you girls. Comin' home in style, you are."

We said good-bye to Mr. Stokes and sauntered regally up to the porch.

"Just jottin' into town," I said. "You know how us social girls live."

"Takin' taxi cabs!" Momma gave a low whistle. "Livin' high on the hog, ain't you?"

Gemma sat on a rocker and patted her stomach. "If we ate like that every day, we'd be turnin' into hogs. I done ate enough to last me a year."

"So it went okay, then?" Momma asked uncertainly. She hadn't been too fond of letting us go in the first place, but Daddy had convinced her that we couldn't hide from everything.

We followed Momma into the kitchen so she could finish her dishes while listening to us tell her about our day. We were in the middle of running down the list of things we'd eaten when Daddy stormed into the house.

"Harley, you're trackin' mud into my house," Momma scolded, but she stopped when she saw his face. "What's wrong now? Someone get hurt?"

Daddy just stood there, one hand on his hip. Then he said, "Sadie, Jessilyn, Gemma . . . you seen anyone in the back fields of late?"

We all shook our heads.

"What is it, Harley?" Momma asked impatiently.

"Somebody done slashed the tires on my tractor, that's what. I just got me them new tires, and they ain't no good to nobody now. And I ain't got the money to go about replacin' 'em." He started to pace the floor, smacking his hat against his leg with every other step. "Who does things like that? Sneakin' onto a man's property and ruinin' the things he works hard for. Who does that?"

Momma sighed and leaned over the sink, staring out the window. After a minute, she said, "Well, what're we gonna do?"

"I don't know." Daddy paced the floor a few more times, and then he looked up at me and Gemma. He could see the worry on our faces, and that made him calm down a bit. He gave us a small, forced smile. "It'll work out, girls. Ain't no worryin' to be done. It'll get fixed like everythin' else."

"But you need that tractor for the farm," I said. "What'll you do if you can't use it?"

"Jessilyn, that ain't your worry. Like I said, it'll all work out." He walked off into the den, and Momma went after him. I could hear them talking quietly as they left.

I sat at the kitchen table, tapping my fingers thoughtfully. I wondered if Jeb had locked me in that shed last night to keep me from seeing him fooling around with the tractor. But then, why would he have told me that he'd locked me in? I'd been wondering about that ever since I found out.

On our farm, we had only five hands altogether, and out-side of Jeb, all of them were colored men who had small, worn homes and large families. But Jeb was alone in the world, and he lived an acre away in an old shack that sat on our property. We didn't even know where that shack came from, but Daddy let Jeb use it for a home, what little there was of it. The lean-to, though, kept some of his personal effects and a few tools he'd brought with him when he came to Calloway.

I believed he'd had plenty of opportunity to lock me in as he'd said, but I couldn't figure out why it would benefit him to do it. Each time I thought of Jeb, I questioned him even more. And each time I thought of that lean-to, I wondered just what he kept inside.

✳

The week before the start of school, Gemma and I were helping in the fields to take some of the pressure off Daddy. He never liked us doing those sorts of chores. He'd always said, "Girls are delicate and they shouldn't be doin' dirty work in the fields." But I didn't mind so much unless it was a scorcher, and this day in particular was only eighty degrees, cool by Calloway standards.

We had no more information about the tractor than we'd had the day Daddy found it beat up, and Daddy was spending most of his time trying to patch the old steel wheels he'd taken off for the fancy new tires. They were bent up and tore up the ground they ran across, but he had no choice. A working farm needed a working tractor, and that was all there was to it.

As we worked that morning, I watched Jeb closely. He gave nothing away and seemed innocent as a dove. I couldn't imagine not being able to trust him, yet that conversation with Walt Blevins kept running through my brain. He'd known about Walt bothering me, and he'd warned him, but I also realized that he'd only warned him for his own benefit, to keep his plans intact. What were those plans? There was no longer any question if Luke was right that Jeb had been hiding something. I had only to wonder exactly what it was that he was hiding. I did nothing but wonder.

By noon, Daddy told us we'd done enough.

"We ain't but got through two rows," I told him.

"You shouldn't be doin' any rows," he said. "Look at y'all's hands. All dirty and rough. You head on in and get some dinner, and if there's any woman's chores to be done, you can help your momma. It'll be gettin' hotter throughout the afternoon, anyhow."

Gemma and I trudged up the path examining the beginnings of blisters on our hands. "Shoot!" I said when I found one on the inside of my finger. "The finger next to it will rub it like crazy."

"Shoulda worn gloves like I done told you," Gemma said.

"I hate wearin' gloves; you know that. Keeps me from feelin' what I'm doin'."

"Well then, don't complain about blisters."

"You wore gloves, and you got a blister comin' up."

"Only a small one," she said in her defense.

"Ain't no comparin' big ones and small ones. You got a blister, then you got a blister. Ain't no difference between the two." I slowed as we neared the old shed and walked over to the lean-to, examining it as best I could in the bright sun. Then I looked around to see if we had any company.

"What're you doin'?" Gemma asked impatiently. "Dinner's gonna get stale waitin' for us."

"Just a minute," I hissed. "You ate two tomatoes while we were pickin', anyway. You can't be that starved."

"Well, what're you pokin' around the shed for?"

I stood back. "What's he got in that thing?" I tried the door of the lean-to unsuccessfully.

"You get your nasty self away from that lean-to," Gemma said. "That ain't your stuff. It's Jeb's."

"It's on Lassiter property."

"So's my trunk, but I expect no one goes diggin' through it."

I tried the door again, tugging harder this time.

"Jessilyn!"

"I just want to know what he keeps in it."

"What for? He ain't done nothin' to you."

"Ain't so sure," I said seriously.

"What do you mean?"

"I mean, I ain't so sure."

Gemma didn't get my meaning, and I didn't expect her to, but all the same I was determined to get a peek inside that lean-to. I found a sort of crowbar in the shed and used it to jimmy the door open, with Gemma flapping at me the whole time.

"You're gonna break the law," she whispered, her arms spread out in front of her like an attorney presenting his case. "That's what you're gonna do. I ain't never known you to be a lawbreaker."

"It's Lassiter property," I remarked again. "Ain't no law breakin' in that."

The door creaked slightly as I opened it. The space was so small you almost had to crawl into it, and I bent down and did a sort of duckwalk inside, the sunlight illuminating its contents. Several crates were stacked in one corner and a pallet lay rolled up in another.

Gemma came in behind me. "Uh . . . uh . . . uh . . ."

"Would you hush up?" I wailed, my nerves already frazzled enough.

"Can't help feelin' the way I'm feelin'. Least one of us has some conscience left."

"Oh, hush!" I took a furtive look out the door, saw no one, and proceeded to work at one of the wooden crates.

"Now you're gettin' worse. Lookin' in a man's things. That's a sin."

"It ain't no sin."

"Sure as sunshine, it is!"

"When you ever seen the Bible say, 'Thou shalt not look in another man's crates'?"

"Don't you make fun of the Bible," Gemma demanded, her face stricken.

"I ain't makin' fun of the Bible. I'm makin' fun of you."

"Well, I ain't gonna let you do it." She grabbed my hands to keep me from removing the top of the crate.

"Leave me be!"

"No!" Gemma argued. "I ain't lettin' you pry into Jeb's things and feel awful about it later."

I leaned my hip into her side, trying to shove her away, but she retained a steady grip.

"Quit pushin' me," she said, breathless from our struggle. "You ain't gettin' me away that easy."

"I want to see inside," I grunted, still pushing her with my hip. "Now leave me be."

"No ma'am! I ain't raised to do such things and neither

were you. Ain't nice to let friends make mistakes like you're gonna make."

"I've made lots of mistakes," I said, "and you ain't been able to stop me those times, neither."

"I will this time." Gemma's voice was strained as she pushed her weight against mine. "You ain't gettin' in this crate."

We were both breathing hard from fatigue, standing with our feet wide apart, digging our sides into each other. Back and forth we'd lean, one of us giving in for a second before pushing back with all our might. We were grunting and groaning, and the crate creaked under the pressure.

I gave the top another tug, and I could feel it loosen. "I've almost got it. Now get off so I can see inside before someone gets here."

"No, I won't. I ain't gonna let you do it." Gemma clutched my hands more tightly, but her hold only enabled me to pull the lid off, and the two of us toppled to the ground as it released.

Gemma started to sputter at me, but she stopped dead when she got a glimpse at what had tumbled out of the crate. Half hanging out was a mass of white fabric, and we instinctively knew just what that white fabric was. We'd seen it up close and personal.

I jumped up and took a closer look in that crate. I dug around and found a matching hood, hollow eye slits staring at us like a demon. "Klan," I whispered, my heart dropping with the realization of what Jeb was.

"You mean we got Klan right here?" Gemma gasped. "We got Klan on Lassiter property?"

My ears pricked up when I heard the voices of some of the men on the path. "They're breakin' for dinner. We gotta get out."

Gemma helped me stuff the robe back into the crate and replace the lid. We flew outside, tossed the crowbar back into the shed, and made it down the path and out of sight without getting caught.

Once we were near the house, I led Gemma off the path toward the cover of some trees. "Don't you tell no one," I said.

"Tell no one what? What we saw?"

"Don't say nothin' about what we saw, and I don't want you tellin' what I'm about to tell you, neither."

"What?"

"Well, do you promise not to tell no one?"

Gemma shrugged like she didn't think I was going to say anything worth sharing.

"What's that?" I asked. "That mean you won't tell?"

"No, I won't tell. Mercy's sake!"

"All right, fine." I took another look around for eaves-droppers. "The other day, when I was goin' to find Jeb for Momma, I saw him in the woods by the top fields talkin' to Walt Blevins."

Gemma looked genuinely puzzled. "What for?"

"Don't know what for exactly, but he told Walt to leave me alone."

"Maybe he saw Walt sneakin' around and took care of him for your daddy."

"Don't think so, 'cause he talked to Walt right friendly, like he knows him. He said that messin' with me would spoil his plans."

"Plans?"

"He didn't say nothin' else. Just said he didn't want Walt messin' up his plans."

"That don't make no sense."

"It does if Jeb's in on all the trouble."

"You in more trouble than you're tellin' me?" she asked with a shake in her voice. I was surprised by the fierce look in her eyes. "You tell me straight."

I paused and then said, "Gemma, you got enough to worry about. You ain't got to be worryin' about me."

"If there's somethin' wrong, I want to know. I been suspectin' you ain't been tellin' me all. Well, now's the time. I want to know."

Tears started to spring to my eyes, and it made me cringe to feel the way I did. I hated feeling the isolation of being a victim.

"What is it?" Gemma asked anxiously. "Tell me."

"I think Walt's gonna hurt me," I blurted out, all the fear of the past days rushing back full force. "He looks at me like no grown man should look at me."

"He threaten you?"

"As much as he could without actually sayin' so."

"Why didn't you tell your daddy?"

"Daddy's got enough trouble. . . ."

"He would want to know."

"No! I don't want Daddy knowin'. I don't want no one knowin'. You promised me. It's between you and me."

Gemma didn't understand me. I could see that on her face. When it came right down to it, I didn't understand me either. But things were what they were, and I didn't have any experience in handling such things. We barely said two words to each other on the way back to the house.

"Your daddy and momma would feel badder'n I don't know what if you ended up dead," Gemma said as we snapped beans for supper that night.

"Hush your mouth," I whispered. "Luke's comin'."

"Looks like your momma's beans are on the menu," Luke said happily as he ambled up the walkway. "And I could smell her honey ham all the way from Miss Cleta's house."

"I know," I replied. "Been makin' me hungry for the last hour."

He mounted the porch steps in one stride and straddled an old straw chair. "Give me a bowl, Jessie, and I'll help you out."

"There's other more important ways you could help her out," Gemma muttered.

I grabbed Gemma's bowl away from her, making her drop a bean onto the floor, where Duke quickly retrieved it. "Gemma's gotta go help Momma in the kitchen," I said with a glare at her, knowing full well that she'd hint enough to have Luke guessing at my troubles if I let her stay out with us. "You can use her bowl."

She sighed and let the door slam extra hard on her way in.

"She seems right sober," Luke commented to me when Gemma had gone.

"She gets that way when she's hungry," I lied.

Luke didn't believe me, I could see, but he was used to me and Gemma arguing about things. He likely figured he'd be better off not knowing what our spat was about.

We had an end-of-summer storm that night in late August, and since there wasn't much nearby lightning from it, Momma excused me from dishes so I could enjoy it on the porch. Gemma volunteered to help Momma since she didn't want anything to do with thunderstorms anymore. So Luke and I sat on the porch glider while Daddy smoked his pipe on an old rocker.

"Ain't too many more nights like this left," Daddy murmured after a particularly long clap of thunder. "Gettin' on to the end of the season now."

"Yes'r," I responded quietly. "Summer's almost gone." Most years, I thought summer always went too fast, but I couldn't say that this summer was one I wanted to hang on to any longer than necessary.

"School startin' soon, Jessie?" Luke asked.

"Next week."

"You happy to go?"

"S'pose I'm just toleratin' it. Ain't like I'll be long on friends or nothin'."

"Now, Jessilyn," Daddy said with a tone that likely didn't even convince himself, "there ain't no tellin' for sure that you won't have friends."

"You been around town lately, Daddy? Ain't no one wants to be our friends." I crossed my arms and said with sincerity, "I don't care none if they don't, neither. If they got worries 'cause we got Gemma, then they ain't worth bein' friends with, nohow."

"That's my girl," Luke said, tousling my hair with a hand that nearly covered the top of my head. His brotherly gesture did nothing to improve my opinion of the current summer.

Another loud jolt of thunder sent Duke cowering underneath the glider with a squeal. Then almost as quickly he came flying back out in excitement as Mr. Tinker's truck rumbled up our gravel driveway.

"What in the . . . ?" Daddy mumbled. "Ain't expectin' to see him tonight."

Mr. Tinker popped his head out the side window and hollered for Daddy.

"What is it, Otis?" he hollered.

"Got some trouble at the Pollard place, and the sheriff's out in Sellers County for a meetin'. Could sure use your help."

Daddy stood and stretched. "What kind of trouble?"

"Same as usual. Old Jeff Pollard's been into the jug too much today, and his missus swears he's gonna kill 'em all with his flailin' and cussin'. You know how she gets."

Daddy shook his head, handing me his pipe. "Stick this inside for me, will you? And tell your momma where I'm headin'."

"You need me to go along?" Luke asked.

"Naw, you stay on here."

"Don't know, Harley," Mr. Tinker said. "Might come in handy if Jeff's all a sight like his missus says he is. He's no small man, you know."

"He ain't so big as the two of us can't handle him. 'Sides, he gets all tottery when he's tight. Won't be able to see straight enough to figure out who to punch."

"No trouble, if you need me," Luke insisted.

"Ain't no harm in a couple more good hands," Mr. Tinker said.

Daddy turned to Luke, who was now standing near him, one hand hanging on to the porch pillar. "Luke, I'd be just as obliged if you'd stay behind with my girls." He lowered his voice. "I'd feel mighty good knowin' they wasn't alone tonight, you hear?"

Luke tipped his hat. "Yes'r."

Daddy's tone and the look on his face when he spoke to Luke made me even more nervous than I'd been. Now I knew for sure that he was scared for us, and my daddy didn't scare too easily. I pulled my knees up to my chin and hugged them, watching Daddy tug his hat down tighter before heading out into the light droplets of rain that had begun to fall. "Be careful, Daddy."

"Oh, I'll be fine, darlin'," he said with a lighthearted smile. "Ain't nothin' old Jeff Pollard's goin' to do to me. He's been a fine neighbor right these twenty years, and he ain't like to do nothin' bad."

I returned the pipe to its place on the mantel and told Momma where Daddy had gone. I stared out the front window, watching the truck leave the house, my heart heavy. I had a persistent feeling of doom these days, like something awful waited for me around every corner. Fear had become my constant companion, and I hated to see my daddy head off into any situation that could be dangerous.

Momma came up behind me and took a look out the window. "That Jeff Pollard. What a sight." Then she went back to her humming and dish cleaning.

I left Momma and Gemma to their busy work and walked out to the porch, where Luke sat tapping his foot.

"Rainin' good now," he told me.

"S'pose." I settled in the seat next to him. "You think Daddy's safe out there at the Pollard place?"

"Don't see why not."

"But his wife says he's bound to kill 'em, Mr. Otis said."

"Aw, his bark's worse than his bite, I'll wager."

"How d'you know?"

"Well, your daddy says so, and what your daddy says is usually right. Besides, Jeff Pollard works at the factory with me, and he seems a right good man. Most decent men don't go doin' awful stuff when they're liquored up."

"But the drink does bad things to people."

Luke looked at me sideways. "How do you know? Your daddy don't drink."

I stumbled a little because I hadn't told anybody about Buddy Pernell's advances at the Independence Day social, and I didn't feel like letting on now. So I just said, "I been to enough barn dances to know what men are like on the drink. It ain't nice, is all."

"No, it ain't nice, but I don't think a basically decent man would kill his family just from bein' drunk. I'd say he's gotta be a mean one to begin with if he's gonna do somethin' crazy like that."

I wasn't so sure I agreed with his theory. "Seems to me when a man loses his senses he's bound to do anythin'. A man shouldn't do somethin' that takes away his senses, the way I see it."

He nodded slowly, thoughtfully. "Well, I reckon you're right about that. A man gets his sense from the good Lord. I guess he should be mindful of keepin' it."

"That's right." I sat there for a few moments listening to the thunder as it rumbled further and further away. "Luke?"

"What's that?"

"You drink whiskey or anythin'?"

"What's that?" he asked again, and I could tell I'd made him a bit uncomfortable.

"I said, you drink whiskey?"

"Well, you got to realize that there's different kinds of drinkin'," he said after a good throat clearing.

"That don't make no sense," I said. "Either you drink or you don't."

"Now, that ain't so. There's a difference in havin' a little taste, like I do now and again, and in gettin' good and drunk on purpose."

"I don't see no difference if it makes you fuzzy, and Daddy says even a little makes him fuzzy, so that's why he don't take it."

"Well, each man's different."

I turned to him, and I'm sure my shock and petulance must have shown on my face. "Luke Talley, you tellin' me you're a drunk?"

"I ain't no drunk!"

"You just told me you have a taste of whiskey some days. Seems to me that makes you a drunk."

"No, it don't! You just hold on to your britches there, little girl. I ain't no such thing as a drunk."

"I ain't no little girl," I hollered, standing up. "And I know a drunk when I seen one."

"Now, Jessie . . ."

"For all we know, you got yourself a still hidin' in your backyard."

Luke stood to his full height and gave me a look that made me shiver. "Don't you go sayin' things like that about me, Jessilyn. You want to have the law on me? I may be many a thing, but I ain't no moonshiner."

He looked at me expectantly as though I'd feel sorry for my words any second, but my idol of Luke had been chipped, and I was fit to be tied. I turned away from him sharply and slammed the screen door open so hard it shook the house.

Momma came walking to the kitchen doorway when I marched inside. "What in the world . . . ? Jessilyn, what've you got a bee in your bonnet for?"

"Luke's a rotten drunk," I hollered, and then I ran up to my room with the vehemence of a woman scorned.

It was about twenty minutes of thinking about the bad side of alcohol before I decided I'd have to see Pastor Landry about my dilemma sometime. Surely a preacher man would have the right answer on such a subject. So it was with a heavy heart and a faded view of my perfect Luke that I wandered back downstairs about eight thirty. I avoided eye contact with him when I found him resting in Daddy's chair in the den.

Momma was sitting by the lamp, her face as close to her embroidery as it could be without poking her eye out with her needle. "There you are, Jessilyn," she said as though I'd never been distraught to find out my true love was a drunkard. "You think I should use sky blue for this pillowcase or cornflower?"

I really didn't care about shades of colors just then, but as I plopped down next to Gemma on the couch, I mumbled, "Cornflower, I guess."

"That's what Gemma said. Cornflower it is."

Gemma was reading her book quietly, but she took time to whisper to me, "What's got you riled?"

"Nothin'," I bit back. "Girl's got a right to get her back up now and again, ain't she?"

"Sorry I asked."

I felt sorry for being so harsh, and I couldn't quite figure why I had been either. But then, I couldn't figure out much about myself those days. Luke tried catching my eye several times over the next ten minutes, but it was no use. I kept my eyes trained so hard on the portrait of my great-grandparents that my eye sockets felt about ready to pop.

At nine fifteen, the clock disturbed the silence to chime once. I was starting to worry about Daddy not being back yet, but one look at Momma's easy expression told me I was probably exaggerating. If there had been real cause for worry, Momma would have been the first person to have it.

The clock wasn't the only thing that disturbed the quiet, though, as Duke started to bark like crazy. There was all sorts of ruckus coming from the back of the house, a mixture of barks and growls with a few yips mixed in. We sat and listened for about a minute before Momma finally said, "Sounds like Duke's fightin' with somethin'."

"We'd better find out," I exclaimed. "He might get hurt."

"Probably just a raccoon," Gemma said with a yawn. "He's done that enough times."

"But what if it has rabies or somethin'?"

"Ain't none of the other ones had rabies."

"That don't mean this one can't. We need to go help him."

"Jessilyn," Momma said, "we can't do much to help him if he's fightin' with a dangerous animal. We can't fight wild animals."

Luke was looking out a side window, so I appealed to him instead. "Can't you get Daddy's gun and see what's happenin'?"

"I'll find out what it is. Y'all stay here inside the house." Luke stuck his hat on, unbuttoned a couple buttons on the bottom of his shirt, and reached inside to pull a pistol from his waistband. I could not believe my eyes. Now my Luke wasn't just a drunkard, he was a drunkard who carried a pistol. Heavens, he was a drunken gunfighter!

My heart leapt as I watched him walk out the back door, but I didn't know if I was more worried for his safety or for his soul. I made a note to ask Pastor Landry about gun carrying too.

The noise had gotten more distant now, and I assumed Luke was having to walk down toward the corn rows to find Duke.

"Land's sake, they make a mess of noise, those animals," Momma complained. "We should have tied him up after supper. Don't know what good we get from that mutt, anyhow."

"Momma!"

"Well, we don't get no affection from him, Lord knows. All he does is eat our table scraps and chase animals."

"But that don't mean we should want him gettin' killed by a wild animal."

"I didn't say I wanted him killed by a wild animal, Jessilyn. Watch your tone of voice."

I said a quiet "Yes, ma'am," but a loud crash at the far end of the room made me shoot up from my seat before I even got settled down.

Momma and Gemma jumped up as well, with Momma gasping, "What on earth? My heavens, what is happenin' in this house?" She raced across the room and pushed my and Gemma's heads down like we were under fire. "Jesus, protect this house," Momma said over and over again as we huddled together on the floor.

I peered out from underneath Momma's arm to see what had crashed through the window. "It's a rock. Just a big rock."

"A rock don't get through a window on its own, Jessilyn. Keep your head down."

Then we heard footsteps on the porch, and the three of us instinctively focused on the front door. The screen door was closed but unlocked as always, and fear struck us as we realized whoever was on that porch had access to our house.

Momma decided to meet them head-on. "Stay here," she said as she rose and walked slowly toward the front door, her head ducked.

"I ain't lettin' her go alone," I told Gemma. "She crazy or somethin'?"

"Me neither," she said.

We followed Momma in similarly hunched positions.

"I said stay back," Momma hissed.

"We ain't bound to sit by and let you go by yourself," I said with determination. "We're comin' too."

Momma didn't say anything more, which surprised me because Momma didn't take any lip from me on a normal day.

We approached the doorway timidly, and when we looked out, we saw an eerily familiar sight. Five men in white stood on our lawn, pointing guns toward the house, calling out to us with curses and wry laughter.

This time, they had come for revenge.

Chapter 19

My heart was in my throat as I stared down those robed gunmen, and I felt naked without Daddy's rifle, like I'd carried one all my life.

"We brought our own weapons this time," one of them said, as though reading my thoughts. "If we's gonna get shot at by young'uns, we may's well be able to shoot back."

"You ain't got no right to be here," Momma said, her voice a mixture of anger and fear. "You get shot for trespassin', let that be on your head."

"See, as we figure it, you folks is the ones trespassin'. We got ways in this here part of the country, and you decided to go against those ways. From our side of seein' things, you made yourselves the outsiders who are trespassin' on our way of life."

I strained my ears hoping to hear Luke returning, but

I heard nothing from the back of the house, not even Duke.

"You ain't got no right comin' on our property," Momma said shakily. "No right! And why don't you take off those filthy hoods and show yourselves, you cowards?"

They stood with no reply, and their silence was more horrifying than any bitter words they could have uttered. The very sight of those white robes flapping in the breeze against the dark of night made my skin crawl. There were several moments of silence as we remained in our standoff, glaring at each other like opponents in a duel.

Then Momma spotted something that made her gasp and start to cry. "Oh, dear Jesus."

I looked around frantically, trying to train my eyes upon whatever it was that had Momma so upset. It took me two passes of the front yard before I saw it. There, coming from around the side of the house, were a sixth and seventh hooded man, dragging a limp form between them. I struggled to breathe as I watched Luke's head bob up and down, his blond hair tousled and sweaty.

"Luke!" I screamed, trying to rip my way past Momma to get outside.

"No, baby," she said, grabbing me around the waist. "You stay here."

I could tell by her voice that she was in tears. Gemma ran into the house for some reason, and I fleetingly hoped she was going for the rifle so we could kill all of them for what they'd done to Luke. "I want to go to Luke. Let me go!"

I struggled and flailed against Momma, finally breaking free and running onto the porch.

"Jessilyn!" Momma screamed.

I could feel her grasping at my shirt as I fled, but I made it to the end of the porch and hopped the rail, landing right where the men who had Luke were standing. They dropped him to the ground, and I ran to him, falling to my knees in front of him.

"Oh, Luke, what'd they do to you?" For all I could see, he was lifeless, his bloodied face displaying no movement. I put my head down to his chest to listen, but I couldn't hear anything. In sheer rage, I jumped up and started pawing at one of the men, ripping my fingernails into whatever skin I managed to make contact with. "You killed him!" I shouted over and over again. "I'm gonna kill you. You hear? I'll kill you."

The man I attacked howled and swatted at me. "Get her off me."

The other man pulled me off like a rag doll, his face against my right ear. "Ain't you done enough killin' for one year?" he asked in amusement. "You're just a regular killin' machine, ain't you, little girl? Well now, I like spunk in a girl, sure enough. And you got spunk."

"If I'm a killer like you say, Walt Blevins, then I ought to have no trouble puttin' a bullet through your heart."

In normal times, Momma would have washed my mouth out with soap for that, but she said nothing even though I knew she must have heard me. She just stayed frozen there on the porch with her hands over her mouth and terror on her face, two Klansmen blocking her path to where Walt stood with his dirty hands on me.

Just then, Otis Tinker's truck came flying up the road, spraying gravel every which way. Daddy was hanging halfway out the window firing a pistol into the air and shouting things I'd never heard my daddy say before.

Walt took a minute to whisper, "This ain't over, pretty girl," in my ear before dropping me like a hot potato.

I crawled back over to Luke, sobbing, while the rest of the group fled. There was absolute chaos in the yard, with Daddy and Mr. Tinker yelling and Momma wailing.

"Jessie!" Gemma screamed. "Jessie! Jessie! Stop shakin' him!"

I realized then that I had taken Luke by the shoulders, shaking him back and forth, begging him to wake up. At Gemma's orders, I let him go suddenly, his head dropping back to the earth with a thud.

Engines roared as the two trucks carrying the Klansmen sped off down the dirt road, and Daddy helped Momma over to where Gemma and I sat with Luke.

Gemma held me as I wept, but we both jumped a mile when Luke jolted up into a sitting position, yelling something about killing someone. He closed his eyes tightly and muttered again, "I'll kill 'em all."

I must have cried out his name ten times, throwing myself over him like a blanket.

"Now, Jessie," Daddy said, "don't strangle the boy."

"I thought he was dead."

"Well, keep that up and he will be." My daddy's face was red with rage, his hands shaky as he grabbed my shoulders, yet he somehow found the ability to tint his tone with light-heartedness. "Come on," he urged as I resisted his efforts to pull me away from Luke. "Go to your momma. I need to help Luke into the house."

I stood reluctantly and watched, with Momma's arm about my shoulder, as Luke got up, wincing in pain with every move he made.

I looked over at Mr. Tinker and said, "You seen what they done, ain't you? They near killed Luke. You gonna arrest 'em?"

"It's right hard to arrest men with no identity."

"They got identity, all right. I can tell you that Walt Blevins was one of 'em, and so was Cole Mundy. I know them voices."

"Jessilyn—" Daddy grunted from the strain of lifting Luke— "I thought we agreed not to get the law into this."

Mr. Tinker went over to help Daddy, ignoring my insistence that the men be arrested.

We got Luke settled on the couch, and Momma gathered her antiseptic and bandages. I followed Mr. Tinker out to his truck, telling him all the reasons he needed to arrest half the men in Calloway.

But he seemed loath to engage in any argument with me. "Jessilyn, you best talk this over with your daddy. Now you head on back inside, you hear?"

"Ain't no use gettin' the law involved," Luke moaned when I renewed my argument inside. "Even if we could for certain identify them, which we can't, they'd get off anyhow. That's the way it works in these parts. Klan gets by with everythin' and anythin'."

"But, Luke, just look what they done to you." I had his hand in mine, and I kept squeezing it. "They bruised you all up. They can't get by with that."

"Jessilyn," he said with a grin, "you're gonna wear the blood right outta my hand."

"Oh, I'm sorry," I gasped, dropping it quickly. "Did I hurt you more?"

Luke put a hand on my cheek and patted it lightly. "I'm gonna be just fine, you can be sure. Don't you worry none about me."

"I always worry about you," I said, tears starting to drip down my cheeks again.

Momma coaxed me away. "You let me fix him up now, and you go put some tea on. It'll settle his stomach." I watched for a minute as Momma worked on him. Her hands were as shaky as the rest of us. "Just look at me." She laughed nervously. "I'm all thumbs tonight."

Gemma and I went into the kitchen together, and as I filled the teapot, Gemma came to my side and whispered, "What'd that man say to you when he had you? He threaten you again?"

"Leave me be. Ain't me you got to worry about."

"I got this whole family to worry about. Now, I want to know what he said to you," she demanded.

I slammed the teapot onto the stove, but her grip on my arm told me she was in no mood to accept defeat. "Fine! He said it wasn't over. That's all."

Gemma shook her head, wide-eyed. "He's got somethin' in for you."

"Everyone in this town has it in for us. What's the difference?"

"But Walt's got it in special for you. He's gonna hurt you, you hear? He won't be happy till he does."

"You promised not to tell no one," I argued. "You best keep it to yourself."

"I don't have to do nothin' that I think puts you in danger. This has all gone far enough, and I'm tellin' your daddy."

"No, you ain't," I said. "You just keep your mouth shut!"

Gemma looked me hard in the eye and tightened her lips before saying, "Not this time. This time, I do what I gotta do." She moved away from me.

But I caught up to her and blocked the doorway. "You ain't tellin'."

"I'm tellin' your daddy," she replied. "I'm tellin' your daddy right now."

"Tellin' me what?" Daddy asked, his sudden appearance making us both startle.

Gemma looked at Daddy and then back at me. "Gotta do it, Jessie. For your own good."

I folded my arms and glared at her fiercely, but I didn't stop her. I knew it was useless.

"Gemma?" Daddy asked. "What is it you're tryin' to say? I want to know what's goin' on in my own house, you hear?"

"It's that Walt Blevins," Gemma said with hesitation.

"What about him?"

"He's been threatenin' Jessilyn."

"Threatenin' her in what way?"

"He's been talkin' to her indecent-like."

"What do you mean, indecent-like?" Daddy leaned down as though getting closer to Gemma would help him understand her better. Then his eyebrows narrowed, and he asked, "You mean he's makin' advances at my baby?"

Gemma said nothing, and Daddy correctly took her silence as corroboration. His face turned violent, and his eyes looked darker than I'd ever seen. The distress this news was bound to cause my daddy was part of what had kept me from saying anything to him, and I eyed Gemma sharply.

"Gemma," Daddy finally said after several seconds of silence, "you stay with Jessilyn as much as you can when you're home, you hear?"

"Yes'r."

"And, Jessilyn, you stay in this house. No goin' out without me or Luke, and no wanderin' in the fields."

"But, Daddy," I moaned, "I'll have nothin' to do."

"Now you listen to me, Jessilyn Lassiter. Ain't no tellin' what that man's capable of, and I ain't gonna have you walkin' into his trap."

"I'll be stuck in this house all day, bored stiff."

"Bored is a lot better'n what you could be if that man gets his paws on you. You stay in this house. You hear?"

I stood there in slight shock, watching everything I'd feared come true.

"I asked you a question, Jessilyn," Daddy said. "You hear me?"

"Yes'r."

Momma came up behind Daddy with bloody rags in her hands. "What in the world is goin' on now? Ain't we had enough trouble in this house for one night?"

"Jessilyn's been gettin' threats and not tellin' us," Daddy bellowed. "Walt's been bein' aggressive with her, and our girl decides not to tell us."

"Jessilyn!" Momma sounded horrified. "What'd that man do to you?"

"He ain't done nothin'. He's just sayin' things, is all."

"I don't care if he's just sayin' things or not," Daddy continued. "Ain't no way you're goin' out of this house without a man with you, and that's final."

Luke joined the fray at this point, his voice weak but strong enough to be heard over the commotion. "Who's been threatenin' Jessie? Is it Walt again? I swear, I'm gonna kill that boy. . . ."

I'd had enough. I couldn't take the loud voices and the chaos any longer, and the very idea of losing what little liberty I had left made my heart sink further still. My nerves broke. "Everybody just stop! You see why I told you not to tell, Gemma?" I asked in tears. "Ain't I had enough troubles this summer, now I got to be locked up in my own house? Walt Blevins, he gets to go around doin' whatever he pleases, and I got to suffer for it. Ain't none of this fair, and I'm tired of all of it. Everybody just leave me alone!" I pushed past Daddy, running upstairs to lock myself in the bathroom.

Gemma knocked on that bathroom door near about fifty times, but I ignored her and put my hands over my ears to block out the noise. For the life of me, I couldn't figure out why she was so worried about getting in there, and I yelled as much at her when she hit around sixty knocks. "What's your fuss? Can't you leave me alone, like I said?"

"You let me in there."

"What for? Leave me alone."

"No! I want in there."

I unlocked the door and opened it just enough to peer at her through the slit. "I got people followin' me near everywhere these days. I should be able to go to the bathroom by myself."

"Now listen here," Gemma said seriously, her hands planted firmly on her aproned hips. "You fixin' to do somethin'?"

"Besides gettin' rid of you?"

"Yes, ma'am. I mean besides that."

"Like what?" I argued, squinting till my eyes were barely open. "Can't do much in this little bathroom."

She leaned closer to the door, poking her nose into the

small space I'd left her. "Now listen here," she said again, like she was my momma or something. "You plannin' on hurtin' yourself?"

For a few seconds I didn't know what she was talking about, but when I realized what she'd meant, I rolled my eyes. "That's right. I came in here to jump out the window."

"Don't you kid about that. I'm serious!"

"If I jumped out this here window, I'd land on the kitchen roof. Most I'd do is twist an ankle." I wiped my runny nose with the back of my hand. "Good grief, Gemma Teague, you do beat all."

"You've been all nerves and jitters lately, and now you're all upset like this. Can't see as how I shouldn't think you might be up to somethin' bad."

"Life ain't so bad I'd kill myself."

Gemma pushed the door until it opened about six inches. I could have kept her out, but I let her open it, figuring I'd put her mind at ease. I thought she was being crazy, but even in my state, I didn't want her fretting about me dying.

"You ain't got nothin' in here you can hurt yourself with, do you?" she asked, stepping into the room, going straight over to the medicine chest.

"Don't think I can kill myself with Daddy's stomach pills," I told her. "They're nearly just candy peppermints, anyhow."

She ignored me and continued to turn bottles around for inspection.

"Ain't likely I can kill myself with bandages, hair oil, or

perfumed powder neither," I said with a sigh. I held the door open widely for her. "Can you leave me be now?"

"I heard of someone that done choked on powder before." Gemma held the bottle up and shook it to determine how much was left.

"Oh, you did not," I said with a smirk. "Ain't nobody ever choked on powder."

"Did too! Old Mr. Donley broke old Mrs. Donley's bottle of rose powder, and he inhaled so much of it he died the next day. It coated his lungs."

"Old Mr. Donley was close to a hundred years old. He died of a heart attack."

"Wouldn't have had a heart attack if he didn't breathe in that powder."

I thought her story was ridiculous, and I was finding her intrusion particularly irritating now. "Just shut on up and get outta here."

We glared at each other, mostly because neither of us liked being bossed around, and here we were doing just that to each other.

"I'm takin' the powder with me," Gemma said adamantly.

I have no idea why I didn't want her to. I certainly had no plans to smother myself with it. But the very idea that she was so certain I might try got me angry. "No, you ain't, neither," I said, grabbing the bottle.

She never let go, and we both had our hands on the powder, tugging away.

"You ain't keepin' it, I'm tellin' you," Gemma growled. "Let go!"

"No! You let go. I was here first."

"Jessie, just let go, and I'll leave you be."

"No!"

We pulled and argued for another thirty seconds, and for the life of me I have no idea how Momma and Daddy didn't tear into us for making such a ruckus. But we stood there fussing, tripping toward each other and then away from each other with each tug on the bottle. That is until I gave it one last good tug that pulled Gemma forward quickly enough to cause powder to fly out of the pinhead-size holes in the bottle, sending a white cloud through the bathroom with a great poof.

We both started to cough, and I waved my hand through the air, my eyes shut to keep the powder out. Gemma dropped the powder bottle into the sink and started shrieking, pushing me desperately. We both stumbled out into the hall, covered in white.

"Quit pushin' me," I yelled when I regained my stability. "You tryin' to kill me yourself?"

"We had to get outta there," she argued. "I ain't gonna let us die like old Mr. Donley."

I shook my head and coughed one more time. "This is the dumbest thing you've ever done," I said, brushing white from my dungarees.

Gemma didn't say a thing. She just cleared her throat

about five times and then let her tongue hang out like Duke when he was hot.

"What're you doin'?" I asked.

"I can't breathe right," she gasped.

"Don't be stupid!"

"I can't!"

"Well, I'm breathin' just fine."

Gemma staggered about the hallway like the sky was falling, clutching her chest.

Her wild actions made me nervous, and I grabbed one of her arms to stop her. "Calm down. You're scarin' me."

"Should be scared," she managed to grunt. She backed up against the wall and slid down to the floor, gasping for air.

Her expression made me forget about how put out I was with her, and I started screaming for Momma.

Within seconds, both Momma and Daddy flew up the stairs with loud footsteps, Luke on their heels, all bandaged and patched.

"What's goin' on?" Daddy looked strangely at my powder-covered face before spotting Gemma on the floor. He squatted in front of her. "What's wrong with Gemma?"

"She can't breathe," I cried. "She's chokin'!"

"On what?" Momma asked.

"On perfume powder."

"Perfume powder?" all three of them asked at once.

Daddy had Gemma's face cupped between his hands, and he turned to look at me. "How do you mean she's chokin' on perfume powder? She try eatin' it?"

"No, we were fightin' over the bottle, and I yanked it, and Gemma went flyin', and then powder just went everywhere, and she inhaled it like old Mr. Donley, and now she's suffo-catin' 'cause it's coated her lungs," I said in one long breath, ending my explanation on a high, screeching note.

"You didn't swallow any powder, Gemma?" Daddy asked.

"No," I answered for her. "But she sucked it up into her lungs."

"Sadie, get the girl a glass of water," Daddy said, dropping onto one knee. "Gemma, take a good breath in, girl, and calm down."

"She can't," I said. "She's dyin', just like old Mr. Donley."

Luke put his arm around my shoulder. "She'll be fine. Don't you worry none."

Momma came back and managed to get Gemma to put her tongue back in her mouth long enough to take a sip of water.

"Old Mr. Donley," Momma said as Gemma drank, "died because he was ninety-eight years old, girls. It had nothin' to do with suckin' in powder."

At the time, it seemed to me that the water had healing properties to it, because after that one sip, Gemma's eyes crawled back into the sockets where they belonged.

"He didn't die from powder?" I asked, my voice calmer with the relief of seeing Gemma's face relax.

Daddy scratched his head and took a deep breath. "I done lived thirty-nine years, and I ain't yet heard of a man who up and died from breathin' in powder."

"Only thing you were sufferin' from," Momma told Gemma, "was worryin'. You're just fine."

We were all quiet for the next thirty seconds as we watched Gemma take a few more gulps of water and start to figure out how to breathe like normal again.

I broke the silence when I realized I'd been in a panic over nothing. "You mean I was all scared and bothered over you for nothin'?" I yelled at Gemma.

"Now, Jessie, hold on up there," Luke said.

"But she had me afraid she was gonna die just 'cause of some stupid story."

"She ain't done it on purpose."

"Gemma, I done told you that was nothin' but a tall tale. You done got me whipped up over nothin'. Ain't I got enough troubles?" I held my hands out in front of me and said, "And look at me! I'm covered in powder 'cause you wouldn't leave me alone." I smacked my dungarees and watched the cloud of white form around my legs.

Gemma took one look at me in that cloud of dust and burst out laughing.

I stared at her. "What're you laughin' at, Gemma Teague?"

She didn't have enough breath in her to respond, and it wasn't much time before Momma, Daddy, and Luke found themselves joining in.

I was livid. "Y'all think it's so funny I got myself lathered up and worried about everythin'? I got too many worries for any girl these days, and the only thing you can do is laugh at me?"

But no one seemed to care much about my nerves, and I stood there in that hallway with my arms crossed, listening to them laugh at my distress.

Finally Gemma stood and came over to me, taking my hands in hers. "Sorry."

When she spoke, a little leftover powder blew off from her lips, and I regarded her frosted face. "You look like one of Momma's powdered cakes with that stuff on your face."

"Bad?" she asked.

"You're 'bout white enough to be a Lassiter." I put my arm around her and said with as much of a laugh as I could muster, "You fit in just fine now."

Chapter 20

School started on a Tuesday that year because the Saturday before had drenched us with steady rain, flooding the creek behind the school. It took two full days to clean the water from the school rooms, so we kids got one extra day of freedom.

From the day Daddy found out about Walt's threats, I had been shadowed every minute, and not because it was thought I would kill myself with perfume powder. Daddy made up a schedule of sorts that would make it possible for me to be accompanied wherever I went. The schedule hung on the kitchen wall and said such things as:

Gemma on normal days:
11 a.m. to 2 p.m. School days: 3 p.m. to 6 p.m.

Luke: Tuesdays, Thursdays:
6 p.m. to 9 p.m. Walk to school on school days.

Momma and Daddy had their own times on the list too. It was a ridiculous list, and it flapped in the breeze that came through the window that morning, taunting me all through breakfast. On that first day of school, September weather had come on the heels of the rains, leaving the air crisp and breezy with ominous clouds that brought a somber atmosphere.

As his scheduled duty, Luke was to walk me to school since it was on his way to the tobacco factory, and Daddy had insisted on driving Gemma because he didn't feel she was much safer alone than I was. I reveled a bit in knowing I wasn't the only one being followed around, although she had it much easier than I did.

Gemma and I had both been worried that morning, but neither of us wanted to say anything. We were quiet from the time we stretched and got out of bed to the time she said good-bye through the truck window. I sadly watched her go, wishing life were fairer and we could go to school at the same place. We could have used each other as allies that day. But then I figured that if life were fairer, my summer would have been easy, Gemma's momma and daddy would still be with us, and Luke Talley would be madly in love with me by now.

Life simply was not fair.

When Luke walked around the corner whistling, I just nodded a hello and shuffled down the porch steps, calling to Momma that I was leaving. I grimaced when I saw the dark red cast of the bruises around Luke's eyes and along his cheekbones, but I didn't bring it up. Knowing Luke, he wouldn't want to discuss it anymore.

We had gone about a half mile when Luke said, "You sure are quiet this morning."

"Ain't got much to say, I suppose."

"Scared about school?"

I whipped my head around. "I ain't scared of nothin'!"

He whistled through his teeth. "Don't go gettin' antsy on me, now. I was just makin' conversation."

I looked at the path ahead of us and kicked a pebble that skipped four times before splashing into a rain-filled hole.

Another quarter of a mile passed before he spoke again. "You be okay at that school?"

"Why wouldn't I? I've gone there every year without any trouble."

"Ain't the same now, and you know it."

It irritated me that he was bringing up a sore subject, but I fought down the inclination to be harsh. Instead I shrugged and said, "Ain't much to be done about it. Things will be like whatever they'll be like, and I'll just have to deal with it."

It was Luke's turn to kick a pebble, but his rocketed about four feet off the ground and sailed ahead into the bushes at the side of the road. "Ain't right a girl's got troubles like this," he said, his voice laced with frustration. "It just ain't right!"

I smiled at the angry creases I saw on his face. The very fact that Luke Talley was upset for me put an extra spring in my step, and though we said little else on the rest of our journey, I enjoyed it thoroughly.

When the school came into sight, I slowed my pace, but we still reached it far too quickly. Most of the kids were already there, talking noisily in groups scattered across the weed-ridden schoolyard. The boys were separated into four groups, the girls into six, and there wasn't one to which I felt I belonged.

I took one deep breath and steadied myself. "Guess I best get goin'."

Luke took me by the shoulders, and though I was tall for my age, he slumped so he could look me square in the eye. "You have any trouble, you get to the teacher and let her know, you hear?"

"You askin' me to tell tales?" I asked with a snip in my voice. "Ain't nobody here that tells tales don't get picked on. Ain't I got enough troubles already?"

"You already got troubles; that's right. That's why I'm tellin' you to get to your teacher if anybody gives you trouble."

I didn't see me doing any such thing, but I smiled at him to make him feel better.

He took my smile as an agreement and stood up straight. "Now," he said, tucking my arm into his, "let's get you on inside."

I hadn't expected him to walk me any farther, and when he started leading me past the groups of girls, I knew he was trying to help me out by being seen with me. There wasn't a faster way to get respect from the girls than to be seen on the arm of a good-looking older boy, and he knew it.

I didn't know if his plan would work, all things considered, but I didn't try to stop him. The way I saw it, even if his plan fell dead flat, it was worth it all the while. As we walked by, heads turned, those of both boys and girls, their interest likely being in more than my alliance with Luke.

I'd always been the tomboy amid the real girls, so I had never attracted much attention from anyone of any sex. I just fell somewhere in the middle of things. But now I was learning what it was like to be the center of attention among my peers. I was quickly becoming sure that I didn't like it.

The bell rang as I mounted the steps to the school, and I turned to look at Luke. "Well," I said, my voice catching in a sort of hiccup. I cleared my throat and continued, "Guess I gotta go in."

"You remember what I said now." He tucked a stray bit of hair behind my ear and grinned. "You'll be fine. I feel it in my bones."

His sweet touch had thrilled me enough that I believed in his optimistic prediction for the first five minutes of being in that musty school, but it only took until I found my seat and got my pencil out to have the trouble start.

"You can't sit there," I heard Matt Cokely say. I thought he was talking to me, and I looked up, ready to challenge him. But I quickly found that he was talking to Cy Fuller's daughter, Missy, who had sat at a desk beside me.

"What for?" she asked.

"You gonna sit next to a nigger lover?"

Even though my heart was racing, I glared at Matt, not saying a word.

Being a little backward, Missy didn't seem to fully understand the boy. More to the point, she probably had no idea why he was talking to her at all, because with his good looks and popularity, he wasn't the type of boy who would normally talk to a homely girl like her. That was the beauty of this prejudice, I was quickly discovering. It spanned a wide range of social classes.

For my part, all I kept thinking was how Missy had sat down next to the girl who may very well have killed her daddy, and I cringed when she turned to study my face. I knew she was mulling over Matt's words, but I imagined she was picturing me with a rifle in my hand, her daddy's blood spilling out on my front lawn. The searing guilt stung like a hornet, and it was all I could do to keep from telling her how sorry I was. Only she didn't know what I was sorry for.

Missy shot me an uncertain look before she moved herself and her things to another seat. I smiled at her awkwardly so she wouldn't think I was mad at her. After all, if I'd killed her daddy, she had every right to keep as far away from me as possible.

Matt simply stared at me a moment more, his head wobbling in a way that I assumed was meant to show me how clever he thought he was. Then he took a seat two rows in front of me.

I had chosen a seat at the back of the class in hopes of attracting less attention, and not one seat was taken on either side of me. Most of the children seemed to have very definite opinions about me, but the ones who didn't followed along with the rest in ignorance.

My teachers weren't much better. Except for Mrs. Polk, my English teacher, each one of them treated me as though I were nonexistent. Whenever I heard a teacher say, "You there," I knew they were referring to me, the "nigger lover" in the back row.

Their rejection of me worked in favor of my education, though. In those first few days, I focused more on my schoolwork than I ever had. When I had my nose in a schoolbook, the rest of the class, their snickers and gibes, all faded into the background.

Each day I spent the dinner break under a willow tree behind the school, while the other children crowded around in groups in the schoolyard. I took one of Miss Cleta's novels to school with me and spent the half hour reading fantastical stories while I ate.

On Friday, I had gone through the looking glass with Alice and was paying no attention to what went on around me when a familiar voice interrupted my serenity.

"I can think of better things for a girl like you to be doin' than readin' stories."

I snapped my book shut as though I were writing in my diary and wanted to keep it from prying eyes, then looked up. Walt Blevins was leaning against a tree about fifteen feet away, his thumbs resting in the belt loops of his pants.

"I can teach you better'n books, little girl," he said with a grin. "Anytime you want to learn, you just come to me."

I packed my things and stood to leave, but Walt blocked my way in an instant.

"What do you want from me?" I asked, my emotions frayed.

He laughed. "Now, you're old enough to know about that. And anything you don't know, I can teach."

I stepped to the right, but he followed, so I stepped back to my left. He blocked my way each time. We were like two clumsy, unwilling dance partners.

"Stop!" I cried desperately after two tries to elude him. "I just want you to stop! What did we ever do to you?"

"What'd you do? Girl, it's people like you who threaten me and every law-abidin' citizen in this country."

"Why? There ain't nothin' we've done that goes against the law. We ain't hurt no one."

Walt leaned in and lowered his voice. "From what I hear, you hurt someone enough that he ain't breathin' no more. And this—" he pulled his shirt aside to reveal the bullet wound I'd gifted him with—"this ain't no beauty mark. As I remember it, it hurt more'n a little."

"You deserved that. You know what I'm talkin' about. I'm sayin' we ain't hurt no one by havin' Gemma with us."

"Well then, that's your opinion, ain't it? That's all. Thing is, it's you and your kind that make niggers out to be the same as white folks, and that ain't good for no one."

"Why not? You give me one good reason."

Walt shook his head slowly, grinning like I was the stupidest thing he'd ever seen. "Girl, they don't belong in civilized society. Ain't you figured that out yet? We white men got to protect what's ours. We made this country, and we ain't like to let them take what's rightfully ours."

"The color of someone's skin don't make 'em any less a person," I argued. "God made us all for a reason."

"But He ain't made us all the same, pretty girl." He took my book and tipped my chin up with it. "Don't take nothin' but one look at you to prove that."

I snatched the book from his grimy hands. "Let me by. I have to get back to school."

"Don't rush off now . . ."

Walt reached for me, and my skin prickled with terror. My entire body tensed in dreaded anticipation and my mind reeled, searching for a solution to my problem. I was so preoccupied by my circumstances that the sudden clang of the school bell made me jump, but it was the very thing that saved me.

"They'll be expectin' me inside," I told him with a broken voice. "You want them comin' out to look for me?"

He backed up and made a motion ushering me by. "Don't let me stop you, princess. I ain't never gotten in the way of good ol' book learnin'."

I rushed to get past him, but he stuck a foot out to stop me momentarily.

"You do me one favor and get a message to your daddy for me," Walt whispered in my ear. "You tell him he best not go pushin' his ideas on other people if he wants his family to keep out of trouble. And you tell that Luke Talley to keep his dirty hands out of my business."

I ignored his words and sidestepped his booted foot.

But he caught me by the arm and stuck his face into my hair. "You have fun bakin' them pies last night? Blackberry, I hear they was."

My whole body froze, prickles racing up my spine.

"That's right. I get good information. You think you's alone out at that farm?" he asked. "No ma'am. There's eyes on you. It just ain't the eyes you'd expect, is all."

I wrenched away from him, but I couldn't take my eyes off his face.

Walt smirked at my terror. "Done got you scared now, ain't I? Well, you can't be too careful these days. You best take my warnin'."

I managed to get my feet to move, and with one last bit of fight, I avoided his grasping hands and ran.

"You just remember," he called as I fled into the school, "I got eyes and ears everywhere. I know what you're up to day and night."

I turned and took a last look at his sneering face.

Walt nodded at me and hollered, "That's right. Day . . . and . . . night."

I whirled back around and tore off into the school. His words had put new fears into my heart. Someone was keeping tabs on me. Someone who could get close to us. The very thought made me ill.

From then on, dinnertime for me was spent inside at my desk.

I never passed Walt's message on to my daddy. I had gone to a place in my mind where I believed if I pretended things were all right, they would be. I had kept secrets before, and the way I saw it, my near-imprisonment had come from those secrets being revealed. I hated being the victim, followed and coddled by those who feared for my safety.

All I wanted was to stop feeling afraid.

By Tuesday afternoon of our second week of school, everyone could tell that we had a good storm blowing in. Summers in Calloway could bring a lot of rain, late summer in particular, and we had become pretty used to it. The gloom moved in slowly throughout Tuesday, and by the time I walked home from school with Luke, the trees were swaying in a steady wind.

Luke carried his hat since it wouldn't stay on his head, and with the wind in my face, I had to work hard to keep up with his long strides. We didn't say much. He seemed solemn, a rarity since Luke was normally cheerful and smiling. But then, he had taken to brooding a bit these days. It wasn't so much that he was unhappy; he just seemed thoughtful, caught up with concerns. We were all like that really, but on this particular afternoon, Luke seemed to be in an especially foul mood.

Several times I glanced at him, thinking of saying something, but I changed my mind each time.

We were rounding the corner to home when he said his first words since hello. "I got a visit at work today."

"Who was it?"

"Don't know. Just found a message in my locker."

"Who from?"

"Didn't say. But it said somethin' about you. Said if I wanted the letter explained, I could ask you. Seemed to me somebody was tryin' to warn me you could be hurt if I didn't watch my step."

I just kept walking, staring straight ahead.

"Jessilyn," Luke said, taking my arm to stop me, "you been bothered by anyone?"

I stared at him, my mouth open with no words coming out.

"I asked you a question," he said. "Have you been bothered?"

I lowered my eyes because I didn't want to tell him, but I couldn't lie to him either.

My actions told him what he wanted to know, and he yelled into the wind, "This is gonna stop. Ain't no reason why good people gotta suffer for bein' right."

I watched him while he ranted, thinking it best to keep out of his way.

Luke paced and muttered and beat his hat until it looked wrinkled and ragged. Then he pointed the hat at me. "You tell me when someone gets on you, you hear me?"

I shook my head at him without thinking.

"What do you mean, no?" he demanded.

"I won't tell you if you're gonna tell my daddy."

"You can't go around keepin' stuff from your daddy."

"I can too! I'm tired of causin' trouble for him. Besides, I know he's been havin' money troubles. He can't keep it from me no matter how much he tries. I know people round here ain't been buyin' from him. We might lose the farm over this." I shook my head adamantly. "No sir. Ain't nothin' more I'm worryin' Daddy with. He's got a pocketful of worries as it is."

"Now you listen here," Luke said, edging up in front of me. "We're all in this thing together. Ain't just you involved here."

"You think Walt Blevins would be botherin' us so much if he didn't have it in for me? I shot him, and now he wants to hurt me back. And what about Cy Fuller? We got worries about the law because of that." A lump formed in my throat at the mention of Cy, and I spun away from Luke to keep him from seeing me cry.

"You ain't done nothin' wrong. Not one thing, you hear? Don't you let that get into your head."

"Stop tellin' me not to worry." I turned to face him without fear of exposing my tears. "Everyone tells me not to worry. Meantime, I ain't allowed to leave the house alone. I look behind me all the time, scared to find someone sneakin' up on me. Ain't nothin' that don't make me scared no more. Nothin'! And every day of my life, I got to wake up thinkin'

I murdered somebody's daddy." My last words tore me up inside, and I started crying a river, feeling like a fool the whole time.

Luke dropped his hat onto the ground and pulled me to him, burying my face in his chest. I about soaked through his shirt with my tears, but he didn't seem to mind. He kept patting my back and smoothing my hair, saying all sorts of nice things to me like, "You're a tough one. You'll be just fine, Jessie girl. Don't you worry now."

Through the wind and my hiccuping sobs, I couldn't hear everything he said, but with my ear against his chest, I could feel the vibrations of his deep voice, and it put me at ease.

Eventually I pulled myself together, and Luke tipped my chin and wiped my cheeks with his handkerchief. "Ain't no reason for you to feel bad," he said. "You let those people make you feel wrong for protectin' yourself, and they've won."

"But I killed him," I moaned. "I got to live with that. I can't never look Cy's family in the eyes again."

"You ain't killed that man. I feel it deep down. Don't you go worryin'. Just don't you do it."

I wiped my face with his handkerchief before I said, "Luke . . ."

"What's that?"

"I meant what I said. I ain't tellin' you nothin' if you don't swear not to tell my daddy."

"Jessilyn," Luke said, dragging my name out in exasperation, "your daddy'll kill me if he finds out I knew somethin' and didn't tell him."

"Walt came to school," I blurted out.

"What'd he do?" he asked, his jaw tightening. "He hurt you?"

"He said his usual things about me, things he shouldn't say."

"Did he touch you?"

"Not really, he just talked." I crossed my arms, my trademark stubbornness returning. "But I won't tell you what he said if you don't swear to keep it secret."

He sighed and pushed his windblown hair back. "It ain't right."

"Then I'll deal with it on my own," I said, charging off toward home.

Luke grabbed the back of my shirt and pulled me to a stop. "All right. You swear to tell me everythin', and I won't tell your daddy nothin'." He pointed at me and added, "But you better not skip anythin', you hear?"

I nodded and wiped my leftover tears with the back of my hand.

"Now, you tell me the rest of what Walt said," he said.

Before I got the chance to, I caught sight of something out of the corner of my eye and glanced over in time to see Luke's hat whipping across the field.

"Your hat's runnin' off," I told him, managing to grin.

"Holy smokes!" he exclaimed, running after it.

I watched him, enjoying every bit of his wild chase. The old tattered hat teased him mercilessly, stopping here and there only to fly off again whenever he got close enough to catch it.

Luke approached me sheepishly once he finally retrieved it, but it didn't take him long to remember our earlier conversation. I spent the rest of the short walk home telling him about Walt, and he spent the rest of the walk getting more and more upset. It seemed we were all in a sort of war in those days.

I took comfort in knowing Luke and I were in it together.

Chapter 21

The brewing storm moved in on Wednesday morning with gloomy clouds and constant wind. I woke up to a darkened room and checked my clock three times to make sure it really was seven in the morning since it looked like ten o'clock at night. My bedside lamp wouldn't work, and the still dimness mirrored the uneasy spirit I'd woken with.

Gemma was sitting on the floor in front of the window.

"What're you lookin' at?" I asked.

"Sky looks funny."

I rolled over and peered out the window. No doubt, she was right. The sky did look strange, dark but with color in it, making the landscape look a sort of greenish gray. "Just a stormy day," I murmured, but I didn't believe my own words. I had a sudden fear that trouble was coming today, and I tugged at one of Gemma's braids. "Maybe Daddy can ride us both to school in the truck. We'd best not wander around outdoors on a day like this." I swung my legs over the side of my bed and padded across the creaky floorboards to get dressed.

Gemma looked at me funny. "What's got into you? You worryin' about somethin'?"

"I'm just makin' a suggestion."

"But you ain't never been afraid of storms before."

I shrugged and tried to pin a nonchalant look on my face. "Ain't no reason to go gettin' wet, now is there?"

"Jessilyn!" Gemma hopped up off the floor and met me face-to-face. "You keepin' somethin' from me again?"

"No!"

"Yes you are. I can see it in your face. Now what's goin' on?"

I knew she'd badger me until I told her what I was thinking, so I just stared at my feet and murmured, "Ain't no good comin' today."

"How do you know that?"

"You know that feelin' I get. Well, I feel it today." I looked at her and tucked a hand against my middle. "I can feel it right here."

I could tell my words scared her because her forehead creased all up and she said angrily, "You best stop all your talk about bad feelin's. They don't do nothin' but build up worries." Gemma slipped her dress over her head and eyed me while she did up her buttons. "You got into fortunes and the like or somethin'? 'Cause if you have, your momma will have your hide. She says that's devil talk."

"I ain't no gypsy!"

"Well then, you're talkin' nonsense. I done told you before you can't see the future."

"I ain't never said I could see the future. All's I said is I got me a bad feelin', and my bad feelin's mostly come true, and you know it."

Gemma studied my face with a solemn expression. "Then don't you go nowheres today. If you're worried about troubles ahead, then you just stay on home with your momma."

"I got school. I can't not go nowhere today."

"I don't want you to leave here."

I stared at her briefly before tugging my shoes on and saying with determination, "I got to go to school today. There's a test." Gemma scowled at me and readied herself to argue, but I cut her off. "Gemma, I done tried not to tell you I had a bad feelin', but you made me. Ain't no way you can expect me to sit still and do nothin' till nightfall."

She turned away from me with a jerk, and I could tell she was angry and frightened.

I ate my cold oatmeal that morning with little interest and met Luke at the end of the walk with nervous butterflies in my stomach. But school went fine, with the exception of the blankness my mind took on once I got that history test in front of me. No one bothered me. In fact, no one paid a lick of attention to me. I was starting to think maybe my bad feeling would come to nothing. In fact, I even got a surprise when Luke showed up to walk me home instead of Daddy.

"Got off a bit early today," he said when he met me in the schoolyard. "Told your daddy I'd be happy to see you home."

Yes sir, things were looking far better than I'd expected.

Luke and I made our way home with ease, chatting like the world was sunny and life was fine even though we had to practically yell over the roaring winds.

When we got home, Daddy was coming out onto the porch, his bag of tools slung over one shoulder. "Goin' to Miss Cleta's to mend her broken fence. Jessilyn, you stay inside with your momma."

"I don't wanna stay inside," I whined. "I been stuck inside at school all day."

"Well, your momma's up to her arms in scrub water upstairs, and she won't be able to keep an eye on you out here."

I felt five years old again, and my face must've showed it.

Luke, as usual, came to my rescue. "I'm gonna fix my old shed door today, Mr. Lassiter. She can come on home with me if she wants. I'll bring her back in time for supper."

His suggestion suited me better than anything anyone could have said, and my frown turned into a smile in record time.

Daddy gave his approval. "Y'all be sure to get back in time for supper. Your momma's fryin' up some catfish, and you know she hates us bein' late on fish night."

Momma took pride in her cooking, and she always insisted that fish "just won't do lukewarm!"

Daddy looked up at the dark skies. "If it's rainin' hard by suppertime, stay put, and I'll come over with the truck to pick you two up. And, Jessilyn, you tell your momma where you'll be."

I ran inside to tell Momma and joined Luke for our walk to his house.

While we were there, I sat on a nearby fence and watched as he filed away at the wood to level the edge of the door. His whole body was tense trying to keep that door still in the whipping wind, but he managed skillfully. My thoughts were full of all the ways I was sure Luke Talley would be the perfect husband and how I'd be the perfect wife. I thought of all the things I could do to help him with his work and all the food I could cook for his suppers, despite the fact that I never did any cooking besides cutting up potatoes and flouring biscuits.

"Jessilyn *Talley*," I whispered to myself with a sigh. "Sounds good."

Luke stopped working and wiped his forehead with his sleeve. "You say something?"

My heart pounded when I realized I'd said my thoughts aloud. "Nope," I answered quickly.

He tilted his head, then grinned. "You bored?"

"Ain't nothin' but bored these days."

"Ain't nobody makin' you sit still all the time," he said.

"Ain't like you can't do nothin' just because someone has to be with you."

"Feels like I'm all tied up." I slid off the fence and plopped into a pile of hay. "Here I am growin' up into a woman, and I can't even go off by myself nowhere."

Luke let out a sarcastic little noise that sounded like he was spitting.

"What's that for?" I demanded.

"What're you talkin' about 'becomin' a woman'? What kinda talk is that?"

I sat ramrod straight, my mouth tightening into one taut line, and I didn't say a word.

Being only nineteen himself, Luke didn't have the sense to quit the conversation, so he said, "Ain't a good idea for little girls to go wishin' to be women. You best just be happy bein' a girl while you can."

I jumped up and put my hands on my hips just like Gemma. "You got nerve, Luke Talley. If I ain't no woman, then you sure ain't no man."

Luke slammed the door shut and leaned one hand against it. "What d'you mean I ain't no man? You see any boys who can live on their own? Ain't no boy that could take care of you the way I do."

"Take care of me? Who needs you to take care of me? I'm grown enough to do whatever I want, and I ain't got need for no babysitter, neither."

He stared at me for a minute and then smiled, shook his head, and returned to his work, his back to me.

I was angry that he ignored me and tired of being treated like a child, and I made a sudden decision that had I been in any proper frame of mind, I would never have made.

Amid the noise of Luke pounding a nail, I grabbed the jacket I'd worn and ran away from the shed and through the woods behind Luke's house. I didn't know where I was going or how I was going to keep Daddy from whipping me for running off, but I didn't care just then. I walked on through the trees that bent and swayed in the wind, dark skies above me threatening rain more every minute. It took me only about ten minutes to regret my decision and have the fear crop back up again, but I'd committed myself now, and returning to Luke with my tail between my legs was no option.

Then it came to me that I was nearing Mr. Tinker's place, and I could ask him to ride me home in his truck.

So I picked my way over fallen branches and fat toadstools, keeping my eye out for landmarks that would reassure me I was heading in the right direction. My skin crawled at the whistling of the wind through the trees, and the creaking of branches and rustling of animals in the brush made my heart race.

Just outside the Tinkers' property sat an old, broken-down barn. When we were younger, Gemma and I would make up ghost stories about that barn. It was ragged and lopsided, its shutters hanging at odd angles, and the wooden boards creaked with any slight whisper of wind. Today was no exception, and I felt tingles crawl up and down my spine when I came upon it, those creaking boards sounding like cracks of thunder to my frightened ears.

I set my eyes on the house off in the distance, determined to make it past the haunted barn to the safety of the Tinkers' back door. Mr. Tinker's truck sat outside of the house, so I knew he was home, and I walked on with quick steps. But when I started past the barn, I heard voices coming from inside, low whispering voices that could have come straight out of one of my childhood ghost stories. I stood still for a moment, every part of my body poised to run. The voices were angry and deep, men whose identities I couldn't determine but whose words I was intrigued to hear.

"I told you to make sure you had everythin' we'd need before tonight," one man said. "I gotta tell you everythin' twice?"

"I did get everythin'."

"Just you can't remember where you put it! How stupid you got to be?"

"Got a lot on my mind these days."

"Shut your mouth up," the other man hissed. "You think a man in my position ain't got nothin' on his mind? I get men to do little things for me so's I can worry about the big stuff. And you can't even get the little things right."

No doubt these men were up to no good, and I knew if my daddy were here he'd tell me to hightail it to the house, but a familiar name caught my attention before I had the chance.

"You know good and well the sheriff ain't settled down

about Cy Fuller yet. We best lay low till that gets forgotten."

There was that name, the one that had taken my innocent summer and laced it with blood and nightmares. If there was someone in that barn who knew what happened to Cy Fuller, I had to know what he knew. It was the only way to answer the burning questions that had seared my conscience for weeks.

"We ain't got time," the other voice argued. "Someone's turned on us, and we gotta take care of it before the law gets on us."

"Like you took care of Cy?"

My heart raced at the words, and I crept nearer the barn, peering around the doorway as far as I dared. Any breathing I had managed to do stopped dead the minute I saw those men fumbling about. Their flowing white robes fluttered in the breeze, giving their murderous words an added sense of evil. One of the men was small, shorter than me, but the other was over six feet, well able to take care of me were he to discover my presence. They wore no hoods, but their backs were to me, keeping me from identifying them.

"I don't want to talk about Cy no more, you hear?" the bigger man ordered. "He was gonna talk, and I had to do what I did. That's that. Don't want no more talk about it."

There was a sense of sweet relief in me mixed with a palpable fear. The man's words made it certain to me that I was no murderer, but there was little reprieve in knowing I was in the presence of one. I desperately wanted to know who it was, not just for my own curiosity, but for the sake of Cy Fuller, who I'd been mourning over those past weeks. In some strange way I'd formed a posthumous kinship with Cy through my guilt, and now that I knew I wasn't his killer, I wanted more than anything to see the real killer pay.

The men stood in front of the broken barn window, and I knew if I could reach it without being seen, I'd get a good look at their faces. Only I couldn't go around the back of the barn because it backed up against the trees. If I was to reach that window, I'd have to make a run past the open barn doors. The two men were still digging through drawers, muttering under their breath, and I decided now was as good a time as ever to take a chance. I took as deep a breath as I could manage, flashed a glance at the hooded men to make sure they were still turned away, and scurried out from my hiding place.

A run that should have taken me ten seconds felt like ten minutes. My legs were like rubber, my mind reeling. Just as I was about to scoot past the threshold, rejoicing inside that I would make it without being seen, I stumbled over a dip in the ground, sprawling on all fours. I felt like a deer caught in the crosshairs of a rifle, and I looked up at them, ready to plead for my life. Both men swung around and landed their gazes square on my face.

I was frozen in fear, gaping at the men who'd put an end to my fears of being a murderess, but I didn't feel triumphant. Instead, I felt as though someone had taken my whole idea of the world and ripped it down the center.

There, robed in white, stood Otis Tinker.

I recognized him at once as the man who had confessed to killing Cy Fuller, and I sat helplessly in the dust in front of him, unable to move. The smaller man took a step toward me, but Mr. Tinker threw an arm across his chest to stop him. Then he said mournfully, "Jessilyn . . ."

But I couldn't listen to anything he would say. It was as though the voice I'd known for so long was coming from a complete stranger, and I found my legs, stood up in one leap, and ran from him. I didn't stop to look behind me, couldn't pause to listen for footsteps. Without stopping, without thinking, I fled from Tinker land. I just wanted to be home, and I wanted to warn my daddy that his old friend was a bigot and a murderer. I was afraid for myself and for my family more than I had been all summer long.

When I was halfway home, I heard my daddy calling my name. I saw him dart out onto the path in front of me, and I threw myself into his arms, gasping for air.

"Jessilyn," Daddy said sternly, "where you been? We've been worried sick." But then he saw my terrified expression and bent over to look straight into my eyes. "What is it, baby girl? What's happened?"

Jeb came walking out of the woods to join us, and I looked at him anxiously. I'd heard my daddy's plea to know what was wrong, but I couldn't reply to him. I couldn't trust Jeb enough to say anything. So I stood by silently, breathlessly, but I could tell that my attitude alone had my daddy scared to death.

"Calm down, baby," he said. "Now, I can see you're upset, but you need to tell us what's wrong. Right now!"

I glanced at Jeb again.

Daddy followed my gaze. "It's just Jeb. You can trust him. Now come on. Tell me what's got you so scared."

I shook my head, gulping in air.

But Daddy wasn't taking no for an answer. "Jessilyn Lassiter, I want truth and I want it now, you hear? You tell me what's been goin' on. Right now!"

I knew my daddy meant business, and for that moment my fear of him overrode my fear of Jeb. "Mr. Otis. It's Mr. Otis!"

"What about him? Is he hurt?"

I shook my head again. "He killed Cy."

Daddy stared at me in shock. "What're you sayin'? Why would you say somethin' like that?"

"I heard him say it. And he knows I know. He saw me," I said hysterically. "He'll come after me now. He knows I know."

I couldn't read the expression on Daddy's face, but I heard the severity of his voice when he said, "You get back to the house with Jeb. I'll go for Luke."

"Daddy, no!" I cried, clinging to him desperately.

"Jessilyn, Luke's out there in the woods by himself lookin' for you, not knowin' what we know, and I gotta find him and get him home."

"Don't make me go with Jeb," I fairly screamed.

Daddy took me by the shoulders and said firmly, "I ain't askin' you to go. I'm *tellin'* you. Get on home with Jeb."

"But he's one of them. He's just like the rest of them. You don't know what I do."

"No, it's you that don't know what I know. Now, I can't stand here explainin' things to you. I need to get Luke and get back to the house with your momma and Gemma."

"But, Daddy . . ."

"You got to trust me now," he said earnestly. "There ain't no other way around it. You got to trust me when I tell you to trust Jeb and get on home with him."

I looked deep into my daddy's eyes, eyes that I had trusted all my life, and as much as I doubted Jeb, I somehow couldn't find it in me to doubt my daddy. I dropped my grip on him and turned to follow Jeb.

Daddy bolted into the woods, and Jeb and I hurried through prickly brush and dead leaves. I made sure to stay a few paces behind to keep an eye on him.

"It ain't what you think," Jeb said to me after several minutes. "I ain't what you think I am. I'm workin' *against* the Klan, not with 'em."

He looked back at me, but I wouldn't meet his gaze.

"I don't trust nobody no more," I muttered.

"Ain't no reason for that, Miss Jessie. Reason I'm here is to be someone you can trust."

I didn't reply. We had reached the outskirts of our property, and I could see my momma standing on the porch, calling out for me. I sprinted past Jeb, running as fast as my legs could carry me.

"Jessilyn, you had us worried to death," Momma said when I reached her. "Just plumb worried to death."

She and Gemma hugged me so hard I could barely get a breath, but I could see they were as angry with me as they were happy to see me alive and well.

"Of all things," Gemma spat out. "Runnin' off like that and scarin' us!"

"Y'all need to get inside," Jeb said as he joined us. "Get on in, now."

"What's wrong?" Momma asked. "Where's Harley?"

"He's collectin' Luke and then comin' on home. But I need to call my boys and get you safe inside right now."

We hurried inside with Jeb giving us a little push to get us started, and I watched him as he went to the telephone.

"What's he mean, 'call his boys'?" I asked Momma.

"Ain't nothin' for you to worry about." Momma stood at the window, staring out in search of Daddy, but I tugged at the back of her dress.

"I got all kinds of things to worry about. Ain't no difference addin' to it. I want to know who Jeb is."

Jeb hung up the telephone and faced me. "I work for the government, Miss Jessie," he said bluntly, his voice making it plain that he was too busy to give much information. "I'm here to stop the Klan, not join 'em. Now, that's that, and I want everyone to stay here and lay low. I got to get back out there, you understand?"

"But you had a Klan robe," Gemma blurted in surprise. "We saw it in the lean-to."

I glared at her for giving away such secrets.

Jeb shook his head. "That's evidence I dug up. Nothin' more."

"Jessilyn Lassiter," Momma said. "You girls were fishin' in Jeb's private property?"

"Yes'm. But we had a good reason to," I argued. "I saw Jeb talkin' to Walt Blevins one day, and he told Walt he had plans. I had to know what he was doin'."

"Walt Blevins is givin' information to me so he can stay out of jail for a federal offense," Jeb said. "That's why I was talkin' to him."

"But he's the one tryin' to hurt me. You just let him go so you can get information?"

"We got bigger fish to fry, Miss Jessie. I came to watch out for you while we gathered information, hopin' I could keep you from real trouble until we had what we needed. Only way to get rid of Klan in these parts is to find reason for federal charges." He tipped my chin up and gave me a reassuring wink. "It's all gonna work out in the end. I promise you that. But right now, things are fixin' to explode, and I gotta go meet my boys and see if we can't round everybody up. You stay put with your momma and Gemma. And keep these doors locked, you hear?"

We all nodded, but I didn't really understand when it came down to it. After Jeb left, I looked at Momma and said, "I can't figure out who to believe no more."

"Jeb's speakin' the truth. He's been here all the time on government business; it's just nobody was supposed to know.

317

Now, why don't you tell me what's been goin' on that's got everyone so riled up?"

I sat down on the couch, my muscles sore and tired, my head swimming. "I didn't kill Cy Fuller."

Momma sat beside me with a sigh of relief, and I knew by that simple gesture that she'd never really been sure I hadn't killed that man.

Gemma came over to sit at my feet. "How do you know for sure? Where'd you hear that from?"

"I heard it from the man who did kill him. It was Mr. Otis," I said, my tone surprisingly calm. It was as though I'd run out of the energy I needed to be hysterical.

But Momma did a good enough job for both of us. "Baby, no! No, that can't be!"

"I heard him with my own ears. I heard him say that he killed him."

My momma grabbed the sides of her head like she didn't want to hear anything more, and she kept murmuring, "Dear Jesus, no" over and over again.

Gemma just sat in shock as I had done when I'd found out the truth.

Footsteps on the porch gave us a jolt, but we realized it was Daddy when he started pounding on the locked door, calling for us to let him in. Momma opened the door, and Daddy and Luke rushed into the house.

"Where's Jeb?" Daddy asked.

"He made a call and then went on back out," Momma said. "He told us to stay put."

Luke looked at me and pointed in my direction. "You and me, we got some talkin' to do when this is over, you hear?"

"What for?"

"What for?" he barked. "You up and run off on me like that and get me all scared over you, and you ask me why we gotta talk?"

Normally his tone would have made me bristle, but he'd said he was scared for me, and amid the chaos, I still found the time to let that flatter me.

"I think we can settle this later," Daddy said to Luke. "Don't you think we got more important things to deal with, son?"

Luke glared at me and tossed his hat onto a table before going off to follow my daddy.

I had my back up a bit, but it didn't matter much. I just settled into the sofa with a sigh, daydreaming about the concern I had seen in Luke's eyes.

It was a lot better than thinking about what was looming ahead.

Chapter 22

The next twenty minutes or so went by in a blur. As I sat on the couch, I saw Daddy and Luke rush from room to room, locking windows and checking doors. I heard Daddy muttering because he couldn't reach the sheriff on the telephone, heard him whispering things to Luke that I couldn't comprehend. Momma sat near me praying, as did Gemma, but I was too afraid to think, much less utter words of prayer. The electricity was still out, and the darkness of the house lent to the wildness of our situation.

Daddy came into the hallway and started to say something, but he never got to say a word. He just stopped and stood there, listening.

"What is it, Harley?" Momma whispered.

"Shh!" He walked methodically over to the pantry. I knew what he was going for. I'd gone for it myself one night not too long ago. Goose bumps popped up over my arms, and I glanced at Luke for reassurance. But Luke was staring sternly out the window, pulling his pistol from the waistband of his trousers.

Putting one finger to his lips, Daddy readied the gun and looked at Luke, nodding toward the back door. Luke went to the door, opened it slowly, and after a good look around, departed through it, leaving Daddy to cover the front.

By the light of the lantern, Momma, Gemma, and I looked like frightened little ghosts, our faces lit by shadows. We stayed still for a few seconds before our curiosity got the best of us, and then we rose and crept steadily toward Daddy, who was holding the front window curtain back a couple inches, peering cautiously through. He saw us approach and waved to us to get behind him.

While Daddy made his way to the door, Gemma and I stared nervously at one another, wondering if my prediction that something awful would happen had come true. All sorts of ideas flitted through my mind, scenes of terror and death. What if something happened to Daddy . . . or Luke? What if we were all going to be trapped inside, burnt to death like Gemma's parents, only this time we would be burnt up by sparks that blew off a fiery cross?

Amid my outrageous imaginings, I was cultivating a sense of doom, as I had felt all day long. My heart raced and then seemed to stop momentarily, and then it would race again.

It seemed hours before Daddy finally opened that front door. It creaked loudly at first and then expelled a long, soft whine. The screen door had blown open and still stood wide, letting leaves and pieces of debris scatter inside. From the top of the doorway, something came flying inward, and my first thought was that it was a bird making his disoriented way into the house. Everyone ducked, and Momma let out a shriek, but the thing didn't come all the way in. Instead it bobbed back out of the house as the wind receded, weaving a drunken path back and forth in front of us.

Despite the strands of hair that had blown into my face, I was able to make out a familiar form, disheveled and lifeless, hanging from a roughly tied noose. "Lucky!" I screamed, dashing forward.

Daddy caught me and held me tight. "Stay back, baby," he said, his voice equal parts authority and sympathy.

I struggled momentarily, but Daddy shoved me behind him and told us to get down and stay down. It was an eerie sight to behold as my daddy pushed aside the body of the small cat in order to peer about the porch, his gun at the ready. Lucky's furry remains swung away and then back as Daddy walked onto the porch, and I watched the cat, mesmerized. He was hung by the neck, a rope holding him aloft, lynched by men who were terrorizing us in the name of civility.

I was sickened by the sight of it, but I couldn't move my eyes away. Like a clock's pendulum, he swung to and fro, his small pink tongue poking out of his mouth. From behind me, I could hear the tearful whimpers of my momma and Gemma. Momma tried to push my head down to keep me from looking, but I wouldn't budge. I was compelled to study the gruesome scene.

Out of the corner of my eye, I saw someone pass by the den window, and I jumped up, shrugging off Momma's restraining grasp, to warn Daddy. I had just reached the doorway when I saw Daddy whip around and aim his gun toward the end of the long porch, where a man stood pointing his pistol at Daddy.

"Don't shoot!" I called, realizing how easily my daddy and Luke could have shot each other in cold blood.

Daddy and Luke lowered their guns, sighing in relief.

Daddy shook his head and wiped his forehead. "Son, that was way too close for me. We should have a sign or somethin' if we—"

He was interrupted as someone came around the corner of the house, bringing the two men to raise their guns again. It was Jeb, his hands flying into the air the minute he spotted Luke and Daddy ready to fire.

"It's only me, Mr. Lassiter," he said breathlessly, his face red and glistening with sweat. He pointed toward the back of the house. "Think you'd better come to the fields with me."

Daddy and Luke went with Jeb right away, and though I knew Daddy would have told me to stay put had he taken the time to think about it, I followed them anyway. Momma hollered after me but gave up and decided to come, Gemma at her heels. My bare feet stung as I made my way across the gravel drive, not taking the usual time to pick my way gently across it, but I didn't think twice.

I ran all the way, and my chest felt raw and hollow when I finally reached the fields. The sight was more than I could believe, an image I was sure would be burned into my memory for eternity.

For as far as my eyes could see, my father's living had been destroyed. The sheds were ablaze, obliterating every object they held within. The crops, as well, were lit to the sky, flames leaping and dancing amid a symphony of pops and crackling brush. We could hear nothing but the roar of fire. With the winds as wicked as they were, our house was completely vulnerable. Daddy, Luke, and Jeb worked feverishly to build a firewall, Daddy shouting at the same time for Momma to put in a call for help. Momma, though, was nearly passed out, bent over in the tall grass crying to Jesus. Gemma was stiff as stone, engulfed in terror. I found my legs and ran to her, pleading with her to call for help in Momma's place.

I have no idea why I didn't think to place the call myself right off, but I knew with one look at Gemma that I would have to. Her eyes were glassy, and up close I could see reflections of the flames dancing in them. I shook her a few times before running to the house, tripping over stones as I went.

I made my way to the front door, but it only served to have me run straight into Lucky's corpse. I screamed and jumped back against the doorway, petrified as his wide-open eyes stared into mine, close, then far away, and then close again as he swung, the rope creaking with each stroke he took. Holding my breath, I grasped the rope, tugging desperately to get him down, tipping my head away from the fur that stroked my face. I struggled to get him loose, and eventually out of sheer terror I pulled with all my might, finally managing to free the rope. The force of the release sent me flying backward with Lucky in my grasp. I dropped him like a hot potato and, realizing I had come here for a purpose, left him on the floor and headed to the telephone.

But there was no operator on the end of the line. It was silent, as was the house. Despite the chaos that was taking place in Daddy's fields, the house was still and eerily uninhabited. There was only me and a dead cat there in the thick darkness.

Or at least that was what I thought at first.

Every once in a while my momma shivers, rubs her arms quickly, and says, "I swear somebody just stepped on my grave." I knew what she meant right then as the hair on my arms stood on end and my face felt prickly. There was something or someone with me. I knew that as surely as I knew no one in those fields would hear me if I screamed.

I turned around slowly, willing myself to look and see what it was that had suddenly inhabited the space behind me.

There in the hallway, illuminated by what little outside light there was, stood a man robed in white, the crisp fabric billowing in the breeze. He was holding the rope from which Lucky hung, as though taunting me with it, but he said nothing. The silence of the scene was more horrifying than anything he could have said to me.

I crept toward the kitchen, grasping behind me in hopes I would eventually run into the countertop where Momma kept her knives. With each step I took backward, he took one forward, the floorboards creaking as he came.

At length he spoke, but it was no more than a whisper, making himself even more ghostly. "You don't want this happenin' to you, do you?" he asked, nodding at the dead cat he held. "You want to end up swingin' from a rope?"

I couldn't reply. I simply shook my head much longer than I needed to. Even though he whispered, I knew it was Walt Blevins, and the very thought of being alone with him paralyzed me with dread.

"Well now, little girls who don't want trouble shouldn't go around shootin' at people all willy-nilly then, should they?"

"You can stop whisperin'," I said with a breaking voice. "I know who you are. Just as I knew you every other time you hid like a coward."

"Coward? I ain't no coward, girl. I'm a patriot!" Walt ripped his hood off, revealing his sooty, sweaty face, and slid Lucky across the floor toward me. The cat's remains coasted to a stop at my feet. "That's right. You oughta thank a man like me for savin' this country for you and yours. If we had a country made up of gutless fools like your daddy, we'd be run over by darkies. How'd you like that?"

Still making my way backward, I ran into one of the kitchen chairs, giving me a shiver of surprise as it jabbed my side. I knew I had to edge past the chair and stumble a few more feet if I was to reach a knife. It was still dark in the house, but with my eyes adjusted to the dimness, I could see Walt studying my face from where he stood no more than ten feet away.

"Now, the way I see it," he said, "I got me a right to stand up for what's best for this country, and that includes takin' care of people like you."

I hesitated before I asked, "What do you mean?"

"What . . . do . . . I . . . mean?" Walt repeated, pretending to consider my question thoughtfully. "You know where the Good Book says 'an eye for an eye'? I figure you put this here bullet hole in my shoulder, so I should be able to get payback for my sufferin', you see? Teach you a lesson, so to speak."

He sauntered toward me, stopping an arm's length away. "Now, let me think what little piece of you I want to take as payback. . . ." He scanned me sordidly. "Take these locks of yours." He tugged my hair hard enough to tip my head backward. "All I got to do is get me a good knife, and I got me a souvenir. But, naw . . . ," he said, letting my hair drop. "Naw, I don't think I'll waste it on your hair. Maybe I want to give you somethin' that hurts a little worse. Give you a taste of what you put me through, eh? How about that? I got me a gun right over there in the corner. Maybe you'd like to know how a bullet wound feels, burnin' and stingin' and bleedin' all over the place. You want to try that instead?"

I couldn't say a word, couldn't move. My hand was frozen by my side, and though I knew that I was only inches away from discovering a knife, I couldn't make myself budge.

Walt took my right arm in his hand and wrung it tightly, burning my skin, and I cried out in pain. "You best save those cries for later," he whispered. "'Cause it's gonna get worse'n that, I can tell ya. You think I'm gonna let a girl make a fool outta me and get away with it? No, ma'am, I ain't used to lettin' that get by. You wanted to play with Walt Blevins, little girl, and now you better ante up."

He pushed me backward into the counter, but though I was engulfed by his huge frame, the movement pushed my left hand directly onto one of Momma's sharp knives. I found my senses enough to wrap my hand around the handle. "Get off me," I said as forcefully as my short breaths would let me.

Walt looked straight into my face and grinned. "I will when I'm done."

That was when I plunged the knife into his right arm, making him shriek in pain. I shoved past him but tripped over Lucky and struggled to regain my balance. As I started to run away, Walt grabbed my hair from behind, pulling me backward so hard my neck felt like it snapped in two. I landed on my back, my head slamming against the floor, and for the next several seconds I felt dazed, my head spinning in confusion. I could hear Walt cursing me, but it sounded distant and muffled. I opened my eyes to find him leaning over me, one hand around my neck.

"I'm gonna kill you, girl," he seethed, saliva dripping down his chin. "Ain't no one here to help you now, and I'm gonna kill you."

His one hand was large enough to wrap around my throat, and I felt my air cut off. I kicked my feet and flailed my arms, trying desperately to find the knife I had dropped. My eyes were wide and unblinking, my mouth as dry as cotton. None of my thrashing budged Walt's burly frame even an inch, and as his hand tightened even more, I knew it was the end. Weary and with a head that felt fuzzy and light, I dropped my arms and legs, almost accepting defeat.

Until I heard the gunshot. One single gunshot that echoed throughout the silence of the house.

I saw the shock on Walt's face, watched as the patch of blood on his shirt grew to become a river trickling down his front. Suddenly I could breathe again, and I inhaled with a screeching gasp as I watched Walt teeter to his left and slump to the floor beside me, his unseeing eyes looking into mine. Coughing and sputtering, I kicked my heels into the floor, sliding myself away from him. From my haven in the corner of the kitchen, I looked up to see Walt's executioner.

His white robe wasn't as pristine as when I'd first seen it less than an hour before. He was wearing no hood, showing me his worn, taut face. I couldn't discern Otis Tinker's expression just as I couldn't understand how one who had betrayed me all summer long could now come to my rescue.

He simply lowered his gun and spit on the floor at Walt's feet. "He gave us all a bad name, anyhow. Traitor!"

Then he walked out and left me alone with the dead.

Chapter 23

I can still remember Daddy's expression when he fully recognized the truth of Otis Tinker. There was a sadness in it that brought tears to my eyes, a sort of heartbreak that I'd had the good fortune to have never seen on my daddy's face before.

For the first time, I knew a little bit about such things. I, too, had felt the strain of broken trust. I'd had a summer of it.

All my daddy could say to Mr. Tinker as Jeb chained his hands together was "Why?"

"You'd never understand," Mr. Tinker said. "You never did."

"I understand more than you like to think," Daddy replied. "It's my understandin' that kept me from becomin' like you."

"There you go again," Mr. Tinker railed. "You act like we're the ones stirrin' up trouble, but ain't you got the sense to see it's you that's got the trouble? Ain't no way we can start lettin' niggers run our country, Harley. Ain't no way we can let that happen and keep civilized." Mr. Tinker's face was earnest, his tone pleading.

I realized he was as certain of his beliefs as my daddy was of his. "You sayin' Gemma ain't civilized?" I asked him suddenly. "My Gemma?"

His face changed when he heard my voice, a sort of softness creeping back in, reminding me of the opinion I'd had of him only a few short hours before. "Honey, you ain't got to think 'bout none of this. It ain't for children to worry 'bout."

I studied him, dismissing his patronizing talk, and walked closer to him. "If I'm too young to worry about it, then how come you let me think I'd done your killin'?"

Mr. Tinker dropped his eyes in a slow, drooping way and stared at his feet. He'd run out of answers. He could look my daddy in the eye, even after all those years they'd been friends, and he could stand up against him sure and steady. But the minute he looked at my eyes that were too young to understand all the darkness that could inhabit a man's heart, he lost some of his swagger.

I asked again, "How come, Mr. Otis?"

Daddy was the first to speak. "Otis don't know why, baby girl. There's a lot Mr. Otis don't know about."

Otis Tinker never said another word to me for the rest of

my days. The law came down on him hard for killing Cy Fuller and Walt Blevins. It hadn't been a colored man he'd killed but two white ones, and for that he was sentenced to pay with his own life. I couldn't help but think of poor Elijah Baker and how he'd suffered at Walt Blevins's hands. Walt had never paid a cent for what he'd done, at least not until the day he was shot through the heart by one of his own. The disparity of it muddled my head. For all my trying to understand some men's minds, I couldn't see any difference in people just for their color. But then I figured I was better off not understanding such things.

The morning after we'd watched Jeb lead Mr. Tinker away in chains, I poked my head out the window bright and early to see my daddy and Luke working their hands to the bone in the fields. I couldn't quite believe the amount of work that would need to be done to restore all my daddy had toiled for over the years. But when I saw Momma there beside Daddy, dirtying the small hands that Daddy had always refused to let see hard work, I knew I had to skedaddle out of bed and do my part.

Gemma was already up, and I could hear her in the kitchen.

I stuck on my overalls and hurried downstairs. "You been up long?" I asked her. "I don't want to look lazy."

"I just got up, and anyways your momma and daddy

don't even know I'm up yet. I thought I'd get some coffee on. They're sure enough bound to like some."

I shook my head and got a few biscuits from the bin to take out with the coffee. "Ain't no way to fix what's been done out there. Just ain't no way."

"Ain't nothin' impossible, Jessie. That's what my momma always said."

I could never argue with anything Gemma told me when it came from her momma, rest her soul, so I kept my mouth shut and spread honey on the biscuits.

When the coffee was done, we put our fixings on a tray and carried them outside to Momma and Daddy and Luke. They dusted their hands on their britches and thanked us for the food, but little else was said as they ate wearily.

After Daddy gulped down his last bit of coffee, he smacked his hat back on his head with a loud sigh. "Gonna take us a couple years' work to get half of this done ourselves. And I ain't got the money to hire more help. I ain't even got the money to pay the men I got."

"We gotta try," Momma told him. "Ain't no other way but to try."

Daddy dug his boot into the ground, scanning the fields critically.

I looked at Luke for reassurance that things would be better than Daddy said, but he just smiled weakly at me, and I could see in his eyes that he felt the same.

I heard Momma murmur one of her impromptu prayers—"Dear Jesus, send us help"—but I didn't quite think it would do any good. We were in a bad spot, and nothing short of Jesus and His angels coming from the sky with picks and hoes would save my daddy's farm.

But God taught me a lesson about angels that day. They don't always wear wings and carry harps. Sometimes they can just be people. People who open their hearts up to do things God tells them to do. I saw some of those angels that morning as I stood with a tray of empty coffee cups. They came from the front of the house, all fifteen of them, carrying tools and wearing gracious smiles. Some were white, some were colored, but they were united by one purpose.

"Ain't got enough hands, as I see it," Miss Cleta said, a basket of baked goods slung over one arm. "S'pose you'll have to let us lend you some."

Daddy took his hat off and stood there with it in both hands, tears threatening his eyes. "Can't pay you a cent. Can't do a thing for you."

"Ain't a one of us who wants nothin', Mr. Lassiter," said a colored man I recognized as Jimbo Turner, a dishwasher at the Rocky Creek Diner. "We's just come to help, is all."

The pastor of Gemma's old church and our pastor Landry stood side by side. Miss Cleta held the hand of Toby Washington, the colored teenager who ran errands for her, in a display that would surely have turned the stomachs of some.

Tears stung my eyes to see them there, our ragtag, multi-colored band of angels, and I stepped forward to accept Miss Cleta's basket. "I best make some more coffee," I squeaked out, my throat tight. And before the tears could come in front of everyone, I rushed past them and into the kitchen.

As I poured more cups of coffee, I said a prayer of thanks. Some tiny part of Calloway had started to heal, and though I didn't yet understand much about prayer, or about God for that matter, I figured I owed my thanks for such a thing.

Miracles didn't just happen on their own.

I remember clear as a bell the day they hung Otis Tinker. He was hung just like many a colored man had been, only Mr. Tinker wasn't innocent as so many of those colored men had been. He had blood on his hands, blood that I had once imagined was on my own. And on that day, a day when Daddy refused to leave the house to witness the final decree, Mr. Tinker breathed his last at noon on the mark.

As the time neared, Daddy rocked on the front porch slowly and methodically, his pocket watch in his hand, watching the seconds tick by. He opened that watch at eleven forty-five, and he sat for the next fifteen minutes staring at it without uttering a word. I sat on the porch steps next to Luke, who was keeping an eye on his own watch, which he had opened and laid on the step between us. Gemma was on the step below me, her back resting against my legs.

By eleven fifty-five, Momma was standing at the screen door, whispering prayers I couldn't understand, but I guessed at what she was saying. She'd be praying for his soul till the very last, hopeful until the end that Mr. Tinker would repent of his ways. "Weren't all of that man wicked," she'd said to me that morning. "Ain't no man with some good in him that shouldn't have a chance of escapin' an eternity of hellfire. He saved you in the end, don't forget."

I didn't have enough of a grasp on the situation to judge one way or another, so I hadn't replied to her declaration. But when I heard her whispered pleas just before noon on that first day of November, I whispered my own prayer for the man I'd thought of for most of my life as a kind, decent person.

Daddy's watch stayed open as the seconds ticked down. But with two minutes to go, he stopped rocking the chair, Momma stopped whispering her prayers and stepped softly onto the porch, and silence filled the air. Luke put an arm around me, and I let my head rest on his shoulder, my heart thumping in time with the watch. At noon, I jumped as the chimes started to ring inside the house like a death knell. Each clang of the clock made my stomach sink further.

The moment the last bell rang, Daddy snapped his watch shut, stood up quietly, and walked over to lay a hand on Momma's shoulder. "I'm gonna take a little walk, darlin'," he said, his husky voice barely audible.

Momma was crying softly, and it wasn't until Luke handed me his handkerchief that I realized I was crying too. Daddy put a gentle hand to my head and then to Gemma's as he walked down the steps beside us, and then he wandered off with a gait that spoke of his heavy heart. He disappeared past the shed and into the woods.

Momma had once said to me, "Daddy takes his thinkin' walks because sometimes a man needs to be on his own to figure things out and find some peace again." That autumn afternoon, I hoped more than ever that my daddy would find some peace amid those half-leafed trees.

We sat that way for a good hour, with no sign of Daddy, not one of us saying a word, likely because no one knew what to say at times like those. Momma had just murmured something about getting the stew started when we heard footsteps crunching around the bend in the road. Luke stood to see who was coming, and I climbed to the top step to see over his tall frame.

I was torn in two as I caught sight of Mrs. Tinker coming into view, her hair pulled tightly away from a tearstained face, the skirt of her black dress rippling in the breeze. Momma gasped and gripped her collar before running past us and down the steps to embrace Mrs. Tinker.

At first I wasn't sure how Mrs. Tinker would take that. After all, we were the ones who had stirred things up that summer. But Mrs. Tinker did nothing but melt into my momma's arms, her sobs coming in long, wheezing exhales. There wasn't a dry eye between the four of us when Momma calmed her down long enough to coax her inside for tea. Even Luke had tears in his blue eyes, and I made a mark in my memory of the first time I saw Luke Talley cry.

Daddy returned within another half hour, and I ran to him when I saw him, my arms outstretched.

For the first time since I was five, my daddy picked me up and held me, even though I was tall enough for my toes to touch the tops of his shoes. "It'll be all right, baby girl," he whispered into my hair.

"Mrs. Tinker's here. She's awful tore up," I said, my voice shaking. "Mr. Otis did what he did, and now Mrs. Tinker ain't got a husband, and her boys ain't got a daddy. Why do people do things that cause so much hurt?"

"I ain't got an answer for that." He set me down and tucked a lock of hair behind my ear. "Ain't no one but God got an answer for that. Best we can do is pray we don't do the same."

"I ain't capable of hatin' like that," I told him adamantly. "I could never hate a body like Mr. Otis hated Gemma and people like her."

"Jessilyn, ain't no man can't get someplace he never thought he'd get to. You let enough bad thoughts into your head, you can end up doin' all sorts of things you never thought possible. Otis let evil into his mind and it took over his heart. We best be on our guard and keep our minds on what's right and true so we don't become things we'll regret."

His words scared me. I wanted to always be able to trust people, to know that good people stayed good people, but I was realizing all too quickly that the human heart is fragile and needs constant attention. I'd seen enough bleakness in my own heart to know my daddy was speaking the truth.

"That's why we all need to know Jesus in our hearts," Daddy said. "Ain't no one else who can keep watch over our hearts like He can. Ain't no one else who can take the bad out and replace it with good. You best put thought to that, Jessilyn. Ain't no more important decision you can make, you hear?"

I'd heard similar words from both my parents many times in my life, but this time they struck deeper. I nodded at him as I always did in response to such talk, but I knew this time I'd be putting thought to it in a way I hadn't before. Life had become too real for me to dismiss the importance of Daddy's words.

In the shadow of Mr. Tinker's death, I took life more seriously.

Maybe that summer was the worst of my young life, but maybe it was also the most important. Time meandered on without Gemma's momma and daddy, and it meandered on without Cy Fuller and Walt Blevins. And just the same it meandered on without Otis Tinker. But those of us left behind viewed life more dearly, felt it more keenly. I'd learned a bit more about God, and I'd seen His powerful hands at work. As I was growing, my heart was changing, and the way I figured it, there were lessons learned in those dark days that would help me for years to come. In fact, they were lessons that would help us all in years to come.

Jeb succeeded in finding the evidence he sought against

the Klan, and the remaining members who had been dis-covered were sent to prison for mail fraud. It seemed the local Klan had an interest in making money, just not in legal ways. I didn't understand all the particulars as Daddy tried to explain them to me, but I was grateful to see them gone, knowing full well that a local court would never have made an example of them as the federal courts did. Still, prejudice in Calloway existed in plain form. Klan activity was only a small part.

We were to see much more of those Mr. Tinker left behind in the bleak days that followed his death. Mrs. Tinker spent much of her time with my momma, and Gemma and I watched the boys while our mommas sewed and cooked together. And every time the boys' wild ways would try my patience, I remembered they'd lost their daddy through no fault of their own, and I'd scold them with less sting in my tone.

Luke still took suppers with us almost every day, and as the brisk autumn evenings turned into cold winter ones, he'd sometimes stay the night on our couch to avoid a bitter walk home. I liked having him nearby. As I was learning to adjust to life as it had become for me, his presence made things feel more stable.

As for me and Gemma, we went on as before, but Gemma was a little less like a momma to me and more like a friend. I suppose that happens between two people when the younger one starts catching up to the older one. I'd been forced to see life from a place I'd never wanted to go, just as Gemma had in her own way when she'd lost her momma and daddy. We could relate better then. We got on well most days and fought a bit less than we had . . . but we still fought. I suppose that, too, is what life is like between people. Some good things, some bad things, a good bit of understanding . . .

And a lot of love.

As I sat on the porch blowing steam into the biting cold of a December night, I glanced over at Gemma, where she sat on the rocker, her knees bundled tightly under her chin. Her face was scrunched up against the cold, her teeth chattering. She hated being cold, but I knew she sat out on that porch because I wanted her to be with me, and her sweet spirit made me smile.

I leaned my head against the porch rail and sighed deeply. The way I figured it just then, my summers may have been full of bad luck, but my life wasn't. And even though Momma told me time and again that there was no such thing as luck, only blessings, I figured as far as family went, I was one of the luckiest girls alive.

Momma opened the front door and looked through the screen at me as though she knew what I was thinking and was correcting my thoughts. "What're you thinkin' about, Jessilyn Lassiter?"

"Just thinkin' about how . . . *blessed* I am," I said, replacing my word with hers.

She smiled at me and tossed her dish-drying towel over one shoulder. "Sure enough," she said brightly, staring out at the leaden sky. "Sure enough we all are."

Momma went back to her dishes, and I turned to share a knowing smile with Gemma. Inside, Daddy's guitar and Luke's vibrant whistle made a sweet melody, and I could hear Momma's hum joining in a bit offbeat. There was a crisp stillness in the air, teasing us with the thought of snow, and I tucked my blanket more tightly around my shoulders and smiled.

"Sure enough, Momma," I murmured even though she couldn't hear. "We all are blessed . . . beyond measure."

About the Author

Jennifer Erin Valent is the 2007 winner of the Jerry B. Jenkins Christian Writers Guild's Operation First Novel contest. A lifelong resident of the South, her surroundings help to color the scenes and characters she writes. In fact, the childhood memory of a dilapidated Ku Klux Klan billboard inspired her portrayal of Depression-era racial prejudice in *Fireflies in December*.

She has spent the past fifteen years working as a nanny and has dabbled in freelance, writing articles for various Christian women's magazines. She still resides in her hometown of Richmond, Virginia.

Discussion Questions

1. The people of Calloway seemed to have a problem with Jessilyn and Gemma's friendship primarily after Gemma came to live with the Lassiters. What made the difference in their minds? Could you relate to Sadie's mixed emotions about keeping Gemma?

2. Take a walk in Gemma's shoes. How would you cope with her combination of loss, fear, and feeling out of place?

3. Explore the sisterhood between Jessilyn and Gemma. In what ways did tragedy make their bond stronger?

4. How do the Lassiters personify the title of the book, and how can we do the same? Why is it so necessary in our contemporary culture to stand up for what is right and true?

5. Despite the closeness of her family, Jessilyn feels alone in her guilt over Cy Fuller and in her struggle with Walt Blevins. Why? How would a relationship with Jesus Christ have eased Jessilyn's burden of loneliness?

6. How does Jessilyn's persistent questioning of her faith point to God's sense of timing and purpose in all things?

7. In what ways does Luke's presence provide a stabilizing force for Jessilyn?

8. Do you think Jessilyn and Luke are drawn together by being the only nonbelievers in their tight little circle?

9. How did Miss Cleta's courage inspire the girls? How did it inspire you?

10. How did Otis Tinker's belief in his "cause" enable him to lead a double life? Do you feel that we're capable of letting this sort of deception creep into our own lives?

11. How do the "band of angels" bringing help to the devastated Lassiter farm show that even the smallest acts of selflessness can make a strong impact?

12. How did the Lord use the tragedy and fear of the summer of 1932 to teach Jessilyn and to bring the characters together?

BRIDGEPORT
PUBLIC LIBRARY

1230194139

CP012